Tales of the Automazombs

Downfall

D1732448

Tales of the Automazombs: Downfall

2nd Edition

© 2019, 2022 Dex Greenbright

Dex Greenbright, Editor, Cover Artist

ISBN: 978-1-0880-3443-9

Tales of the Automazombs
Downfall

Contents

THE RULING DEAD

By Dex Greenbright

Prince Ashford burst through the doors into the hall. A trio of servants hastened in behind him, intent on preparing him for the ceremony whether he wished it or not. The Prince swatted away a particularly forceful woman who had been one of his personal attendants since birth.

"If I am to go down to greet the Empire's subjects, I must at least wear the Colors!"

A portly advisor stood in the doorway, gasping for breath. The Prince was busy pulling articles of clothing off their hangers and knocking over displays in his search for the royal outfit.

"Your Highness! Please calm yourself. This is a shining moment for humanity, not just Teraltis."

"This is the governor's idea, isn't it? He wants to prevent us from wearing the royal garments so that we don't overshadow him. He's a fool, Corwynn. This is just the sort of thing we need to prove to the world how mighty Teraltis is. He won't matter in the long run; this is *our* moment of glory! We will retake all of the plagued lands."

"I wouldn't be too sure about retaking the lands entirely. Something doesn't feel right. Governor Frigenz isn't one for ceremonies. Still, it was your father's idea not to wear those old robes."

The Prince stopped and turned to face Corwynn. Ashford's mouth tried to form words and failed. The servants took advantage of his sudden stupor and quickly fitted him with a gold and silver embroidered vest. When Prince Ashford's voice returned, his words all tumbled out at once.

"My father? I didn't think..."

"No, you didn't. And now you will be late. I've arranged for a second zeppelin. You should arrive after the opening ceremony, but before the Emperor's speech."

"Of course. Thank you, Uncle Corwynn."

The Prince's bow was almost imperceptible, just a quick dip of the head to apologize for his brashness. The old man bowed deeply in return and huffed off toward the office of the Advisors Council. Ashford looked down at the servant who was pressing a slate-colored jacket into his hand. She was young, no more than seventeen. Her skin was tan, and she wore a braid of long, bronze hair down her back.

"You're new."

"Pardon, my lord, yes. I started a week ago. My name is Jaena"

"You are not from Teraltis. The correct way to address me is 'Your Highness.'"

"I beg your pardon, your highness. I'm Aadoburi, from a very low family."

Aadobur. It was not unheard of for the lower classes to flee in an attempt to better their station. Perhaps when he was Emperor, the relic country would finally be liberated from its archaic and backward traditions. If the whole world were Teraltian, there would be no need to defect for a better life.

He accepted the jacket while the other two servants shined his shoes and brushed a speck of dust from his pant leg. The finishing touch was a silver and emerald coronet. He may not have the robes, but he would look as majestic as possible.

With his preparations complete, Prince Ashford sauntered down the marble corridor to the palace's private airship port. When he reached the ship Corwynn had arranged, he heard someone clear their throat behind him. He turned to find the three servants waiting patiently. He had forgotten to pick which of them was going to attend to his needs during the trip and ceremony. He gestured toward the new girl and ascended the ladder into the airship's main cabin.

Jaena pointed to herself in obvious disbelief. The other two servants nudged her forward in answer. The girl beamed. She gathered her skirt and quickly followed after the Prince.

* * *

Jaena's heart felt as light as the airship's balloons. Everything she had worked for had finally paid off. She was attending royalty. If she played her cards right, she could save enough to send any child she might have to a university. Merchants and artisans were well respected. She beamed as the view of Caelspyr shrank away, outside her tiny window. If only her mother could see her now.

Even more exciting was the ceremony the Prince and Emperor were attending. The palace staff had been talking about the reports for days. The Teraltian Automazombs in the old capital had finished their task. The city and the surrounding farmlands had been cleared of the plague. Other cities had reported similar results. The landbound were saved. There had been other rumors, dark whispers of riots and madmen, but Jaena guessed these were simply people who were desperate to return to their beloved city. The Teraltians she knew claimed it was the most magnificent city on Eysan.

She stared out her window at the wondrous scenery, wishing the trip landward was longer. Jaena could watch the world drift past from an airship window forever. In just under an hour, she spotted wrought iron structures ahead. They drew closer to the airfield, passing one of tallest buildings she had ever seen; she counted fourteen stories as they flew down the wide avenue.

The street was filled with people cheering for them and for the Emperor. Larger figures that gleamed with metal appendages stood stationed at key locations. Jaena pressed her face to the glass; those had to be Automazombs! Most citizens on the ground gave the Automazombs a wide berth, but a few stood by the grotesque machines or even touched them.

Maxwell, the zeppelin attendant, walked up to Jaena.

"Hideous, aren't they?"

Jaena blushed.

"They saved us. I suppose they earned the right to be hideous."

"Don't trust 'em, though. I've got an uncle who..."

Jaena tuned out his nay-saying and turned her attention back to the scene outside. So long as Prince Ashford didn't require her, she would enjoy the experience.

The avenue ended in a large park square lined with trees. The Emperor would make his speech facing a statue of the first D'alori Emperor. The swelling crowd jostled for a better view of the stage. A few citizens had even climbed onto the marble statue for a better view. As the Prince's zeppelin neared the stage, Jaena could see the Emperor walking up to the podium. The zeppelin descended slowly in a secure airfield just off the square's north side, surrounded by palace guards. Governor Frigenz sat at the far end of the stage. His face was pale as he sat, uneasily tugging at the hem of his coat.

As Emperor Falkoun reached the podium, the crowd roared wildly. Prince Ashford shoved his way past Jaena. He insisted on being outside with his father. His ship was landing far too slowly. He shouted at the captain to open the doors. The captain pulled the controlling lever, though they were not yet landed. Prince Ashford raced down the ladder and jumped to the ground.

With the doors open, Jaena could hear specific phrases from the crowd more clearly. Some praised the Emperor; others condemned him for retreating to the clouds. Everyone was restless. She couldn't quite see, but it looked like an Automazomb was moving within the mass of people, too. While she was not accustomed to such ceremonies, she was certain that the tension in the air was more sinister than could be usual. As the Emperor reached the podium, the shouts near the back of the square became more insistent and violent.

The Emperor ignored them, or didn't notice, since the statue was blocking his vision of that part of the crowd. But Jaena saw the crowd lurch. There was a struggle. The fight quickly spread toward the stage. Palace guards and city soldiers moved to quell the violence. Jaena watched the scene nervously. Why weren't the Emperor and Prince leaving? She backed away from the open door and wished she hadn't been the attendant chosen for this trip.

Screams cut the air above the roiling crowd. Jaena peered through one of the zeppelin's round windows. Citizens fought with soldiers and guards as much as one another. The statue was being torn down as frenzied citizens attacked those who had climbed the sculpture. The damage they were capable of, despite being unarmed, was astonishing. They fought until their hands bled and still kept going. It was as though they didn't feel pain.

The Emperor retreated toward the airfield with his men and Prince Ashford. More soldiers and guards formed a barrier between the crowd and royalty. The first wave of the throng were easily rebuffed, but there were too many. Jaena squeezed her eyes shut as an angry citizen broke through the line, only to get stabbed by a guard's electrified halberd.

The guard captain shouted to his troop. Any guards who had not yet fallen to the crowd pulled back to protect their ruler. A handful of men rushed the Emperor's guards. Jaena saw one madman bite a guard on the arm. Another guard quickly beheaded the attacker. More and more of the mob surrounded the fleeing men. The blood-soaked governor was whisked away through the park by his assistants.

Prince Ashford and Emperor Falkoun were separated by the pressure of the mob. Guards grabbed the Prince and shoved him back aboard the airship. The zeppelin captain was already taking off. Prince Ashford loudly protested, insisting that he should be on the ground protecting his father.

Jaena couldn't see the Emperor amid his guards and attackers, but she heard his agonized cry. The Prince's guards still on the ground jumped to the Emperor's aid, ripping away the layers of crazed men and women. At the bottom of the human pile, the Emperor lay bruised and bleeding.

At this sight, Prince Ashford flew into a rage. No number of servants could stop him from sliding back down the ladder and helping the guards lift his father onto the zeppelin. As they ascended, the grounds below shifted and seethed with the movements of the ever-growing riot.

* * *

The palace was blanketed by an eerie silence upon their return. The Emperor's wounds were even more severe than they had initially appeared. Emperor Falkoun was quickly sequestered in his chambers. The only ones allowed entrance were family and doctors. Corwynn had been in several times, taking full advantage of being both an advisor and the Emperor's brother. He sent for every doctor and healer on Caelspyr.

Prince Ashford paced outside his father's room. They had been tricked! The whole ceremony was a plot to kill his father – and probably him as well. Was Frigenz in on the plot? He had looked overly nervous. What did he hope to accomplish? Without the Emperor's guidance, Teraltis would fall into ruin – or worse – civil war.

Ashford turned toward the door. He would be expected to sit at his father's bedside. As his hand reached out, it trembled and he pulled back, horrified by what he expected to find. How could Teraltis carry on without Falkoun the Great? How could the gods threaten to take his father so suddenly? No. Father needed him. He had to be strong, a reflection of the Emperor's strength. Ashford once again tried to steel himself when the door opened from the inside. Corwynn emerged in a hurry, pulling Ashford in his wake.

The Prince leaned close to his uncle and questioned him in a low whisper.

"How is he?"

"Not well. The attack brought on an illness. He sleeps now, but when he is awake he coughs blood and has a violent temper."

"The doctors have a cure, right? They know what this is?"

Corwynn paused in his stride. He glanced around the hall to make sure none were listening. When he felt secure, he continued walking, though more cautiously than before.

"Your Highness, your father has every doctor, herbalist, alchemist, and faith healer we could find in that room with him. None of them have an answer and he is worsening. All they know is that it is not the plague, at least as we know it. It may be time to think of your ascension to the throne."

"Have them try harder!"

"Prince Ashford, if your father dies…"

"I won't let him!"

"Now, Ashford, think reasonably."

"My father's irreplaceable to this country! How do you think it will look if I take the throne after a mysterious illness kills their beloved ruler? They will cry murder!"

"Perhaps he can survive this illness, but if he doesn't…"

"Make certain he does survive, Uncle Corwynn, or perhaps I will blame the death on a power-hungry brother."

Prince Ashford stormed off, leaving his worried uncle caressing his throat. In uncertain times such as these, even falsely accused regicide could earn a man a visit to the executioner.

* * *

Over the next few days, the Emperor grew steadily worse. His fever raged despite the cooling herbs. His appetite diminished; though he would chew mindlessly at anything placed before him, he consumed none of it. His temper was so uncontrollable that soon it seemed they were locking the Emperor in, rather than locking intruders out.

On the fifth night, in the middle of a blood-coughing fit, the Emperor collapsed. The doctors checked his vital signs and, determining he had none, called for his brother.

Corwynn came in and stood at the back of the room. The Emperor looked a wreck. His final hours must have been excruciating. His healing team sat near, exhausted and with heads hung low. The Aadoburi servant girl was cleaning up after the Emperor's sickness. She was young, but quiet and diligent in her task. In the silence, the only thing that could be heard was the girl's scrubbing brush.

Scrub, rinse, scrub, rinse, empty the bucket. Scrub, rinse. *Groan.*

Everyone in the room jumped at the unexpected noise. It had come from neither the doctors nor the girl. Before confusion began to overtake grief, a more insistent moan was heard, this time coupled with movement – from the Emperor's bed.

The doctors and other healers excitedly gathered around. It was a miracle! The Emperor had pulled through! The doctor marking vital signs must have been incorrect. The physicians took notes and congratulated one another on saving their ruler's life.

The Emperor slowly sat up and looked at the men and women surrounding him. His skin was pale and his eyes bloodshot. A trickle of blood from his earlier coughing escaped his lips as he opened his mouth as if to speak.

One of the doctors leaned closer to hear the words of the Emperor. The others looked on expectantly. There was a long, heavy pause followed by a quick lurch forward. The Emperor tore the doctor's ear off. The Emperor's victim tried to call for help, but was silenced by a second bite to the throat.

The medical team panicked. A few ran out of the room, one stood paralyzed, others screamed. Corwynn and two doctors kept level enough heads to restrain the Emperor before anyone else was hurt.

Prince Ashford burst into the room. The doctor who had been attacked lay in a pool of blood on the floor. The servant girl was backed up against the wall, superstitiously gesturing protective wards. The Emperor writhed in his bed, arms and legs tightly bound to the bedposts.

Ashford stormed over to Corwynn.

"What happened?"

The more composed doctors checked the Emperor's vital signs again. They looked at one another and then back at the readings.

"Your Highness, Emperor Falkoun is dead."

Price Ashford watched his father tug at the restraints. The Emperor's head lolled wildly as he snapped blood-covered teeth at anyone that went near him.

"Are you mad? Dead men don't move or call out in pain! Why is he restrained? Do we pay you healers to torture?"

"Ashford, wait!"

Corwynn grabbed the Prince's arm, reaching to untie his father, and pulled him sharply away as the Emperor bit the air where his son's hand had been.

A healer woman cautiously stepped forward.

"The Emperor moves, but has no heartbeat. He attacked a doctor and was restrained. If you give us time, we will find the cause of this new condition."

Prince Ashford was livid. He broke free of his uncle's grasp and confronted the healer woman.

"I would ask if time would allow you to bring back the dead, but it seems that's already been done. You will have no more time, healer. Get out."

As they argued, the mauled doctor twitched and rose up beside them. His movements were awkward and disjointed. He slowly shuffled toward the Prince, his mouth hanging agape as he moaned. The servant girl grabbed a nearby vase and threw it at the pale, unblinking doctor. It was only a small distraction, but it gave Corwynn enough time to pull his dagger and plunge it into one of the man's bloodshot eyes. The doctor crumpled to the floor. He didn't move again.

Corwynn straightened up and took a deep breath.

"Well. It appears there are grave decisions to be made. Ashford, I think the healers should stay. I have many questions, and they might provide the answers. Nobody is to speak of this to anyone outside of this room."

Ashford followed his uncle out, but stopped when he saw the servant girl.

"You. You were on the airship when my father was attacked."

"Yes, my lord."

"It's '*Your Highness*'." Prince Ashford slowly pressed the words out through gritted teeth. He towered over the girl. "Jaena, isn't it? You are hereby sworn to secrecy. You must never breathe a word of these events to anyone."

"I… of course, your highness."

"Good. For your sake, and that of any family you have, you had best keep quiet."

* * *

Jaena's shaking threatened to spill the red waters of the cleaning bucket. She had stayed to clean up the doctor's blood and bits of flesh. The healers took the body away to a Scholar building to study it. The Prince's threat echoed in her mind. She felt as if the Imperial guards were watching her more closely.

She made her way to the west kitchen. They butchered meats there. Nobody would notice a girl emptying bloodied water into those sinks. She cracked the door open. Nobody was inside to become suspicious. Jaena breathed a sigh of relief and hurried in. She held her nose as she emptied the cleaning bucket. The pieces of flesh were quickly turning gray. As the foul muck chugged out of sight, the girl looked at her soiled hands. A testament to the terrible secret she now kept.

In the middle of scrubbing her hands raw, the kitchen began filling with other servants. Jaena rushed to remove the remainder of the pinkish stain and made for the door. Everyone was talking about the Emperor's locked doors and the suspicious shouting coming from within. Gossip had spread quickly about the attack at the ceremony. Wild theories about coups and conspiracies were thrown about.

She recognized a blonde woman near the table. They had been paired up on quite a few tasks. Jaena quickly turned her head away and reached for the door. If she could get out without incident, then maybe everything would be fine.

"Jaena? Come, girl! Don't be shy!"

Jaena closed her eyes tight and cursed silently. She cautiously turned to face the group.

"Oh, I'm sorry Bridgett. I'm just tired."

"Nonsense! It's not yet midday. You only need to eat something. Join us!"

The others stared eagerly and waved Jaena over. It didn't look like she had a choice. She smiled as graciously as she could manage and joined the others.

"So, girl, what do you think went on in the Emperor's chambers?"

"Oh, I really couldn't say."

Maxwell, the zeppelin attendant spoke up.

"But, you went in there, yes? You have to have seen or heard something."

Jaena winced. If anyone threatened her secret, it was him. He'd been the one to give her a cleaning bucket.

"I... I really didn't. I cleaned up the sick and left."

"That's the bucket there, though, isn't it? How is it still wet hours later?"

"I found other spills. I didn't finish until recently."

Bridgett chided him.

"Stop pestering the girl, Max!"

"Sorry, it's just, I'm not used to all this not knowing."

Another woman chimed in, hands on her hips.

"It's the plague, I bet. Thought we cured it, but it's back and this time none will survive."

The uproar from this speculation was explosive. Those who agreed were panicked and those who didn't were loudly arguing their counterpoints. Nobody was looking at the Aadoburi girl anymore. Jaena took this as a perfect opportunity to slip away.

She shut the door soundlessly behind her. The argument in the kitchen was muted here in the hall, but it would still be obvious to any passersby that something had the servants worried.

A tall pair of guards swiftly stalked toward Jaena. They each carried an electrified halberd, an ornate pole with a dagger on the end that would both stab and deliver a nasty shock. Jaena turned away from them and started walking. One of the pair sped up and cut her off, using his halberd to bar the path. The second guard came up behind so that when Jaena tried to back away from the guard in front of her, she bumped into the other. The man she had bumped into spoke in a low growl.

"Prince Ashford told us to keep an eye out for a ruckus amongst the servants."

The other guard was a lean woman of the northern regions, Irenorn judging by her blond braids. She continued barring the path and narrowed her eyes at Jaena.

"He also said that if something did happen, you were likely involved."

The male guard placed a heavy hand on Jaena's shoulder.

"You need to come with us."

* * *

10

The Emperor's palace on Caelspyr had not been built with interrogations in mind. Nobody had been sent to a dungeon in over a century and anyone suspected of wrongdoing could easily be transported to the courthouse by the rail system. But this matter was much too dangerous and much too private for the courts to hear.

Corwynn rubbed his forehead above his eyes as the servant girl was led to the repurposed bedroom. The window coverings let only the faintest orange glow through. Shadows dominated the old advisor's face.

"What did you tell the staff about the Emperor? I need to know if this can still be contained."

"I said nothing! They only had guesses."

"Which were? The more helpful you are, the better things will be."

Jaena fidgeted in her ornate chair.

"An attempted coup, a war with the landbound, or…" Corwynn motioned for her to continue. Jaena bit her lip. "…or perhaps the plague has returned to kill us all."

"You saw that… thing. That's not the plague. But we need to quell these wild theories."

"Pardon, Your highness, but how? The servants are accustomed to knowing everything that happens within the palace. Without details, they will keep guessing."

Corwynn pulled on the end of his moustache.

"They cannot know the full truth, but they can be given enough answers to satisfy."

* * *

The next day, the advisors held a secret meeting. Several servants were kept on hand to attend to the nobles over the course of the day. During this meeting, the Emperor and the current situation were discussed at length. Corwynn, as head of the Advisors Council, presided over the meeting, steering the conversation and hoping this plan would work.

His story began that Governor Frigenz had plotted with a group of Irenorn separatists, using the ceremony as a trap. Corwynn looked around the room, content at the general acceptance of his words. There was no doubt that it had indeed been a trap, though who had set it and why was a mystery. The story continued with the Prince capturing one of the plotters. The captured separatist was sequestered deep within the castle for interrogation. Any noise heard from that room was the interrogation, which could be happening at any and all hours. Only authorized personnel would be admitted.

Many were concerned about the Emperor after the attack. Corwynn explained that the Emperor fell ill from a poisoned blade. The Emperor moved to a more private room to aid in his recovery. A counterattack would soon be launched on the separatist base near Irenorn Prison. The "Iceberg" and the surrounding land held so many criminals it was an easy tale to believe.

Only a few advisors knew the truth, so the story served to placate both the palace staff and the Council. With the story told, they discussed their options. Caelspyr itself was armed only against small attacks. The Imperial Army regimens from both Caelspyr and Dantus would have to be deployed. If that failed, there was some talk of a privately-run task force renowned for handling difficult situations.

Corwynn offered to send out the orders himself, privately noting that he would have to bar the others from giving any orders without his permission. Quelling a false uprising in one's own country only worked if no real shots were fired.

By evening, the meeting's gory details had been relayed amongst the servants. The prisoner was secured in a room several floors below the Emperor's now-empty chambers. That area, clearly identified by the noises of the prisoner being interrogated, was to be avoided for security reasons. There was no danger of the truth being exposed.

* * *

There was a small celebration in the southern wing. Maira, a sweet kitchen maid, was getting engaged. Jaena joined the rest of the servants for a night of revelry. When she heard Maxwell talking about the prisoner, she decided she would have to keep an eye on him. She followed him out the door to the hall. A gardener named Jakob joined her, saying that a stroll would do the three of them good. Jaena did her best to keep the two young men out of trouble, but when they decided to wander drunkenly into the halls, that task grew increasingly more difficult.

It didn't take long before they passed the "interrogation room." Guards had been posted in front of the door. One of them sneered in disgust at the servants stumbling through the main hall. Jaena shrugged apologetically as she tried to guide her companions to a more appropriate side passage.

Once away from the guards, Jakob leaned heavily on Maxwell's shoulder.

"Did you hear they're anti-sky as well? If the coup succeeded, they'd have us grounded in those plague-ridden lands. No more floating islands. Do they even worship D'alor?"

"But the coup didn't succeed. They'll finish off those separatists and everything'll be fine."

"I still say we go in there and show that bastard true Teraltian loyalty."

Jakob pressed his fist into the palm of his other hand and grinned.

The blood drained from Jaena's face.

Maxwell glanced around the corner at the guards and then meandered back to his friend.

"We can use the service hall to get in."

Jaena stammered an objection as she tried to pull her companions away by their shirtsleeves.

"I…I imagine it's locked."

"They never think about us. And the door blends seamlessly with the walls. Why would they even remember it's there?"

"But what if… we find more guards inside. We'll be caught!"

"Oh, calm yourself, Jaena. The guards talk as loosely as the advisors. There's nobody posted beyond the two out front. And do you hear any interrogations right now? No."

"Max is right. Now let's show that fiend Teraltis can't ever be stopped! Let's go!"

"I… No! No, I won't go. You shouldn't either! It could be dangerous."

"It'll be fine. Besides, if there's trouble, we'll protect you."

Jaena stood frozen. She had to warn someone. No, they'd say she was in on it. Her whole family would be in danger. Could she manage to stop them herself? Both were taller and stronger and they obviously weren't going to listen to reason. It would be so much easier if she could just tell them.

While she struggled with her thoughts, Jakob shouted back as he ran off into the dark.

"If you change your mind you know where we'll be!"

Jaena weighed her options again – certain death from a guard's electrified halberd or probable death from an undead Emperor? She ran after the others and prayed for safety.

The space was once a suite for favored guests. A small antechamber and a bathroom large enough for a comfortable tub and toilet took up the front third of the suite and provided a bit of buffer between the main hall and the occupant. The rest of the space was a bedroom, with the servants' entrance discretely placed in a corner, camouflaged as part of the wall and usually obscured by a large wardrobe. However, as the three of them entered the room, Jaena saw that the bed had been removed, as had the other furniture. It seemed Emperor Falkoun had little use for them since he died. And came back. In place of furniture, there was a large post in the center of the bedroom. Attached to it was a heavy chain that led to a shadowy corner against the far wall. The men stumbled ahead, slurring out an old war song.

Jaena doubted the other two had enough wits between them to recognize this as a place of danger. She hissed to Maxwell, hoping to the gods the Emperor was incapacitated.

"They must have moved the prisoner. There's nothing here. Let's leave!"

"Somebody's on the end of that chain. It's got to be him."

Jakob walked through streams of moonlight as he neared the far wall. His foot nudged the thick chain. There was a quiet shuffling in the darkness ahead. He lifted the chain, whispering threats at the shadows as he yanked the prisoner into view.

"Try to take down our Empire? Rotten scoundrel!"

The chained monster stumbled out into the dim light. Even with hollow eyes and torn, sallow cheeks, the Emperor's ghastly visage was instantly recognizable. Maxwell took a cautious step forward, but Jaena clutched his arm and tugged him back. Emperor Falkoun cocked his head to the side as he shambled closer.

Jakob dropped to his knees instinctively.

"Y-your Imperial Majesty! I…"

The Emperor's lower jaw sagged open. A low gurgling moan was his only response.

Jaena shrieked out a warning, but it was far too late. With fingers like claws and teeth like knives, the Emperor shredded Jakob. His terrified screams had the guards rushing in halberds first, ready to subdue all intruders. Jaena recognized one of them as the woman who had led her to questioning days prior.

The Irenorn woman's fierce glare let Jaena know she remembered as well.

"You!"

14

Jaena, still locked onto Maxwell's arm, staggered back. Her feet began running before her mind had a chance to catch up. The guard shouted after them.

"Servant girl! Get back here!"

Jaena raced through the service halls with Max in tow. More guards were called to the room while the Irenorn guard chased after the escaping servants. Jaena's eyes watered as she raced in no particular direction. Prince Ashford had made it very clear that she would be in danger if anyone discovered the Emperor in his current condition. She had to flee. She had to escape from Caelspyr.

Maxwell kept glancing back. He was still drunk.

"Jaena? What just happened?"

His voice snapped Jaena back to the present danger. She released her grip on his arm and muttered an apology. She immediately regretted letting him go.

His feet were now as firmly planted as his demands for answers.

"What was that?!"

"That was the Emperor. He's become something evil."

"But... we need to warn somebody! Jakob was just--"

"Eaten. But, no! Guards chasing us means they already know. We have to get out of here. We'll be killed if we stay."

"Killed?" Max squinted angrily down the hall they had just run from. "You're wrong. This is just a drunk's dream. Let me sleep this off and forget the whole thing."

The shouting of guards grew louder. They didn't have much time. If they were going to escape with their lives, she had to snap a very groggy Maxwell out of his stupor. She called his attention, readying her hand at her side. When he turned to face her, her hand met his face with an astonishing force. It wasn't kind and Jaena felt sorry for doing it, but the sudden stinging pain had worked.

Max jerked at the sound of the guards.

"*Oh gods*, what're we to do?!"

Jaena nervously watched the shadows as she considered their options.

"You're an airship attendant, right?"

"That's right."

"Did I hear that you're training to become a pilot?"

"Almost done. Well, with the basics."

"It will have to do. Let's head for the palace port."

"Are you insane? You're talking about stealing from the Emperor."

"The Emperor is dead. He won't notice. The only ones who will already want to kill us."

Maxwell stood silent for a moment before heaving an exaggerated sigh. Jaena nodded quickly and once again tugged her accidental accomplice forward.

* * *

Prince Ashford was roused from his slumber by an aggravated Corwynn. The stout old advisor was fuming as he paced around the room.

"Your fears about the girl were well-founded, Ashford. And there's more dire news as well."

"How bad is it?"

"One dead, but now a half dozen guards know more than they did, or should."

"The guards are well trusted. Where is the girl now?"

Corwynn groaned in frustration. This situation was spiraling out of control with all the speed of a man kicked off Caelspyr's outer rim.

"It seems she found a pilot. One of your airships has gone missing."

Prince Ashford's face twitched.

"She escaped? A girl who has information that could bring down the Empire is gone?"

"I've dispatched the enforcers in our fastest cloudskippers to hunt them down. But I have more dire news yet to relay."

"What could possibly be worse than exposing father's... condition?"

"The Inventors Guild has studied the samples from the Emperor and that doctor. It seems the doctors were only half right when they said it was not the plague."

Ashford covered his mouth and nose with his sleeve, his eyes wide with fear.

"Don't tell me we've been infected."

"It seems fluid-borne now. We should be safe unless his blood or saliva – if he has any – get into our bodies. The real trouble lies in the chemical traces."

"What does that mean? What chemicals?"

Corwynn pursed his lips.

"*Automazomb* chemicals. The plague has combined with the very chemicals meant to cleanse."

"So, what of my father?"

"The Inventors Guild recommends a long-term study in their labs."

Ashford stiffened.

"No. I can't let him be tortured like that. He is still the Emperor!"

Corwynn tried to comfort his nephew by placing a hand on his shoulder.

"Prince Ashford, I'm sorry, but he's not. Your father, my brother, died that night."

"I cannot let him suffer. A zeppelin will bring him to the old capital. If there is anything of my father left, he will be happy there with his people. If this disease came from the ground, let the ground keep it."

Corwynn could see the look in the Prince's eyes. It was the same uncompromising Imperial gaze his brother had while calling for additional troops to defend the desert border. There would be no arguing.

"And what will you do, Your Highness?"

"It seems I have no choice but to claim the throne. And you - I trust you will do your best to help me gather up the pieces of the Empire when it shatters."

* * *

Jaena paced around the control bay, circling Maxwell into dizziness.

"Can we outrun them?"

"Cloudskippers? They're made light and fast. We're in a zep, a transport ship."

"Yes, but, you can outmaneuver them, right? Does this airship have guns?"

"I haven't even mastered the basics yet. And no. Just… leave me be!"

She blew out a nervous breath and went to the window. They'd made it as far as the Kalahn Sea. Everything about the view she loved on the way to the ceremony looked ominous now. The clouds were thick around them. Every now and then she spotted the dark shapes of four cloudskippers. They were closer every time. The zeppelin jerked left, tossing Jaena about the cabin.

Jaena raced back to the pilot's chair.

"Is that them? Are they shooting at us?"

Maxwell pointed to a cloud system ahead, dark as night.

"Storm winds. Flying into that cloud is our only chance. Those cloudskippers are too light to fly reliably in there."

Lightning flashed. Jaena steadied herself.

"Is there anything I can do to help?"

"Watch for them. Tell me the location of any cloudskippers you see. I'll do my best to dodge them."

The zeppelin flew into the storm cloud. Jaena returned to the cabin, ready to warn Maxwell of any danger. Storm winds raged around them. The zeppelin was buffeted about the sky. Her stomach was churning even more violently than the winds surrounding them. She was almost sorry she had escaped at all. The future she had worked so hard for was gone. Jaena shrieked as a cloudskipper emerged from cover only to be blasted by a lightning bolt arcing toward the ground. The smaller airship's engine burst with yellow and white sparks.

Another two cloudskippers appeared to their left. Jaena shouted to Maxwell, who responded by sending the zeppelin into a nosedive. Jaena grabbed onto an iron strut so she wouldn't tumble forward. Below them was the great sea, vast and cold. Bullets zipped past the window; the cloudskippers had followed them and had opened fire. Maxwell pulled up at the last second. One cloudskipper crashed into the waves. The other was right on their rudder.

Jaena jumped at the sound of wood splintering and metal clanging. The cloudskipper behind them was too close to miss. She smelled smoke. She glanced at the control bay. Maxwell was yanking on the steering column with all of his strength. They were losing altitude. Jaena could see the Shunniran city of Usoma on the horizon.

Maxwell pointed to the sliver of land ahead.

"Don't worry, Jaena. I've got family in Shunnira. We'll be protected."

"You have to land this ship first."

He attempted a laugh to calm her fears, but the clouskipper behind them continued its assault. The zeppelin shuddered, caused Maxwell's hand to slip. His laugh turned into a gasp and Jaena gripped the walls until her knuckles lost their color.

"Max?"

"Hold on!"

Maxwell's tongue was wedged firmly at the corner of his mouth as he put all of his weight into controlling the helm.

Jaena shrieked.

"Max!"

"I said hold on!"

She braced herself. The cloudskipper's next attack pierced the zeppelin's balloons.

18

The impact itself was quick. The ship smacked the water, smashing windows and flooding the small cabin. Jaena kicked her feet in the rising water, but her long skirt slowed her down. Maxwell abandoned his post. Together, Max and Jaena thrashed their way toward the nearest broken window. It was a desperate battle; the seawater flooding in pushed them back further than they moved forward. There had to be another escape. If they didn't find a way out soon, the ship would be too deep for them to make it to the surface without running out of air.

"Is there any other way out of here?"

"Well, not unless we go through a balloon, but that thing's not filled with oxygen."

Jaena tilted her head up. The balloons! Then she studied the cabin. The curved port windows could hold a decent amount of air, if they were pointed the right way.

"It must still be somewhat inflated, or we would be on the seabed by now. If we can tilt the ship, maybe we could get that intact window facing upward. That will save a pocket of air. We can hide there until the enforcer thinks we're dead and gives up. The sea didn't look so dark below us. I think it will be relatively shallow."

Maxwell stared at her for a second, stunned, then gave a quick nod. "Worth a shot."

They trudged through the rising waters to a wall of gauges, valves, and levers. They worked at the control board, angling the submerged rudders and fins that now attempted to position the cabin relative to heavier currents than mere air. Jaena heard a loud bubbling noise out the port side and felt the ship listing beneath her. It was working! The two pushed the heavy equipment to the port side and quickly clambered up the slanted floor toward the starboard windows.

Thankfully she'd been right about at least one window being intact. Around them, the airship gurgled and groaned as it gave up its struggle against the waves. The water rose and covered them to their necks, but the angle they'd arranged the ship in kept the large pocket of air from streaming away in little bubbles. They huddled together as the zeppelin sank and settled on the sea floor. The air grew stale, but Jaena held Maxwell fast. The Emperor's men wouldn't give up that quickly. Not with what she knew.

What felt like an hour passed before Jaena and Maxwell swam for the surface. She was grateful the zeppelin had crashed within sight of land. They surfaced a ways off shore for a quick breath and to check for danger. The cloudskipper was gone. Shunniran ships now patrolled the skies, apparently disturbed by the sight of Teraltian enforcers at their border.

Jaena and Maxwell each took a deep breath and swam underwater again. They did this several times; they didn't risk being seen until they emerged beneath a wooden pier. Jaena was thoroughly exhausted by the time she reached shore. She clutched the soft sand between her fingers as she crawled out of the tide. Maxwell was close behind. The two sat on the beach catching their breath.

A hundred horrid thoughts raced through Jaena's mind. She had to find a way to warn her family about Prince Ashford. They would have to go on the run. She might never see them again. And what of the Emperor? That doctor he attacked and killed rose again. She feared the same would happen to Jakob. She had to do something before this new horror spread further.

Jaena staggered to her feet.

"You said you have family here? Could they help me send a message? I can't keep the Emperor's secret any longer."

* * *

Deep in the heart of Caelspyr, a machine was clogged. A pair of pipeworkers approached the machine with boxes of tools.

"Bet you it's a dead rat. They always try to drink from the wastewater stream and get caught. Filthy creatures."

"Alright, I'll take that bet. This here's palace wastewater. I say some Imperial idiot's dumped their trash. Loser buys drinks."

The first worker adjusted a valve revealing a glass viewing port. The other looked inside. The thing stuck in the pipe looked like gray meat and a lot of blood.

"That's no rat."

"It's not? Damn. Let me see."

As the first worker leaned over to look, his hand accidentally turned the valve further. A dull crack could be heard within the machine and the edges of the viewing port started leaking. The second worker covered the gaps as best he could with his hands while his partner grabbed a sealant. The meaty clog responded to the leak by settling further into the machinery. The added pressure only worsened the leak. Pink water and bits of the clog sprayed everywhere. The second worker sputtered and gagged.

"Hurry up with that stuff!"

His partner spun around, sealant tube in hand. The man underestimated the slickness of the spill and fell forward, cracking his nose on a small metal pipe. Fresh red trails joined the pinkish-gray chunks on the ground. He staggered to his feet and once again hurried to finish the task. With the leak stopped, the two drenched workers pulled a large red lever that would send the clogged water away from the drinking water cleansing system. The first worker caressed his broken nose and looked up at his partner.

"I think I'm definitely going to need that drink now."

The other worker coughed, spat out a gray-pink gob, and nodded.

VESPYR LOVES COURTNAY

By Jessica L. Lim

Vespyr Alyn had never been one to subscribe to such notions as suddenly and deeply falling in love with someone she hadn't even met, but then she saw him.

It was a random encounter. They were on the skyway between Astria and Beylr. Vespyr had managed to obtain one of the highly coveted seats when he entered her carriage. She looked up from her daily bulletin and there he stood. He took no notice of her, but she definitely noticed him. He looked resplendent in his dapper gray suit; his dark blond hair styled in the latest fashion, which complimented his finely drawn, handsome face. She could not see his eyes then, but she imagined them to be piercing regardless of color. He carried himself confidently, not hunched tiredly like many of their fellow passengers, and she was instantly attracted to him.

The idea stunned her; she found men attractive, of course, but she had never reacted to one so viscerally. Her initial astonishment gave way to intrigue. She found herself staring at this man. She started to wonder who he was; what his job was; who his friends were; what he did in his spare time. She looked back to her bulletin quickly when the beautiful man turned toward her gaze, desperately hoping her embarrassment was not written all over her face.

He moved to the door right before D'alynic Station. Vespyr's body seemed to take on a life of its own as she stood to stand beside him. His attention was focused on the door; she stared at his reflection in the glass. If he found her intrusive, he made no indication.

When the skyway came to the stop, the object of Vespyr's attention moved through the crowd swiftly, deftly weaving his way through the throng of other commuters. Vespyr had never been very good at making her way through a crowd without bumping into someone or another, but somehow she found herself skilled enough to navigate her way with confidence.

Suddenly, she stopped. She had been so focused on following this man that she didn't realize what was happening. When she took in her surroundings, the buildings were all wrong. Crowds streamed around her as they bustled about a busy shopping and financial district. Vespyr was still three quarters of an hour from her stop. What had she been thinking? Following this stranger off the train had been the most impulsive thing she had ever done.

With a heavy sigh and a shake of her head, she turned on her heel and walked back to the D'alynic stop. This side trip cost her an additional thirty minutes. She was definitely going to be late. Vespyr cursed herself. Her foolish whim prevented her from being able to go home and change before dinner, as she would have preferred. Not only would she still be in her work attire, her sister Alina would probably order something spectacularly vile for her.

An hour and a half later, Vespyr arrived at The Palace Hotel. The architects who designed the building tried to mimic Teraltis's temporarily abandoned D'allori Palace, crafting it in marble. The stone was used in only one other building in the skies: the Royal Palace on Caelspyr. The hotel seemed to glitter brilliantly against the dark, smoky sky. The interior was just as lavish with its gleaming alabaster walls, vaulted ceilings, sparkling chandeliers, and marble floors. Patronizing the Palace Hotel for any reason at all implied a certain amount of prestige.

Since Vespyr and Alina were such good customers, they often had their pick of tables. When it was just the two of them, Vespyr was happy to be tucked away in a corner. But whenever Alina was showing off, they were always in the center of the dining room.

Which is where Vespyr found her sister tonight; she could hear her sister's tittering laugh rising from the center of the dining room. Vespyr nodded brusquely to the maître d'. Were it any other time, she would stop to chat with him or at least offer a polite word, but the consequences of her little misadventure put her in a bit of mood. That, and the fact that her dinner companions for the evening were some of her sister's more boisterous friends.

"Hiya Ves," Kevan greeted cheerfully. He was perhaps one of the few friends of her sister's that she could tolerate. Even if he did insist on calling her "Ves".

She smiled politely. "Lovely to see you again, Kevan," she replied cordially, sitting in the chair he pulled out for her. She nodded to the others seated at the table. She recognized them, but she sometimes had trouble keeping track of Alina's ever-rotating entourage. She doubted it would matter since she would most likely be talking to Kevan all evening.

"We haven't had a chance to order yet," Kevan explained. "You're saved from whatever poison your sister would have ordered for you." He proffered a glass of wine, which she accepted gratefully.

"What kept you?" Alina asked.

Vespyr had no intention of revealing her folly to all those in attendance so she simply used work as her excuse. "You work too much, Vespyr," some friend commented, as if this socialite would know. To herself, Vespyr thought most of Alina's friends wouldn't know a good day's work from an Infected.

She still couldn't believe there were people in the world who got away with not working. After the Outbreak, the Emperor had decreed that every person living on the Floating Cities should concentrate their efforts on sustaining civilized society. Many of the working-class people privileged enough to obtain life on the Islands found their place in the Undercity, maintaining the intricate cogs and gears that kept their new worlds afloat, while citizens in Vespyr's social class found work with the Artificers or the Inventors Guilds. The attitude seemed to be if you didn't live to work, you didn't deserve to live. Everyone was all too aware of what could happen to you if you braved the world below.

25

Food was ordered and served, and the wine flowed copiously. All the while, Vespyr managed to give the appearance of paying attention. Really, she was remembering her brief encounter with her beautiful stranger. At one point, while talking with Kevan, she thought she saw Him amidst the sea of faces in the dining room.

"What's wrong?" Kevan inquired, noticing the sudden shift in her expression. He tried to follow her gaze, looking for the object that captivated her.

"Sorry, I thought I saw someone I knew," she said quickly. She reached for her water and took a great gulp.

Vespyr took her leave of the dinner party not long after that. For some reason, she was mildly shaken by her sudden vision of her stranger. Perhaps a good night's sleep would remedy her temporary insanity.

* * *

It didn't. If anything, sleep caused the visions to be more vivid. Her brief encounter, if she could even call it that, replayed in her mind's eye to a more fulfilling degree. This time, when the man of her dreams (literally and figuratively) entered her carriage, the seat beside her was vacant. He sat beside her. He was close enough that their sides touched.

She awoke more flustered than when she'd gone to sleep.

During her morning skyrail commute, she caught herself looking up expectantly when they approached D'alynic Station. Much to her disappointment, she did not see her beautiful stranger enter her carriage. Suddenly, an idea struck her: if he was not on *this* car, perhaps he was on another. Again, her body moved of its own volition, going from carriage to carriage, one end of the train to the other. Unfortunately for her, she did not see him again that morning.

Vespyr went to work in a strangely dour disposition. *Idiot*, she berated herself. *What is the matter with you? Since when do you become obsessed with someone you've never met?* She decided to put her beautiful stranger from her mind. It had been a once in a lifetime sighting, and there was absolutely no sense in fixating on it. Coming to terms with the reality of the situation, while not particularly pleasant, did marginally improve her day at work. (It was work, after all.)

26

Vespyr worked in the Liaison Office, a government agency created by the Emperor's Privy Council post-Outbreak to communicate between the High Council and the Inventors. It certainly wasn't a boring job; there were meetings with various councilors of all social statuses, translating or transcribing a multitude of documents for one group or another, and even observing cure simulations (although these meetings were usually for her superiors).

"What's with you, Alyn?" Her co-worker and friend, Kalin Rhys, appeared beside her as they went through security check.

Vespyr heaved an exaggerated sigh. "Oh, you know, I have that meeting with Lord Vanmir this afternoon. I'm not entirely convinced I will be able to persuade his lordship to withdraw his proposal."

Kalin winced sympathetically, "Yes, his lordship is one of the more delusional of the aristocracy. His brilliant plan?"

"Some cocktail of drugs that would inoculate humans against the plague. It's not completely ridiculous, but his methods of testing are not wholly ethical."

"Shoot someone up with these mystery drugs and send them Below?"

Vespyr nodded. "I'm not saying the idea hasn't been bandied about before," she admitted, "but to be sanctioned by the Council? Could you imagine the nightmare that would happen if the news hawkers caught wind of it?"

"And Lord Vanmir is the sort of man who wouldn't give a damn about that." Kalin shook her head, "It's a wonder he hasn't caused more trouble by now."

"That we know of," Vespyr noted. "I'm counting my blessings that I don't have to deal with him as regularly as his staff. Can you imagine the kind of stress those people must have?"

"I shudder to think," Kalin replied wryly. "You have plans after work? I was thinking we could go to the tav for a few drinks."

"That sounds like a splendid plan. Ahmetz knows I'll probably need it."

The day didn't go as badly as Vespyr had anticipated. She didn't have to deal with Lord Vanmir as directly as she thought. Thankfully, she was not the only person who thought his drug concoction would not be readily accepted. She did, however, have to compose a flattering communiqué expressing the Liaison Office's gratitude and appreciation for his hard work. It was a fair trade as far as she was concerned.

Her next project was not as exciting, but it was tedious. Her superior dropped a file at her desk from Inventor Erlich, a delightful but somewhat doddering old gentleman with almost indecipherable handwriting. His latest report either suggested swanskin or zomb-kin were beginning to appear near the Shunniran capital. While some part of her hoped for swans, she knew the elegant creatures were not as common as they once were. Unless they were Zomb swans. She squinted at the writing some more. Could Erlich have meant Automazomb swans?

Rubbing her eyes, she decided she needed to get up and look at something that wasn't scrawl for a while. She wandered over to the common area and made herself some tea.

Some of her co-workers were also in the vicinity. She chatted with them easily about the state of the world, various projects, and even a little gossip.

"I'm telling you," She heard one fellow, Jarvis, say, "there's something quite odd about Lord Mudassame's youngest daughter."

"Why? Because she has the good sense not to dance with someone like you?"

This comment earned a few guffaws. Vespyr didn't hear Jarvis's reply, though. She had never cared much for the social politics part of the job. She was poised and educated enough to fit in when she was required to attend social events with the Liaison Office, but with the exception of her weekly dinners at the Palace Hotel, she kept a low profile.

Vespyr was grateful when Kalin came around to her office at the end of the day. "You might have to guide me out of the building," she remarked. "I'm fairly certain I've gone blind."

Kalin chuckled, "Who's handiwork were you looking over?"

"Have you ever read Inventor Erlich's writing?" Kalin shook her head. "Not only has his writing deteriorated to scratch, but he also slips between Ancient and Modern Teraltian."

"You would think for such clever people they would use Guild Standard."

"That would make our jobs too easy." Vespyr stretched, allowing her cramped muscles to uncoil from their previously contorted position. "Just the two of us?"

"If that's all right with you?"

"Certainly. After dinner with Alina last night, I could definitely go for a quiet evening."

Vespyr and Kalin wandered down to Rosilyn Tavern, a chic yet cozy little establishment with dark wood paneling and lit with soft lights. It was a favorite of theirs because it was never full to bursting like some of the louder, more colorful tavs they sometimes went to with their co-workers.

A few patrons were at the bar when they arrived, white-collar workers much like themselves, and a group of scholars situated at a corner table, their bright green tunics and gratuitous gesticulations giving them away. Vespyr and Kalin found a table along the wall that was still intimate enough to have a conversation without others accidentally listening in. Not that it was a great concern to have their discussion overheard, but neither woman was fond of eavesdropping.

"Hiya ladies," Rosie greeted cheerfully when she arrived at their table. She dropped off a bowl of bread and oil. "Whatcha havin' tonight?"

"What sorta brew ya got today, love?" Kalin's dialect always slipped when she was around Rosie, who was from the same borough of the Middle City. Vespyr was always amazed at how easily Kalin could transition from one tongue to the other. It was a talent that made Kalin a valuable member of the Office since she could put the Lower staff at ease.

"Got us a lovely dark 'un tha's been brought in from Kibou if'n ya wanta sup."

"Grand." Kalin looked to Vespyr, "Wine for you?"

Vespyr smiled, "A glass of red, please."

"One of these days, I'll have you drinking something heartier," Kalin declared once their drinks arrived.

Vespyr laughed. "Not likely unless you want to put me out of commission for two days. Brews always give me headaches."

"You just need to acclimate yourself to them," her friend advised.

Their conversation drifted to the job, as was habit. Both women needed to vent a little about their projects or assignments away from the office. But Vespyr and Kalin were friends as well as co-workers.

"How was Alina's rotating cadre of lickspittles?"

Vespyr tilted her head slightly, "Not as bad as I was expecting. I mean, Alina invited some of her more colorful friends, but Kevan was there to keep me sane."

Kalin's eyes sparkled mischievously, "Oooh. Kevan. Isn't he one of your sister's cuter friends?"

"What, you want me to set you up?"

"Not for me, dummy. For yourself. You need a love life."

"With Kevan? He's like a brother!"

"Okay, then if not Kevan, you should let me set you up with one of my friends. I know a fellow who…"

"No!"

"One of my lasses, then?" Kalin's brow furrowed in puzzlement, "Huh. I thought for sure you were interested in chaps…"

"I like men just fine!" Vespyr said quickly. For as empty as the tav common room was, she suddenly felt like everyone was listening to their conversation. She drained her glass and then gestured to Rosie for another one.

Kalin's lip quirked. "What's with you?" she asked. "This topic doesn't usually make you so thirsty."

"I just…don't want to talk about relationships."

"Who said anything about relationships? I just mentioned maybe setting you up on a date. One date, not a binding ceremony or anything."

Vespyr toyed with her empty glass. "Yeah," she said, at length. "I suppose you're right."

Kalin's clasped her hand over Vespyr's companionably, "Seriously, it's just a date or something. There's more to our lives than the Liaison's Office. You haven't dated seriously since what's his name."

"Gareth."

"Whatever. You should have some fun."

"Well…"

"You know what I mean." She leaned in surreptitiously. "So what kind of fellow am I scouting for? Ridiculously handsome? Sensitive and thoughtful? I don't even remember what Gareth was like."

"He was nice," Vespyr offered.

"That's all you can say about him? Well, I knew there was a reason I didn't care for him. Or remember him for that matter."

Vespyr found her mind drifting back to the skyway and the beautiful stranger. His suit, the way he stood, the disposition she imagined him having. She sighed dreamily and said, "Someone who displays confidence and class would be lovely." before she can stop herself. She cleared her throat and clarified, "Someone who looked… er, he *would* look like someone my parents would have approved of."

"Okay, that's something. So, a moneyed individual. Classy, impeccably dressed…"

Vespyr blushed.

"You're making me sound like a snob."

"Not a snob," Kalin argued, "you just have standards. There's nothing wrong with that."

* * *

Unsurprisingly, Vespyr left the tav in a more pensive mood than she'd arrived, which somewhat defeated the purpose of the outing. Her stupid conversation with Kalin brought her mystery man back to the fore of her mind; his face a vivid vision as if he stood in front of her, close enough to touch. "This is absurd," she muttered to herself, physically shaking her head as if it would make a difference. "Since when did I obsess over a stranger?" Her sister Alina was more likely to become infatuated with someone she hardly knew. Her sister ran with the social elite and often fickly favored some upstanding citizen she'd never met based on hearsay.

That wasn't Vespyr. Vespyr preferred to think things through. Even her relationship with Gareth had been properly founded and nurtured, even if it did fail in the end. But perhaps Kalin's chiding had some merit. Perhaps she should indulge in a fling. It would certainly make things interesting.

She was so absorbed in her thoughts that she didn't realize she'd walked as far as Doran Station, a fair distance from where she began. "The second bloody day in a row I do something stupid." *Great, and now I've picked up talking to myself as well.*

The skyrail was moderately full when she stepped onto the carriage. There were still a few seats available here and there so it wasn't necessary to make a quick dash in. She rifled through her folio for a document to peruse on the way home.

"Doors closing," the conductor called. As with any public transport, there was always someone who managed to squeeze him- or herself between the narrow gap of the rapidly closing doors. Vespyr was rarely one of those people, but she'd seen others get clipped or trapped. It became her habit to never look up at the closing door if she could avoid it.

And yet, on this particular occasion, she chanced to watch none other than her mystery man deftly slide himself inside the carriage. She squeezed her eyes shut momentarily thinking the alcohol had suddenly induced visions. But when she opened them again, she was not mistaken. Her beautiful stranger had indeed come onto her carriage for the second time.

For someone who narrowly missed being squished by two metal doors, he was remarkably unruffled. He wasn't fazed, as if dashing onto the skyrail was a regular occurrence, a well-practiced dance. Today, his suit was a tailored dark blue with snowy white cuffs peeking out, clasped together with silver links in the shape of a gear-and-flask. It was a handsome, dignified way to declare he was a chemist of the Inventors Guild.

Today, she could see his eyes; they were just as intense as she imagined. He scanned the crowd, his gaze quick to shift from one person to the next. *Gods, does he see me staring?* Quickly, she looked back down at her notes. When she felt it was safe to look up again, his eyes had passed her over. Something about that saddened her. How could he dismiss her so quickly?

"This isn't something you can simply ignore." He spoke. Her beautiful stranger actually uttered words. Seven words in a rich baritone timbre.

A gentleman a few seats away from her audibly groaned, "Dammit, Endros, we're out of the office. Can't you let it rest till tomorrow?"

Endros strode toward the man purposefully. "Clearly not, Merchell, or I wouldn't have chased you onto the rail." He pulled a packet from his own folio, "These aren't going away just because you leave. You have to give them more than a once-over. We can't possibly…"

"Mind your words, sir," Merchell warned in a tone that demanded acquiescence. Vespyr watched, awed, as Endros and Merchell seemed to square off. The fierce, hazel eyes of her beautiful stranger met the equally unrelenting eyes of Merchell.

"Next stop," Endros replied.

Merchell's eyes narrowed. For a moment, Vespyr believed he would refuse. "You're making a mistake, Cortnay Endros."

"Not nearly as big a one as you would be making, my lord Merchell."

"The next stop will be Taylor Street."

"After you, my lord," Cortnay Endros gestured.

The two gentlemen moved to the doorway. It was only then that Vespyr had a good look at Rickard Merchell, Lord Advocate of His Excellency's Council. She knew the man well, having met him socially and having dealt with him through the Liaison's Office. He frequently had the ear of the Emperor—through the Prince Regent, of course—a fact that often annoyed his fellow councilors, especially since his title was a courtesy and not hereditary nobility. His "peers" often found it degrading to have to be subject to his authority.

But the fact that her beautiful stranger spoke to a man as important as Lord Advocate Merchell in such a manner that would get most men arrested wasn't what captured her interest. No. She was more interested in the fact that her beautiful stranger had a *name*.

Cortnay Endros. His name is Cortnay Endros. Why did that name seem so familiar?

· * * *

Vespyr would learn why the name was so familiar the following day at the office. She received yet another request for consideration from Lord Vanmir. The name that leapt off the page was *Cortnay Endros, Lead Chemist.* Cortnay worked for Lord Vanmir? All this time she'd been dismissing these reports and requests, and she could have…

Wait. What was she thinking? She dismissed these requests because they were unethical! *Not* because the research was unsound. With an audible but unintelligible sound of derision, she threw the request aside.

"What's got you this time, Vespyr?" Kalin appeared at her doorway, two steaming mugs of tea in hand.

"I *just* sent Lord Vanmir a communiqué yesterday afternoon. Not even a full cycle has elapsed and I've got another request for consideration."

"Well, you can't say he doesn't care," Kalin quipped.

Vespyr took a sip of tea. "I have half a mind to take a meeting with him anyway to say to his face he's ridiculously immoral."

Kalin laughed out right. "I'd pay to see that! I can just picture you putting his lordship in his place. Speaking of meetings, we've got one right now."

Vespyr gave every appearance of attentiveness during the daily management meeting. But in truth, her mind kept wandering back to Lord Vanmir's request. It wouldn't be completely out of the realm of possibility to feign interest in his research, or at least meet his team. That wouldn't be wholly unethical on her part, would it?

She somehow managed to go through three other reports and requests while still thinking about Cortnay Endros. She ate lunch with her co-workers – she even participated in a lively debate about new tariffs – while still thinking about Cortnay Endros. She conducted a presentation on Inventor Erlich's findings on the current state of plants Below to three of her superiors while still thinking about Cortnay Endros.

When she left work that evening, she had Lord Vanmir's request tucked into her folio. She resolved to give this new request some serious attention. Not work-attention, no, that wouldn't be right. But afterhours, on her own time, that was taking initiative. She would not treat Cortnay Edros's work the same way Lord Advocate Merchell did. She would give it the proper attention it deserved.

"The next stop will be Doran Station."

Doran. Cortnay has gotten on the skyrail at Doran. Vespyr did not look up when the doors opened and the rush of passengers entered the carriage. She did not want to appear too desperate. There was also no guarantee that he would even use the skyrail again today. And even if he did, he might get on another carriage all together. She would not walk up and down the skyrail again. No. She would stay right where she was and casually scan the crowd.

Verdellen was with her. There by the door stood Cortnay Endros. He did not appear as intense as he had the day before when he confronted the Lord Advocate, but he did not seem relaxed as he had the first day she saw him either. He stood like a man who spent many hours poring over potions and formulas (or perhaps she just projected that upon since she knew his occupation). He wore a suit of dark olive, a color that did not always compliment people but seemed perfectly acceptable on him.

Vespyr convinced herself that it was propriety preventing her from walking up to him. Of course, she had never been one to strike up conversations with strangers on the skyrail. She could do so if the spirit moved her, or when she was forced to at a work social function. But speaking to Cortnay Endros shouldn't be a whim or small talk. It should be official business. She also convinced herself not to follow him as he got off at D'alynic Station. (She did watch him exit the carriage and tracked his movements until he disappeared into the crowd.)

After he left, she pulled out Lord Vanmir's request for consideration, pressing it close to herself, as if holding it close was the same as holding her beautiful stranger.

* * *

Despite Vespyr's former resolve to put her beautiful stranger from her mind, the gods intervened. Yes. It was the work of Verdellen or Ananya...perhaps it was all the gods working together! Whatever the reason, Vespyr now believed that thinking about Cortnay Endros was not a complete waste of time.

She went home that evening and ate her supper while reading over Lord Vanmir's request. He seemed to tone down his initial proposal and now suggested using animals to conduct his experiment. This option was certainly more tolerable than the idea of rounding up "volunteers" (most likely from the Undercity). It was still disquieting, of course, but definitely more tolerable. In her new communiqué, she expressed her appreciation on behalf of the Liaison's Office but this time she included clarification questions. How would the animals be acquired? What sort of control group would he use? How could he be sure the effects on humans and these animals would be the same? Vespyr made sure to send the message through the pneumatics directly lest it be misplaced or lost.

That evening she dreamed of Cortnay Endros. They were once again on the skyrail where they first met. She complimented him on his work with Lord Vanmir. He was pleased she gave it the green light.

"Of course," she answered, "it is the closest thing we have to a solution." She knew it was a gross exaggeration, but he was too beautiful to deny. He smiled brilliantly. "The skyrail is hardly the place to discuss this in greater detail," he noted. "We should find a place with a bit more ambiance, perhaps a bit more privacy?"

"That would be delightful."

They ended up at The Palace Hotel. It seemed Cortnay was an even better customer than Vespyr and her sister since they were conducted to one of the private dining areas. The menu was picked out: a starter of mixed greens sprinkled with almonds, a honeyed roast fowl, venison served in hollowed out black bread, potatoes baked in cheese sauce and topped with bacon, a dessert of lemon cakes and coffee.

Cortnay spoke passionately about his work and his studies. He believed there was a chance to reclaim Below within the Emperor's lifetime – something others scoffed at since it was a poorly kept secret that His Imperial Majesty had been in poor health after the attempt on his life by Irenorn separatists.

All the while, Vespyr listened attentively, asking questions when appropriate, laughing at well-timed jokes. It was not difficult to act naturally around Cortnay Endros. He was charming and charismatic as well as handsome. He was good-natured and passionate about the world. He was perfect.

* * *

Vespyr went to work in the most jovial mood; there was far more warmth to her salutations and a bright smile upon her lips. This isn't to say that she was always cold to her co-workers, more that she tried to be amiable but professional. Today she was downright friendly.

"If I didn't know any better, I'd say someone got lucky last night." Kalin dropped a file on to Vespyr's desk. "I guess you don't need me to set you up with anyone after all."

"Oh stop," Vespyr rejoined weakly, a faint blush coloring her features. "Can't I be in a good mood once in a while?"

"Sure," her friend agreed, "Once in a while. But I've known you for a few years now, Vespyr, and I don't think I've ever seen you like this. Not bursting with good cheer. You don't usually gush until we're alone. Even Jarvis asked me if I knew what was up with you. So spill."

Vespyr schooled her features, but the smile would not be quelled. "There's nothing to spill. I just had a really good night's sleep."

"If you say so, love," Kalin conceded, her expression dubious.

After her conversation with Kalin, Vespyr put a conscious effort to appearing normal. It was not too difficult a task, but every so often, when she remembered Cortnay, a wide smile broke out. Somewhere in the back of her mind there was always Cortnay. It's what got her through the day.

She hoped to see him again on the skyrail that evening. Unfortunately, Cortnay Endros did not appear at his usual station. Vespyr was surprised to realize she was actually disappointed. She had been looking forward to seeing him all day. With a heavy sigh, she pulled out her daily bulletin to read for the rest of the journey.

Vespyr felt strangely deflated when she keyed into her apartment. After running on such a high all day and not actually seeing the object of her desire, she was drained. She did not put him from her mind, however. No. If the gods deigned to cross their paths it must be for a reason. Just because she did not see him today did not mean she would never see him again. That thought cheered her somewhat.

Of course! Cortnay was probably working late with Lord Vanmir or at his lordship's request. He was very hard working and conscientious, after all. And she did just send Lord Vanmir a communiqué last night regarding his most recent request. They were probably answering her queries this very evening.

Satisfied with this knowledge, Vespyr no longer despaired. She did not need to see Cortnay Endros every day. Absence makes the heart grow fonder, as they say.

* * *

It would be three days' time before she would see Cortnay Endros again, though every night she dreamed of him. The dreams started out rather professionally; they discussed his project and even the state of some of the other projects they both knew about. Sometimes they would talk about His Imperial Majesty and the rumors circulating throughout Court regarding his health. Eventually, they would spend the remainder of their time together as any pair of lovers would.

These dreams were peculiar to Vespyr. She could scarcely recall any of her other dreams as vividly as she could these dreams of Cortnay. Likewise, she didn't know she could dream the same type of dream sequentially. Perhaps this was another sign from the gods that their union was meant to be. Why else would Cortnay Endros seemingly permeate every fiber of her being?

Lord Vanmir had yet to respond to her initial communiqué, which she found somewhat unlike him. Of course, every other time she had to deal with him she rejected his requests. Perhaps his lordship was suggesting to Cortnay that he take a meeting with her personally to work out some of the problems she saw. Oh, she hoped that he was not insulted, her Cortnay. No. He would not interpret her inquiries as incompetence. He would see them as intelligent concerns from an intelligent woman. (They had already discussed some of these issues, just not yet in person.)

Three days after she took Lord Vanmir's request to review, one of her supervisors stopped in to her office.

"Did you approve this?" Loral Niall placed Lord Vanmir's file in front of her.

"It's not approved," Vespyr explained. "But I did send him feedback regarding it."

Loral arched a brow, "I didn't think you thought much of Lord Vanmir's experiments."

"This one seemed different. I think it has potential."

"If you're sure…"

"I wouldn't have considered it if I did not think so."

"Of course not," Loral agreed. She knew Vespyr Alyn to be one the Liaison Office's most critical employees. She did not take anything lightly when it came to requests. "Be sure to let me know how this one pans out. I'd be curious to see if it works."

Vespyr nodded dutifully. Kalin spoke to her about her brief meeting with Loral later that evening. Apparently, Kalin overheard Loral talking to one of their other supervisors.

"Did you go over their heads, Vespyr?"

"I would never!" she exclaimed, aghast.

"Well, Loral seems to think so. You usually send Lord Vanmir's requests through her office, and this time, you just sent him something directly. That's how they found out about it, you know. Lord Vanmir wanted to confirm with them that this was actually being reviewed."

"Bureaucracy," Vespyr sighed.

"If I didn't know better, Vespyr Alyn, I would suspect you were trying to move up in the world."

She was honestly surprised by Kalin's comment. "What do you mean? I'm just doing my job."

"In all the time we've worked together, I've never known you to disregard protocol."

"I did no such thing!" she protested. "It was completely informal. I just wanted his lordship to know that were he to clarify some things, we might take his request more seriously." Vespyr looked panicked. "Do you think I should speak to Loral more formally tomorrow? I honestly didn't think I was overstepping anyone's authority. Usually I…"

"Okay, okay," Kalin assured her friend. "I'm sorry if I gave you the wrong impression, love. It was just a curious situation that seemed rather unlike you."

Vespyr weighed Kalin's words on her rail journey home. Had she let her love for Cortnay affect her work? How could she have done such a thing?

"The next stop will be Doran Station."

Vespyr looked up sharply. Doran Station. Cortnay's station. Cortnay worked nearby. She knew the address. Perhaps she should go and speak to Lord Vanmir and explain the situation. To give a poor impression of herself did nothing to impress his lordship of her sincerity, nor her professionalism.

Compelled by propriety, she disembarked from the skyrail at Doran Station. Lord Vanmir's workplace was a few minutes' walk from the stop.

She made it all the way to the guard's desk before she realized she was being absurd. "What in the name of Ananya am I *doing?*" she muttered under her breath. "This would only make things more complicated!" With a huff, she turned on her heel and saw the most beautiful thing she could hope to see.

Cortnay. He was standing by the entrance. He must have come some other way, for she knew if she'd seen him she would not have passed him so casually. He was speaking with someone she assumed was a colleague. From her vantage point, he was speaking far more respectfully to this individual than he had with the Lord Advocate.

"Was there something I could help you with, miss?"

Vespyr barely acknowledged the guard. "No thank you," she answered brusquely. The object of her desire was leaving! He must be off to the skyrail! She quickened her step across the foyer to keep sight of Cortnay. He walked with his colleague some of the way before parting from the other by the station. She looked at her timepiece. It was a quarter past the hour. Perhaps this was the reason she hadn't seen him in days; he'd been taking the rail an hour after hers!

She followed her dream lover to the platform, watching him from the corner of her eye. She was not bold enough to stand right beside him; that would be too forward, despite their many meetings in her dreams. She was but two people away from him, though. She was still close enough that if she wanted to, she could reach out and touch him.

When the train arrived, she boarded one person after Cortnay. She smiled, delighted at his chivalry, as she watched Cortnay approach an open seat, then offer it to a female passenger once he realized she, too, had hoped to sit down. Cortnay seemed content to stand. With the rush of people boarding the carriage, Vespyr ended up right next to him. Right next to him! And she did nothing to manipulate this arrangement.

Thank you, Verdellen! She offered silently. She once again schooled her features into a mask of indifference, but inwardly she was elated to be so close to her dream lover.

It was not her moment, however, to make her dreams play out in reality. Especially after being questioned by Loral Niall and cautioned by Kalin. She resisted the urge to bring up Lord Vanmir and his request. Instead, she contented herself to be in Cortnay's presence. She memorized his features; he was even more handsome than she remembered. She inhaled deeply (but subtly); he smelled of expensive cologne and a hint of the chemicals he probably worked with. She "accidentally" brushed against him when the flow of people shifted at Taylor Street; he was solid but gentle (as she brushed against him, he did not tense but rather absorbed the contact). This encounter reaffirmed what she already knew to be true: Cortnay Endros was perfect.

* * *

Since that day, Vespyr paid even closer attention to her work. She did not want to give anyone the wrong impression again. She did end up speaking with Loral Niall and two other colleagues regarding her communiqué. Vespyr explained that Lord Vanmir's persistent submissions were a distraction from their goal. The regularity of them and the equally regular dismissals might soon overlook a real solution. Why not critically review his submission and offer more efficient feedback that would benefit both parties?

No one could find fault with Vespyr's presentation. She was even complimented for the thought. She was relieved that her work was no longer considered greedy ambition.

Lord Vanmir's case was not her main project, though. She remained on the primary team, but since the Liaison's in-house inventors were now reviewing the proposal more seriously, she would not be needed as a consult until later in the process. She was pleased she was able to help Cortnay, but at the same time she was disappointed because it meant her formal meeting with him would be at a much later time.

Vespyr took to staying at the office a bit later than usual. The only way Kalin could coax her out anymore was if she stayed later herself, and even then it was no guarantee. When Vespyr would beg off yet again, Kalin could only shake her head and quip about her friend's sudden inspiration. "I guess I was wrong," she remarked, "with the hours you put in there's no way you could be seeing anyone."

A slow, secret smile pulled at Vespyr's lips. *I see someone quite regularly,* she thought. *Every night in fact.*

When the evening chime sounded, and the night watch was beginning their rounds, Vespyr took her leave of the office. She walked to the station leisurely, so she wouldn't catch the skyrail *too* early.

Tonight, Vespyr decided. *I'll speak to him tonight. It will be like any other time we've spoken.* She'd seen Cortnay on the train for the past fortnight. Sufficient time had passed and it was time to make her dreams come true. She would have a few of Lord Vanmir's plans in hand when she would "accidentally" bump in to him. He would gallantly help her pick up the papers and realize they were familiar to him. That would get them talking. There was only a slight edge of unprofessionalism to it – having important files like that out could lead to disaster – but Cortnay would recognize she was dedicated to finding a solution, even if it meant continuing work on the skyrail.

Vespyr checked the documents obsessively since sitting down. Cortnay seemed to favor the second-to-last carriage (she'd walked the length of the skyrail in search of him a few times); she couldn't stage exactly where this interaction would take place (if only there weren't so many people on the train!) but she could ensure the opportunity would be there. Best case scenario would be the two of them sitting together; scanning the carriage it was still a possibility since there were indeed open seats, but Doran Station was a popular transfer point and heavily populated.

"Doran Station." The skyrail announcer's voice had never sounded so sweet.

The usual rush of people flooded the carriage. Unfortunately, there was someone absent from the crowd. The adrenaline that coursed through her body now fueled panic. *No. I had a plan. I had a good plan.* She promptly abandoned her seat. *Check the other cars. It will be okay. Actually, it will be better. I can drop the papers in his presence as I'm looking for a space in the carriage. Yes. It will be more plausible this way. Why didn't I think of this before?*

Vespyr went through the train twice before deciding to abandon her search. *I must have missed him.* Then she brightened. *The next train! Maybe he was running late!* There were still a few more stops until the end of the line. She decided to get off the next station and try the following train. Vespyr walked up and down the next two trains before her shoulders slumped dejectedly. *I missed him. How could I miss him?*

She had spent nearly an hour on the skyrail and had yet to make her destination. Vespyr composed herself. She would not let this setback get her down. If this was not the time and place to make formal introductions to the love of her life, then so be it.

It was late. She did not want to go home. Not alone. It was the middle of the work week. She had canceled the last two dinners with her sister. Vespyr knew Alina would still be at the Palace. With every appearance of a consummate professional, she boarded the skyrail back toward the city centre. She would not let her disappointment consume her; she would not indulge in self-pity.

"Miss Vespyr, lovely to see you again," the maître d' greeted cordially.

"And you," she replied, smiling.

"Miss Alina is dining in the Clifton Room this evening."

Vespyr arched a brow; and the gentleman explained: "She dines with his lordship the Lord Advocate this evening."

"Of course," Vespyr said absently.

The maître d' gestured for Vespyr to follow him. He conducted her through the crowded dining room towards the private rooms in the back. These rooms were usually reserved for the Palace's elite guests. It was rumored that His Royal Highness the Crown Prince dined there on occasion.

Alina and the Lord Advocate were laughing when the maître d' ushered her in to the room. "Miss Vespyr Alyn," he announced. It was an old-fashioned practice, but the Palace Hotel prided itself on tradition.

"Vespyr!" Alina cried happily. From the sound of it, she was a little tipsy. "I didn't think I'd see you again for a while!"

"I decided it's been too long, sister," she explained, leaning down to kiss Alina's cheeks. The Lord Advocate was already on his feet by the time she righted herself again.

Vespyr proffered her hand to him, which he kissed. "Good evening, my Lord Advocate. It's nice to see you again. How ever did my sister convince his lordship to join her?"

"We met the other night at one of Lady Mudassame's elegant soirees. Can you believe his lordship has never dined here? I deemed it a travesty and insisted that he join me one evening, and wouldn't you know it? Tonight's that evening!"

Vespyr could not help but smile at her sister's enthusiastic story telling. At least the Lord Advocate wasn't in Alina's circle of ever-rotating gentleman callers. Or if he were, his lordship was at least a contributing member of society.

"Did you want to order dinner, miss?" the Lord Advocate queried, gesturing for his bodyguard to fetch a waiter.

"You are too kind, my lord. A small dish would do."

More food and drink was ordered and more stories were recounted. Vespyr had apparently been living under a rock and needed to know all that was happening in the glittering social circles her sister frequented.

"Why haven't I seen you at any of these events, Miss Vespyr?"

"Please, my lord, Vespyr is fine. As for why I haven't been seen socially, well, I regret that my work keeps me much occupied."

"Ah, that's right! You work for the Liaison's Office."

Vespyr smiled, "Yes, sir. It does not always afford me the time for much else."

"I can't believe that's true," Merchell countered. "Even the various councils have the time to kick back once in a while."

"I'm not one for parties the same way Alina is," she answered.

Her sister laughed, "I usually have to trick her into coming out with me. And even then she may only stay for an hour. I keep telling her she'll never meet anyone that way."

Vespyr smiled at Alina. At another time, she would have blushed or chided her sister for embarrassing her in front of other people. But Alina had no idea of her newfound love. Vespyr could not speak of it, either. Not yet, anyway.

"Have there been any new cases you can speak of, my lord?" Vespyr inquired, trying to deflect attention from her.

"Not much of note, really. Crime still exists at a time of such crisis; I suppose it is a testament to how society will continue to function despite the world falling apart."

Vespyr nodded along, thinking of Cortnay's work on a plague cure. There too, society continued to press on. It made her optimistic for the future.

"If everything continued to crumble then that would well and truly be the end of the world. But there is some hope."

"What are you referring to, sister mine?" Alina asked. "Any new developments?"

"There are always developments," Vespyr said. "Whether they come to anything is the tricky part."

Merchell snorted, "The Inventors are always coming up with ideas, but rarely real solutions."

Vespyr quirked a brow. "My lord?"

"I'm sorry," Merchell answered. "I've just been having some issues with a friend of mine."

Vespyr thought back to the day she learned Cortnay's name. Were her lover and the Lord Advocate friends? "Are you permitted to expand upon that?"

Merchell poured another glass of wine. He regarded both Vespyr and Alina critically before explaining. "Only that I have a good friend working for someone on the Inventor's Council. I worry that his ethics will become compromised if he continues to expand upon his theories. He is a good man, truly. But his dedication to solving the world's problems sometimes clouds his judgment."

"'Dedication' doesn't sound too terrible, in fact, I would call it admirable. And if it brings about a solution..." Vespyr added hesitantly.

"The cost may be too much."

"An outbreak of the plague in the skies would be too great of a cost. Anything short of sacrificing good lives might be a necessary evil to protect the whole of humanity."

Alina stared at her sister incredulously while the Lord Advocate merely raised a brow. "That's strangely callous for you, Vespyr."

"Is it?" she answered, "I don't know. Perhaps it is simply that my eyes have been opened to other possibilities, harsh though they may be. I'm sure the good Lord Advocate has seen the same reports and the like as I have. There are no longer many options left for us. We must do *something*, and unorthodox theories may help us find the right solution." Vespyr directed most of this to Rickard Merchell. She wondered at his lordship's reaction. Would he remain cordial to an acquaintance? Or would he not bother with niceties?

Merchell regarded Vespyr, his expression unreadable. Vespyr had verbally sparred with Inventors and Councilors alike; his lordship did not intimidate her, as he would have expected. After a taut few moments, he smiled coldly. "There are many evils in this world, Miss Alyn. Horrors as we were never meant to see have become a reality for us. I have the same hopes that any of us: a world free of plague, a future for our children and the generations to follow."

It was a diplomat's answer. Vespyr herself had used such words to placate various officials and colleagues; it came with the job. How could she expect anything less from a man in a similar position? Still, she was defending Cortnay. She knew she was defending Cortnay. Cortnay needed her to fight for their position.

Alas, she took too much time coming up with the perfect retort. Alina, who had been watching the short and fraught exchange nervously, finally had the opportunity to change the subject. "Well, I couldn't have said it better myself. More wine, my lord?"

The Lord Advocate's blank expression morphed. "Splendid," he answered pleasantly, proffering his glass to Alina.

Vespyr clenched her teeth. She could not bring it up again. Well, she could, but she lost steam. She lost this one. But hadn't lost all. There was still hope. She rose from her seat delicately. "My lord, my dear sister, I regret that I must take leave. I have a few things I need to take care of at home." She dipped her head to his lordship, "It's been a pleasure."

His smile was smug. "The pleasure was all mine, Miss Alyn."

Vespyr departed gracefully. She had intended to storm out of the room, but her anger gave way to determination. Now more than ever, she wanted make hers and Cortnay's vision a reality. Together they would be able to put his lordship Rickard Merchell in his place.

She caught the skyrail back to the Liaison's Office. She presented her pass to the evening checkpoint. It was rare for anyone to be in the office at this hour, but it was not unheard of. She hadn't been kept in the loop regarding the Vanmir project. It was protocol. There would be a formal presentation at a more critical point in the process. But she knew where she could find the reports.

Vespyr went to her office first to consider her options. She could speak with one of the security personnel and ask for a key… but they would probably ask questions. Could she risk it? No. There had to be another way. She checked the time. It was a little after midnight. The cleaning crews must have gone home by now. Oh! But they leave their keys in the janitor's office. Perfect!

She went to the common area and located the handtowels. She grabbed them by the fistful and stuffed them into a wastebin. Then she found a mug and filled it with old coffee. She brought it back to her office and threw it on the ground. "Dammit!"

The noise caught the attention of one of the security guards. He appeared within minutes of her dropping the mug. "Miss Alyn?"

She looked sheepishly, "Sorry. I'm a bit off-kilter this evening. I'll just go and get some towels to clean this up."

'George', as his nametag indicated, nodded. "Did you need any help?"

"I should be fine once I get some towels," Vespyr answered.

"I'll be on the floor if you need anything else."

Vespyr went to the common area once again. She was sure to make a lot of noise while she was there. She slammed one of the cabinet doors to the point of almost breaking it off its hinges for good measure.

George appeared again. "Miss Alyn?"

"Wouldn't you know it, George? There aren't any bloody towels here." She sighed heavily, heaving her shoulders for good measure. "I don't suppose you could let me into the janitor's closet."

"Of course, miss."

Vespyr followed him down the corridor. He unlocked the door and stepped aside to allow her into the room. She scanned the room for the towels she was supposed to be there for as well as where the cleaning crew kept their keys. She spied one left on the desk.

She stepped over to the corkboard hanging above the desk. "I've never been in here before," she noted.

"I can't imagine you'd have need, miss," George observed. He'd been standing in the doorway waiting for her to get the supplies she needed, otherwise she would have just taken the keys outright.

"I suppose not." As she turned to face him she surreptitiously slipped the keys into her pocket. Crossing back to where the towels were, she retrieved a bundle and stepped out. "Thank you, George. You've been a great help."

He eyed her curiously, "I just opened a door, miss."

She smiled sweetly at him. "That may be, but it's one I needed opened. And I couldn't have done it without your help."

George returned the smile, though it looked more polite than friendly. "Let me know if you need anything else, miss."

"You'll be on this floor?"

"I'm almost finished here and then I have to go upstairs. But if you want me to stay…"

"No, of course not. I wouldn't want to keep you from completing your rounds. But if I needed you…?"

"If it's not an emergency, I'll be back in about half an hour. But if you have any cause for alarm, there's the call button right at the entrance."

"You know, I never knew what that was for. The things I'm learning about my own office. Well, thank you again, George."

They parted ways. Vespyr took her time cleaning up the spilled coffee and replacing the towels. She also took care in making the common room look no different than it had earlier. (She may have been a little overzealous in her search for the "missing" towels.)

Once she was confident the security guard had gone, she hurried over to Loral Niall's office. The reports would most likely be on Loral's desk. At least, she hoped they would be. It was a major project, so it wouldn't still be in the planning stages.

She rifled through a few papers that were left out in the open before turning to the ones in the file sorter. There! She grabbed the file and returned to her office. Vespyr was surprised to realize her heart was pounding as if she'd just run a mile. First, she tricked a security guard and then she stole a file from her colleague. Her relationship with Cortnay was bringing out a whole new side of her. It was actually quite exhilarating.

Vespyr closed her eyes and calmed her breathing. Now she would find out just how much longer she and Cortnay would have to wait until they could meet again.

The very first document of the file contained all the necessary data she needed. Each project was graded in levels from one to five, five being the least likely for a project to receive priority. Only a few proposals ever got rejected once they made it past the screening phase. She looked to the bottom line: Level 5

Level 5! Their project was only a Level 5! How could that be? Vespyr started to leaf through the various documents to find out more. She took no notice to the passage of time as she read page after page of the report, scrutinizing each notation and making notes of her own. The concerns didn't seem to be such great detriments that the whole project had to be ranked so lowly on the scale. There was a slight problem with funding; Lord Vanmir had pedigree but he lacked the depth of wealth needed to purchase the amount of chemicals and materials needed to complete the serum.

And of course, the biggest concern: test subjects. They had conceded to animal trials, which didn't need so much Imperial approval. She saw in the notes that the animals were showing signs of improvement. But that meant now they were back to the same problem as when Vespyr first came across the file. How in the world were they going to test the serum to find out if it works?

Prisoners from the Iceberg made the most sense. They were already cast out from society. That did not mean they should be treated as non-humans, but surely there could be volunteers from the prison. Perhaps if offered a reduced sentence?

Vespyr felt positively drained after reading through the file. How many more setbacks did she and Cortnay have to endure until they could finally be happy? She returned the file before anyone came into the office to begin the workday. She did not feel like working herself, so she took the day off. She desperately needed to see Cortnay.

* * *

"Feeling better?" Kalin stood in the doorway with an expression of concern.

Vespyr looked up from reading a request for the Inventors to build a detection device to uncover new sources of fuel without help from the (potentially infected) landbound workers. Not that she'd absorbed anything she read that morning. She had taken the last two days off to try and recover from the horrible disappointment she'd uncovered. She could not bring herself to see Cortnay despite her own deeper desire. How could she face him knowing she had failed their cause so miserably? She should have pursued the project's status more aggressively, she should have tried to find the funds herself, she should have—.

She forced a smile. "Much, thank you." She gestured to the various piles sorted on her desk. "Now I just have to catch up on all these requests."

"Do you need any help? I'm strangely ahead of schedule at the moment."

Vespyr considered Kalin's offer. If she handed off a few of the files, it would give her more time to work on hers and Cortnay's project. "I would really appreciate that. How many would you be able to take?"

Kalin entered the office fully and started to sort through some of the folders on the desk, picking out at least ten files. Vespyr calculated the time expenditure and figured it would take her friend the rest of the day to sort them out. "I'll check in at the end of the day to see how you're doing."

"Thanks."

Once Kalin was out of sight, Vespyr put aside the project she'd been working on and opened her desk drawer to retrieve a separate folder. She started her own work file on Cortnay's work. She did not claim to have a completely eidetic memory, but she remembered enough of the information to try and sort out how to resolve the issues. The first thing she decided to tackle was the funding. Vespyr was certain she could speak to Kevan, whose father was a prominent businessman with deep pockets and incredible influence in the corporate circles. If they had enough sponsors, that should subsidize the cost of production. She composed an informal communiqué to Kevan, keeping the content selective. She was informative but she didn't want to necessarily include the real reason the project was "on hold".

Next, Vespyr took on the test subject problem. Her superiors foolishly ruled out the use of felons…which probably also took the displaced dregs of the floating cities out of consideration. She scoffed to herself. She was certain Cortnay's serum worked; they were not endangering these castoffs of society. *Why worry over it? If it were this easy we wouldn't be at a Level 5. Think, Vespyr. What are you missing? I mean besides humans to take this serum. There has to be a way. We're so close!*

Who were the ones whose situations were dire enough that this solution might appeal to? Those already infected, or those in quarantine… these people were truly wretched. *Wretched and desperate. Yes! That's it! Loral and the others hadn't thought of this possibility. I must bring it to their attention at once.* Vespyr checked the time. She still had a little over a quarter of the workday left. She could put a presentation together and deliver it; admittedly, it wouldn't be the best one of her career, but she needed to make this project a top priority for the Liaison's Office.

She sent out a quick memo to the people involved. *I can do this, I can do this, I can do this. The sooner I get this done, the sooner I can be with Cortnay. Oh Cortnay. When you see how I've solved our problems you will be so proud.*

During the last hour of the day, Kalin returned with the files she'd taken from Vespyr earlier. "How's it going with you?"

Vespyr grinned. "Brilliant. I think I may have solved a problem one of my projects has been having. If I can convince Loral and her team of making this alteration, I might have a Level One."

"Really? What's the project?"

"If I told you that, you might try to steal it out from under me," Vespyr answered with a laugh.

Kalin regarded her quizzically. "Since when are you so concerned about such things?"

"This is really important to me, Kalin. I just don't want to jinx it. You know how it goes."

"Uh, sure." Kalin plastered a smile on her face, one Vespyr saw through easily. *She doesn't understand. Of course she doesn't understand. She doesn't have her entire life and happiness on the line as Cortnay and I do.* "When's the presentation?"

"In about ten minutes."

"Ten minutes? But it's nearly the end of the day!"

"I know. Sorry. I gotta run. Maybe I can meet up with you at Rosie's later? You know, to either celebrate or commiserate. What do you say?"

Now Kalin smiled genuinely. It had been weeks since they'd hung out together after work. "Count on it."

"I'll send you a message later. Wish me luck!"

Vespyr stood outside the conference room nervously. She hadn't been this nervous over a presentation since she first joined the Liaison's Office. Then again, nothing has ever meant so much to her before. After about six minutes of shifting her weight, Loral came to the door to retrieve her.

Since she was the head of the committee, Loral was the first one to address her. "I must confess I was very surprised to receive your memo, Vespyr. I didn't think you were this involved with Lord Vanmir's request."

"I was the one to bring it forth if you remember," Vespyr answered pleasantly.

"True. I guess I didn't realize you were apprised of the internal reports."

"Not as such, no. But since it's been weeks since I was briefed, I figured there might be a few concerns regarding the project. I thought I would present some ideas that might allay some of the Office's hesitance to really push this forward."

"How very…insightful of you."

"Shall we begin?"

No one could fault Vespyr for her oral communication skills. She did indeed cover some of the concerns the committee had regarding Lord Vanmir's proposal, and she had some interesting suggestions as to how to deal with these potential problems.

"Thank you, Vespyr," Loral said cordially once Vespyr had finished. "You've given us much to think about."

Vespyr stared only for a moment, processing the comment. "What does that mean exactly?"

"Lord Vanmir's project has been put on hold by order of the Lord Advocate."

"*What?*"

The committee members gave her an odd look; Vespyr Allyn rarely voiced uncalculated reactions.

"The project's lead chemist thought the bureaucracy process was taking too long," one of the others offered. "He took it upon himself to further things along."

"Further things along?" Vespyr echoed dumbly.

A stout man with an Inventors Guild emblem grumbled through his moustache, "Took his own concoction to test."

"Tristifir," Loral warned.

Vespyr swallowed hard. The nervous excitement that fueled her started to drain away. "Did it work?" Her voice was as weak as she felt, but she managed to keep upright.

"We don't know," Loral answered. She sounded exasperated. "As I said, the Lord Advocate has put a hold on the project."

"If you knew this, why did you let me bring this presentation to you? If everything's on hold…"

"We don't know what happens now. It's in our best interest to keep our options open. And if this drug does work, then we'll want to move forward. You've just helped us keep this project on the table."

Vespyr wasn't entirely sure what happened next. There were some vague words of "good job" that she could decipher above the buzzing in her ears. Somehow, she managed to return to her office. *"Took his own concoction to test."* That was just so Cortnay. Of course he would take matters into his own hands. She'd taken too long moving things forward that he must have believed she'd failed him.

I should have gotten in touch with him! Told him to be patient. What if…?

Wait. Loral said she didn't know if it worked. He might be okay. No. He must be okay. If something had happened to him, I would know.

"Of course, you didn't know about him taking the drug," a little voice inside her head chided.

No. If something drastic happened to him, I'd know, she corrected herself. *He's fine. The Lord Advocate is just taking precautions. Because they're friends.*

Vespyr decided to go to Cortnay's office. She had to speak to someone who knew for sure how her beloved was doing. *He's fine, he must be fine, I would know, I would know, I would know!*

The same guard she'd encountered the first time she stopped by Cortnay's workplace greeted her again. "Can I help you, miss?"

She smiled. "Yes, I'm here to see Cortnay Endros. I'm with the Liaison's Office."

Something in the guard's expression shifted from impassively professional to sympathetic. "I'm sorry, miss. Mr. Endros isn't here."

"Do you know when he'll be back? It's a rather pressing matter."

"Do you know Mr. Endros well, miss?"

We're in love, you fool! Of course I know him well! Vespyr wanted to shout. But instead: "Of course."

"I'm very sorry to tell you this, but I don't think Mr. Endros will be returning for some time. He's been quarantined," he explained quietly.

Vespyr blinked. "I see."

"Is there anyone else I can direct you to?"

"No, thank you."

Vespyr exited the building woodenly. *Quarantine.* The weight of that word had a peculiar effect on her. She should have been undone with the reality that something happened to Cortnay. She should have dissolved into tears the moment the word left the guard's lips. And yet, she managed to walk out of Cortnay's office of her own power.

She bypassed Doran Station. She could not bear to take the skyrail at that moment. *All our plans, our future…* In her dejected state, Vespyr was not quite paying attention to what she was doing or where she was going. Not that she cared any longer.

Stop it, Vespyr Alyn. You stop this right now. Quarantine does not spell death. Quarantine is just a precaution. No. No, I see now, quarantine is the next step in his plan. Cortnay improved upon my own thought to test those in quarantine. Now he can prove this preventative works! That's why he took the drug himself. He knew it would be safe.

Renewed by this revelation, Vespyr found the nearest skyrail station to take her to The Docks, where she was likely to find the Quarantine Ship. She had to let Cortnay know she was still devoted to him and their cause. She had to see him.

The Quarantine Ship was not marked as such, but it was rather evident which one it was by the armed guards and individuals clad in "Plague-resistant" suits milling around the dock.

She walked up the gangplank with a confidence borne of love. She flashed her Liaison's Office ident badge. "I must speak with Cortnay Endros. He was brought here recently."

The first guard eyed her curiously. "You understand that if he was brought here, he is a risk to Caelspyr."

"I understand that he is a patriot and that I am here on official business. Now, if you detain me any longer I will be forced to bring this matter before the Lord Advocate."

The guard simply nodded. The Liaison's Office alone was enough to get Vespyr to the first checkpoint at the very least. Throwing in Lord Advocate Merchell would just help speed the process along.

Vespyr was brought before one of the doctors in charge of the ship. "You're from the Liaison's Office?" he confirmed.

"Yes. I am here to see Cortnay Endros."

"I see." He inspected her ident badge. "You don't have clearance to be here, Miss Alyn. I assure you that Mr. Endros is being well taken care of and pass along any message you may have for him."

"I have clearance to be here, sir. In fact, I belong here."

"I thought you were from the Liaison's Office."

"Yes. I oversaw Mr. Endros's project. Do you understand the nature of his containment?"

"I know he was working on something for Lord Vanmir."

"That *something* is the reason I'm here. I need to be quarantined."

The doctor recoiled reflexively. Vespyr would have been insulted under different circumstances. But she knew what she had to do. She had to see Cortnay. If this was the only way, then…

She was escorted away by two plague-suited individuals. It took nearly a full hour for Vespyr to be processed by the doctors. There was an interview where she explained the nature of her business on the Quarantine Ship. "I've been working on the same project as Mr. Endros."

"Why weren't you detained at the same time?" This doctor spoke to her from behind reinforced glass.

"I was not at the laboratory that day. I was at the office. I needed to finish some business with the other liaisons."

"How do you know you've been exposed?"

"For the same reason you know Mr. Endros has been."

"You took the same drug?"

"Yes, of course. How else were we to test that the cure works?"

"You don't know that yet."

"I do. I know it works."

Vespyr's vehemence caused the doctor to flinch slightly. *These doctors have no backbone*, she decided, *to be frightened so easily.*

Since the doctor had no reason to dismiss her, he nodded to one of her suited escorts and she was taken to a shower room. Two nurses scrubbed her down thoroughly before dousing her in some strange liquid she assumed was a disinfecting agent.

In the next room, she was given a plain hospital gown. A different nurse took detailed notes of her physique and any other possible anomalies she could detect. Nothing out of the ordinary was found, of course. Still, since Vespyr voluntarily quarantined herself, it had to be believed that there was indeed something wrong.

Vespyr regarded herself critically in the mirror. *Hardly flattering*, she decided. *But Cortnay will understand. I couldn't very well see him in a ball gown. No. Such appearances aren't important to either one of us.*

As she followed her guards through the first level of the Quarantine Ship to the First Stage Room, she started to feel nervous. *Finally, I'm finally going to speak with Cortnay. I must tell him everything we've accomplished and how proud I am of his sacrifice. I can't believe he went and had himself confined to this ship just to ensure our project was a success! Such a noble man.*

The door slid open. She started to feel queasy. *Gods give me strength.* She steeled herself and stepped through. The room looked like any hospital ward: clean, bright common area with individual iron beds. There were curtains that could be drawn around the beds if need be with all the medical paraphernalia one could expect to be visible. The doctors and caregivers all wore thick, oiled canvas suits. For the first time since seeing them, Vespyr wondered vaguely how protected they actually were.

She scanned the room. It was not a very populated ward. This cheered Vespyr; not because it meant that Caelspyr was relatively clean of plague so much as because it meant she and Cortnay could easily seek out privacy if need be. They had much to talk about and she didn't want everyone knowing their business.

Cortnay was sitting by one of the beds in the far corner of the room reading. He appeared calm. *And why wouldn't he be? He had the cure! No, he was the cure, incubating the concoction that would save all of Eysan. While others pace and fidget and argue with the doctors, my Cortnay remains collected.* She beamed at him. The rush of adrenaline compelled her to run to him, but she resisted. *He is setting the example. I must be as serene as he is.*

Vespyr crossed the room. Everyone and everything else melted away as she approached her beloved. *We're finally together, my love.* Her footfalls alerted him to her presence. He looked up at her curiously; his beautiful, intelligent hazel green eyes were as keen as they were the first day she saw him.

"Hello," she said hoarsely. She cursed her voice for betraying her.

He crossed his arms and glowered.

"Who are you?"

Messages in Flame

By Dex Greenbright

Noulam rolled a layer of herbs into the softened wax. If the folk wisdom held true, it would fill a room with healing essence when burned. He cut the wick, then placed the candle on his best display shelf.

He liked to think of himself as the best candlemaker in the sleepy little town on the southern shore of Shunnira. Truthfully, his was the only such business now. There had been another, but that business died when its owner succumbed to the plague. That was when Noulam first offered healing candles. They provided comfort to the townspeople when nothing else could.

When he'd finished the next day's inventory, Noulam kept the stove hot for one more. He retrieved a squat, lopsided ball of wax with half a dozen wicks. He lovingly dipped it once, twice, extending the old candle's life another night.

At twilight, he left his shop. He greeted his neighbors on the way to the beach. They, like himself, had stayed despite the rumors of metal monsters from the north that devoured all in their path. Teraltian fairy stories did not scare him as much as the thought of abandoning his beloved.

His feet sank into the soft, wet sand. Palm fronds swayed in the warm breeze. From his beach on the mainland, Noulam could see small points of light springing to life all over distant Djimbuk, where those in the city lit lanterns and those in villages like his own lit candles. The wild isle rose from the ocean like a beautiful emerald. Ayotomi waited for him there. The quarantine had trapped his beloved on one side of the water, and he on the other.

Noulam lit his candle with a long match. The little flames grew until they joined together as one. He waited for the sky's last pinks and oranges to be snuffed out by a blanket of indigo.

A light appeared across the water. He imagined his beloved's soft skin taking on a rosy glow from the fire. Then, the light went out. It came back a moment later. Out, lit, out, lit. Their own personal code. Her parents had been very strict when they were young; in response, the lovers sat on their rooftops, sending secret expressions of longing in glowing code.

"I cannot wait to see your face again, my love."

Noulam waited until he saw the ending signal, then covered and uncovered his candle.

"A week more. Then nothing will separate us again."

"How are you? I heard rumor of new trouble on the mainland. Is it sickness?"

"I am well. Fairy stories. Nothing more. The plague has left for good this time."

Noulam sprinkled a powder over the flame, turning it red. It was a kiss, in the form of fire. The light across the water flashed purple. An embrace. He'd run out of that one since the local chemist had run west with the other cowards. The only one he had in abundance was the green they used when a parent came snooping; it signaled caution. He kept it with him to remind him of their history. He patted the leather pouch and grinned. It was a good history.

On the third to last day of the quarantine, smoke arose from the forest. At first, Noulam thought it was travelers building campfires. But it was white like steam, instead of the dark smoke of burning wood.

The next morning, a hunting party was selected to investigate. The party's leader, a butcher by profession, shoved a revolver into Noulam's hands.

Noulam protested.

"I've never carried a weapon in my life."

"You are strong. Help me keep the village safe."

"But…"

"We'll return before dusk, friend. Come."

The party followed the hum of an engine as they headed deeper into the forest. A sudden grinding of metal frightened a flock of birds. They took flight. Someone turned and ran. Three others rushed toward the sound. Seconds later, their screams split the air. Noulam gripped the revolver and prayed to the goddess of flame to keep him safe.

The mechanical sounds rumbled louder. Two strange men burst from the underbrush. Their bodies were a patchwork of flesh and machine, all of it splashed with blood. Both had powerful, gleaming jaws and churning mechanisms in their chests. Their eyes glowed with menace. Metal monsters indeed.

Noulam staggered back. His gun went off. The bullet ricocheted off the monster's arm. More of the hunting party took aim. One monster was struck in the head. The glowing eyes flickered, but the beast never slowed its attack.

The butcher switched to using his gun as a club. Others joined him. They worked together to rip off one of the creature's arms. One man got his shoulder mauled, another's neck was sliced by metal claws.

Noulam had an idea. Surely the monsters would burn and he always carried extra matches. He used one to ignite a fallen palm frond. He rushed the second creature, setting its head and torso alight.

The smell of burnt flesh filled the area. Taiye, the village's best fisher, helped Noulam fend off the monster until the fire burned through to the engine's inner workings. A foul, green fluid leaked onto the ground. The creature finally collapsed into a charred heap on the forest floor.

63

The rest of the hunting party had the other monster pinned and were attacking its legs. The beast continued to try and bite them, until the butcher punched the jaw so hard it came unhinged. Noulam ended the fight with another makeshift torch.

The hike back to town was quiet and mournful. Stretchers carried the wounded and dead.

The butcher held his bloody arm tight.

"A wall. We must build a wall, so no more of these things can attack."

The fisherwoman scoffed.

"We should run."

Noulam's thoughts lingered on the attack.

"Let's all sail to Djimbuk. The quarantine will be lifted in two days. Once we are over safely, we can tell them about the metal monsters."

There were more nods of agreement than arguments against the plan.

They arrived home just as the sun set. The villagers mourned their dead and helped the wounded to the clinic. Noulam fetched his candle and headed to shore.

He was careful to preface his tale with the assurance that he was safe, and the beasts were killed.

"You must not tell anyone."

"Automazombs. We've gotten those pamphlets too. If they are real, people need to know."

"Wait until I come to you. Then we will warn everyone, together."

The next day, Noulam made a set of candles infused with spices popular on Djimbuk. If he was going to move his business, he would need something to sell. He spent the rest of the day packing.

While filling a box with finished candles and a bag of green powder, Noulam heard a commotion outside. He leaned out the shop door. Several townsfolk were racing down the street toward the center of town. He spotted a familiar figure and shouted to her.

"Taiye! What's going on?"

The fisherwoman turned. She'd been crying.

"The wounded... they've gone mad!"

"Mad how?"

"They're attacking everyone they see." She gave him a knowing, fearful look. "Their skin is as gray as those creatures."

Noulam froze. Was that possible? The Automazombs had turned his neighbors and friends into more like themselves? Taiye continued down the road. Noulam grabbed a handful of matches, some candles to hold the flames, and ran to help.

The streets around the clinic swarmed with people. Family and friends tried to reason with the wounded and restrain them. Any who got near were bitten or worse. The peacekeepers tried next to subdue and when that failed, slew the wounded-turned-enemies. Similar to the Automazombs themselves, the deathly gray villagers kept moving despite what should have been fatal wounds. They kept killing.

Noulam lit a candle as he spotted the butcher in the crowd of attackers. The man greeted Noulam with a gurgling moan. Blood stained the butcher's mouth and his son lay at his feet. He was the first to burn.

"Zia-novalla give you rest, friend."

Those who survived being mauled by their neighbors soon became violent as well. They shouted and fought with anything that came near. Noulam feared that with enough time, everyone he ever knew would become a hungry, gray monster: kin of the Automazombs.

There were so many infected now. Noulam backed away. He couldn't fight them all. Not so ill-prepared as he felt. This was a job for an army, not a lone candlemaker.

He abandoned the fight and ran for the dock. He would take a boat, row to Djimbuk and wait for the quarantine to fall. He would go to his beloved Ayotomi and together they would warn everyone about the danger of the Automazombs.

Taiye cut him off. Her arm was bleeding. Bitten. She panted and twitched.

"Noulam! You could have stopped this!"

Noulam stepped back. There were others with the fisherwoman. Ten, maybe more. All wounded. Out of their minds.

"You don't want to do this. I'm your friend. The Teraltian monsters are to blame."

Taiye advanced on him, yelling. She didn't seem to have heard anything he said. His ex-neighbors followed her voice to the dock and joined in blocking his escape.

He thought next of swimming. The waters between Djimbuk and the mainland were rough and treacherous. He couldn't cross it directly and if he tried swimming along the coast to the next town, they could simply follow him along the shore.

Noulam held the lit candle in one hand and matches in the other. He was low on options and the others were closing in. If he only couldn't reach a boat, maybe he could still make use of one...

The ramp to a large fishing boat lay just beyond Taiye's group. A strong, wooden ship, one that would burn bright and serve as a warning well into the evening.

He pushed his way past his enraged neighbors. The clawed at his arms and neck and back. One man spat and swung at him with a boat paddle. Noulam ducked, red spittle spraying his face, and kept running.

He needed the fire to build quickly and brightly, so he went below deck. Noulam touched his candle to crew bedding, frayed ropes, old crates, anything that looked like it could burn. He found alcohol in the galley and poured it all over the floor.

Taiye and the others confronted him before he could apply flame to the liquid. There was no escape. Noulam struck all of the matches. Tears blurred his vision as he fought. His attackers grabbed and punched and bit even as he set their clothes on fire. They didn't notice, or they didn't care.

He threw the candle and matches down, igniting the alcohol. His last act was to reach into his pouch of chemicals and toss green powder in the air. It landed on his attackers, on the burning slats of the boat, on himself.

Pain consumed him as the fire consumed everything. But he could see the flames take hold of the fishing boat. They blazed a brilliant green. Noulam closed his eyes. *I will see you again, my love, in Zia-novalla's embrace.*

FALLOUT

By Victoria Bitters

Rich people did not get scared or worried or happy. They got bored or angry or smug. Djermay had never seen real fear or worry on a wealthy person. Even if they showed you all their teeth and made little whickering noises, they still seemed to mostly be laughing at you, more so that you knew you were beneath them than for the actual fun of it.

Djermay had been studying the moods of rich people – nobles from afar, merchants and other people who got their money from a point a lot closer to the laboring classes, from up close – for his entire life. He felt he was pretty well qualified to make this observation. Djermay's newest master would say that he had 'gathered a wide array of data points to support his hypothesis'. While not a rich person himself, Master van Gremphe had to talk to them a lot, which is probably why he talked funny.

The reason why Djermay had, for years now, been technically working for someone who was not a rich person – and therefore not actually paying him, unhappily – was because of the scariest rich person Djermay had ever seen.

Djermay didn't hate rich people. Yes, they were awful and you should never turn your back on one, but it was just one of the ugly truths of life that, in order to live, you needed money. In order to get money, you had to work for someone who had enough money to trade for labor so that their own life would be easier. If you worked long enough for people who were rich enough, you might become a rich person yourself, so there was no point in hating them.

He'd never seen a rich person who was so cold, though. Master van Gremphe worked for the scariest rich person ever. The rich person had decided that Djermay would be working for Master van Gremphe. She announced that right after Djermay had watched her shove his last master – a real gnat-eater called Thimar Havahkno – off of a dock below the flying capital city of Caelspyr, with nothing but 5,000 meters of empty air to catch him. Djermay sure wasn't going to argue with a crazy rich person.

Havahkno had been twice Djermay's size and liked to push around everyone he could. The scary rich person was actually a little smaller than Djermay these days, but she pushed a lot harder than Havahkno.

Djermay didn't even want to know her name. He was a little concerned that she might be like some creature of Chaos that showed up when you said something like "It sure is a good thing Scary Rich Killer Woman isn't here right now." Like in those old Haak-style plays, where the monster sneaks up on the hero who thinks he's safe and everyone in the audience is screaming warnings and pointing but the hero doesn't hear them and gets attacked.

Popular culture – and life – had taught Djermay the value of never letting down your guard. And always assuming the worst of rich people. Still, Master van Gremphe's rich person was a whole new level of worst. Djermay wasn't ashamed of the fact that he hid whenever she came in the lab. Sure, it could get uncomfortable after an hour or so, especially since his last growth spurt. But if she didn't see him, she couldn't throw him off of the dock. Probably.

Today, he was supposed to be hammering out some flat pieces of a metal that was way too bendy. It would never hold anything heavy up, but Djermay didn't criticize and he didn't ask questions. If you asked questions, sometimes you got answers you didn't want, so the safest thing to do was keep your head down (but not your eyes because, again – never trust a rich person).

He'd gotten maybe ten pieces done before the doors burst open and the scary rich person sauntered in. Djermay didn't yelp and break for cover. No. He quietly set his hammer down and casually bent over like he was going to pick something up from the floor – and then scuttled on hands and knees until he reached the cabinet under the sink, which was furthest from the door. He carefully opened the cabinet, slipped inside, squishing himself around all the pipes and sharp-smelling bottles, and eased the door shut. And then he waited until the talking stopped and the lab doors slammed again.

Djermay was almost grateful that the crazy rich person never entered or exited a room without slamming something.

When the doors slammed and he gave the rich person enough time to be sure she wasn't going to change her mind and come back, Djermay squirmed out from under the sink as noiselessly as he could manage, and walked back over to his stupid metal hammering station as if everything was normal.

Master van Gremphe probably rolled his eyes, but he was far enough from being a rich person that Djermay was okay with turning his back on the man. Master van Gremphe was kind of stuck with the crazy rich person, too. From what Djermay could understand of Havahkno's last attempt to push someone around, Master van Gremphe had made some enemies and, sensibly, had run away and hidden. He had lucked into a more spacious hiding spot than Djermay, but he had to stay hidden for longer. And he had to deal directly with the crazy rich person.

Djermay had briefly thought about the reward that Havahkno seemed to think would be paid if Master van Gremphe was turned in to the authorities, but snitching for money wasn't really Djermay's field of expertise. He was good at boring manual labor and exciting bouts of running away, but turning in criminals usually got you beaten up by other criminals, at best. In this case, it would also probably get him thrown off a dock.

And Havahkno really was a gnat-eater, so he could easily have gotten the information wrong about how much the reward was and even if there was a reward.

Havahkno had wanted to make the scary rich person marry him more than he had wanted money, so even if there was a reward, it probably wasn't that much. Because who would choose to marry the crazy rich person if he had a better choice? Gods, Djermay's balls just shriveled right up, thinking about the horrors that rich person would probably unleash on any man dumb enough to take his pants off with her around.

When he finished with all the stupid metal pieces that had been given to him, Djermay looked around for Master van Gremphe. He was messing with his chemicals again.

Whenever Master van Gremphe poured liquid into other liquids or into little glass pans – and then wrote and wrote and wrote about whatever happened or didn't happen – he wore a big mask that covered his whole face. There was a part with holes that went over his nose and mouth and oversized goggles that could be adjusted on the sides covered his eyes. The goggles made Master van Gremphe's eyes look huge and sometimes different colored pieces would slide over them. Djermay hated it when the color was red. It kind of reminded him of that time, several years back now, when the crazy rich person set a plague-eating monster loose in the lab. It also made Master van Gremphe look gross, like his eyes were bulging out and bleeding.

Djermay stayed at his workstation and scuffed his feet loudly. He didn't want to startle Master van Gremphe and have the jumpy man throw chemicals on him again. Some chemicals just stank but others stung and Djermay was a quick learner when it came to not getting burned the same way twice.

Master van Gremphe looked up after a minute of this and flapped his hand in an annoyed sort of way. Djermay waited another few minutes, then started tapping the bits of metal against each other. He didn't really want another stupid job to do, but he also didn't want the scary rich person to notice him *not* working on her monster.

Djermay was very much opposed to the crazy rich person having another monster – or 'mechanical', or whatever she and Master van Gremphe wanted to call it. She'd gotten a broken plague-eater and put it back together, then turned it on and wandered off, leaving it free to eat Master van Gremphe and Djermay. Djermay hid but he could hear the monster going after Master van Gremphe. There was screaming and crashing sounds and the *fwomph* and *sizzle* of things on fire. At the end, the crazy rich person came back and decided to smash the monster. Then she wanted a new monster built. Djermay disapproved, on principle. The woman clearly couldn't make up her mind about what to do with a monster. Also, Djermay didn't want to be eaten.

71

But he couldn't exactly point that out to the scary rich person and then there was his whole policy about not asking questions. Instead Djermay just made his eyes really wide at Master van Gremphe and shook his head when the man tried to explain this task or that. Djermay didn't really want to know how winding lengths of wire around metal pegs or hammering out stupid pieces of metal were going to result in another monster. Or 'prototype'. Master van Gremphe kept increasing the number on the 'prototype version' – they'd make one, then the crazy rich person would break it.

Anyway, eventually Master van Gremphe stopped mucking about with chemicals or writing about mucking about with chemicals and Djermay stopped making annoying noises. Everyone benefited. Master van Gremphe gave Djermay a packet to take to the regular docks. When Master van Gremphe sent him on an errand outside of the lab or the crazy rich person's house, Djermay sometimes wondered if he could just... not come back. Would anyone come looking for him? Maybe the big northern man who looked like the crazy rich person's enforcer. Better to not rock the airship.

Djermay did appreciate his new master giving him tasks that took him out of the lab, even if the regular docks made him nervous. At least they weren't the scary rich person's personal dock. He still had nightmares about that place. Djermay would appreciate these excursions more if he had coin to spend while he was travelling through the city. Instead, he had a patch on his coat that was some rich person branding or something that meant "let this servant go anywhere without paying, but keep an eye on him". If Djermay dwaddled, he'd get some guard or other coming up and asking him where he should be. But as long as he kept moving briskly, no one asked him to pay the train fare or made him turn out his pockets when walking into a fancy building or anything. Djermay could even get stuff without paying if it was on the list he handed to a shopkeeper. Unfortunately, he couldn't even read Master van Gremphe's squished, blobby writing, much less forge it, so he couldn't add anything to the lists and the man never seemed to order food or ale or cheroots or anything fun that Djermay could skim.

When he had to go to the markets in Undercity, Djermay made sure not to linger, anyway. There were more and more restricted and quarantined sections. One would get cleared and two more would get locked down. The restricted zones were where rebels were said to have been caught plotting. No one was allowed in or out without a good reason. They'd be searched and questioned going both ways, no matter what patches they wore. Not worth the hassle, for most folks.

Restricted zones were all over the city. The quarantines were all in the Undercity, so far, but the surface folks – who got their supplies and utilities from things running smoothly in the Undercity – were getting plenty fretful. The quarantines were most common at the lowest points and there were rumors that if too many people got sick in one of the outermost sections, that section wouldn't be switched out – as the modules-on-tracks the Undercity was built on were designed to do, so everything stayed connected, water and power and trade all flowing on – but the section would just be... dropped. Sometimes the whole city shivered and you could even see the piece falling away, from the Rim. When it was announced that rebels had damaged a section of the city too much to be sustained, you had to wonder. You also had to wonder a little about what it must be like on the ground, to suddenly have a city block drop on you. Probably not fun.

After he dropped off the packet to be mailed to some weird ground outpost in the foothills of the Itu Mountains, Djermay took the long way back to the scary rich person's house. When he couldn't put it off any longer, he returned to the lab. Verdellen, goddess of Luck, must've been having Her monthly courses, though, because Djermay didn't see the scary rich person was already there until he was already all the way in the room. She was being weirdly quiet, for her, drawing something while Master van Gremphe looked over her shoulder. They were angled around a middle row counter in such a way that Djermay couldn't hide under the sink without them having a good view of the cabinet. They were busy, so maybe he could go back out...

The big northern man, who was some kind of butler to the crazy rich person, appeared in the doorway, just as Djermay was trying to back out through it. Verdellen's piss.

With no good hiding spot or exit, Djermay kept his head down and went back to the station with the stupid metal pieces. Maybe he could pretend to work on them again. Or... polish them or something. He didn't really want to make noises that caused the scary rich person to look at him.

Keeping half an eye on the pair poking at their schematics or whatever, Djermay eavesdropped blatantly.

"Yes, I know it does poorly with rough terrain. That's why I told you to put electranum-powered stabilizers here and here," the crazy rich person punctuated her tetchy lecture with stabs at the paper.

"We can't get any standard gimbal sets, much less electranum. The district we usually deal with is under quarantine," Master van Gremphe replied. "We'll have to construct our own gyros, from scratch, and scrap the idea of repulsors entirely, given the shielding materials we currently have. Unless you find it productive to burn a hole through your mechanical's chassis. Again." Master van Gremphe sounded frustrated and sarcastic. Djermay relaxed a little. Everything was normal, then.

The district they were talking about was pretty high up. Pretty unusual for a quarantine, though a lot of the rebels were supposed to be hiding with – or were – engineers. There'd been plenty of times when the quarters the engineers had warehouses in were restricted. The scary rich person brought an engineer into the lab, once, back when Djermay had first been dragged into this mess. Djermay thought the engineer had something to do with the monster that tried to eat Master van Gremphe, so he kept an eye on her, but she didn't seem to be actually crazy, just weird. She also asked a lot of questions, which Djermay had his views on. But she asked the scary rich person things like "Why would you think this was a good idea?", which, okay – fair.

"Quarantined? Not just restricted? Hm." The scary rich person got one of her expressions. Djermay stopped fiddling with the bits of stupid metal and tried to figure out if he'd be better off ducking or trying to dodge around the big northern man.

The big northern man did one of his quiet coughs that was apparently some kind of polite version of "pay attention to me, if you're not too deep in the crazy place." The scary rich person sort of waved her hand at him, but he took a step forward – okay, so maybe Djermay would be able to get around him after all – and did the cough again.

"What," the scary rich person didn't even make it a question. The big northern man just looked at Master van Gremphe and then at Djermay, while he was trying to ease around the counter casually. Djermay froze again.

"Say whatever it is or go away, Jaff." The scary rich person ignored the big northern man after that, talking mostly to herself, or maybe Master van Gremphe. "Quarantined sections are deserted, apart from the sick people. More physical barriers, but less of a mob to navigate or negotiate with..." She hummed again, thoughtfully.

The big northern man breathed out in a way that was almost a sigh.

"Lady, I wished to remind you of the excursion that your family – *just* your family – had planned. To visit Dantus. You leave today and expect to return after a week or two."

The crazy rich person raised her eyebrows and dropped her chin, looking at the big northern man from under her brow. Then she tossed her head and waved her hand at him again.

"My family... honestly," she sighed. Pitching her voice higher, she did more hand waving, this time with both hands. "*'Oh nooo. There are signs of siiickness on the capital ciiity. We must fleeee!'*" The crazy rich person rolled her eyes. "It's not the dreaded plague – that's been confirmed through every possible channel. All those fanatical people who got themselves infected studying the plague died off years ago. There have been seasonal bouts of something or other for ages – since the last emperor took himself off to recover, its been practically fashionable to take ill and abandon the city. I thought Mother and Father looked down on that sort of posturing as 'presumptious'. Well, the rest of them may want to flee, but I have my work to complete – work that is actually advancing our knowledge, both of mechanical possibilities and, thanks to Doctor Grumpy-" The scary rich person paused to slap Master van Gremphe on the shoulder. He winced and Djermay appreciated being out of reach even more, as she continued, "- My work is even capable of counteracting the oh-so-frightening plague."

Djermay had been impressed by this claim, when he first heard it, but it turned out that what the scary rich person meant by 'counteracting' was 'burning so insanely that nothing, not even the plague, is left behind'. Burning had been tried in the earliest days, Djermay had heard, but he doubted anyone else would have gone to the lengths the scary rich person did. He wouldn't be surprised if she tried to set fire on fire. And succeeded.

The big northern man stared back at the crazy rich person, almost-sighed again, and left. Djermay started easing toward the door again, but the crazy rich person looked at him. He looked at the counter in front of him. Okay, nuts and bolts, spilled everywhere. He could pick these up and sort them. That was important, right? Maybe he would earn a little credit with Grandfather Qua, god of Order, and gods knew Djermay could use some divine intervention. *Very busy, don't mind me, don't throw me off a dock.* The scary rich person stayed where she was, in the way to the door, but started talking to Master van Gremphe again. It sounded like they were putting together a list. A list would take Djermay out of the lab, if they settled on a different district with the supplies they wanted. Djermay would even take a couple rounds of restriction screening relatively happily, at this point. Anything to get away from the scary rich person.

A lot of boring talk later – with the crazy rich person pacing around, but never actually getting enough out of the way for Djermay to sneak or even just run out – the door opened again. The big northern man came back in, looking just the faintest bit frustrated. He told the crazy rich person that the rest of her family was gone. The crazy rich person ignored him.

"We can't continue without these supplies!" the scary rich person was saying, jabbing the list at Master van Gremphe like she wanted to skewer him on the paper. Master van Gremphe almost didn't flinch, but he looked kind of annoyed, too. Then the scary rich person spun sharply on one foot to look at the big northern man speculatively.

The big northern man quickly said "You'll be wanting to send your prototype out as soon as it's done, I presume? With your family away, it will take longer to negotiate a blind eye for the departure of a specialized shipment. I shall begin immediately." Then he bowed to the scary rich person and left. The scary rich person made a face, but didn't call him back. She turned back to Master van Gremphe, who leaned back against a counter and raised his eyebrows. When he leaned back, the paunch he was growing really stood out. The scary rich person made another face that was pretty much the same one as before, but with more pouting.

"How do you still manage to get out of the way of all the debris that crops up during the first rounds of testing with a belly like that?" the crazy rich person complained, glaring at Master van Gremphe's middle like it was personally holding up her stupid plan. Master van Gremphe just shrugged, which made his stomach bobble a little.

The crazy rich person huffed and said "Fine. I'll just collect the supplies myself. 'Quarantines' are easy to evade, after all." Master van

Gremphe looked squeamish. He really was scared of getting sick, which was fair enough – the crazy rich person kept sending her monsters out and then hauling them back in, mostly broken, with 'samples'. The samples were mostly of other monsters, but sometimes there were... bits. Of people. The crazy rich person made Master van Gremphe help her do tests on them and it sounded like the bits were not from the monsters that were made from dead people, but bits from probably not-dead-yet-at-the-time people. Djermay wouldn't want to do tests on bits from people that monsters had eaten, but Djermay didn't really want to do tests on anything. He would really just like to get paid. And not work for the crazy rich person. Both of those would be great.

Djermay was clearly thinking about plagues and monsters too hard because he almost missed the change in the scary rich person's expression when she looked over at him. For one thing, she looked *at* him, a thing that Djermay had managed to keep to a bare minimum over the last five or so years.

"Well, I'll need someone to carry the supplies while I deal with whatever logistical concerns we may encounter. You, boy – you'll come with me."

Djermay froze, screaming on the inside. Tie a knot in Grandfather Qua's testicles, the scary rich person was talking to him. Even worse, the scary rich person making him travel with her – *alone*, no witnesses or fellow victims to maybe distract her. This was so bad Djermay couldn't come up with an appropriate level of cussing.

The crazy rich person seemed to take stunned, motionless horror for absolute agreement, because she just nodded and started digging through a cabinet next to the door. Master van Gremphe winced apologetically and handed Djermay something from the counter behind him. It was the mask with the bulging eyes. "She'll want to go by a... back route. You won't have to sit through the quarantine interrogation. But, to be on the safe side, keep the mask on the whole time you're in there. And after you get out. We'll hose you down when you get back." Master van Gremphe weakly patted Djermay on the shoulder. Djermay just stared at him.

When the crazy rich person waved for him to follow her, Djermay didn't really have a lot of options. He'd seen how fast she was – if she decided he was moving too slow or not following orders well enough, she *might* stop with just hitting him harder than a woman should be able to hit.

And he *might* be lucky enough to not be near a sudden drop when she hit him. But he didn't want to count on any mercy from Verdellen, given how the day had gone so far.

The 'back route' was on a train, over some barricades, through a bunch of dark tunnels and rickety catwalks – all the Undercity shortcuts that Djermay had grown up in, before he got bumped up to 'servitor' to Havahkno and then walloped back down to 'helper' to Master van Gremphe.

Finally, the scary rich person swiftly unscrewed a grate and they emerged in a quiet warehouse district. Djermay quickly pulled on the stupid mask, his vision shrinking – he didn't know how to fiddle with the lenses to improve it – but the air at least was better. The filter in the mask blocked out the industrial and sewer smells they'd encountered all along the way and the oily and metallic smells that Djermay associated with this district. The official barricades were probably a few streets away, in either direction. No one was in sight. The neighborhood – which should be yammering with machinery in use, workers inside, patrolmen outside, and random people just passing through – was almost quiet. There was just the whistle and metallic moans of the winds on the exposed Undercity buildings and distant sounds of the rest of the city.

The scary rich person led him a block in one direction and half a block in another, stopping at a warehouse with shivering, corrugated walls and a thicker metal door. She pulled out a couple of picks and had the handle turning in just a couple of minutes. Djermay was mildly impressed, but mostly depressed – you couldn't even count yourself safe from the scary rich person if she was on the other side of a locked door.

The crazy rich person hauled open the door – and then slammed it back shut as a groaning figure lunged from the darkness. Djermay made a sound that absolutely was not a scream and made it almost a meter before the crazy rich person caught him by the collar, strangling him a bit before he stopped trying to run. Much too calmly, the crazy rich person said "Not the front door, then."

She still had a hold of his collar, so Djermay couldn't exercise his common rutting sense and get away from the place with a maybe sick, probably crazy, and definitely creepy person who jumped out at people. Instead, he stumbled after the scary rich person as she led him to the support lattice that let the warehouse – with its relatively thin walls – sway with the wind and the movement of the city, but would get in the way of anyone who tried to cut through the accordioned metal.

Djermay really hoped the scary rich person didn't want to cut through the wall. The gaps in the lattice were not big enough for either of them to fit through. But she started climbing instead, up to the roof, where there were smallish windows and openings just covered in mesh wire, for ventilation. The scary rich person smoothly pulled a small hammer pick out of her jacket and smashed the window, knocking out the rest of the cheap glass with a little smile on her face. Like she was only happy when she was breaking something. Djermay shuddered.

The crazy rich person slung herself through the gap, with a slight *clang* indicating that there was something to land on. Djermay dithered. Maybe he could just stay here and ferry the supplies back to the ground? That was still much too visible, in case any guards patroled the district, but it was still probably better than going inside.

"Come inside!" barked the crazy rich person, popping back out of the window and almost scaring Djermay into letting go of the lattice. She grabbed his arm and hauled. Anxious not to be flung to the ground, Djermay scrabbled sideways on the lattice, trying not to lose a shoe or a finger. Landing awkwardly on a rusted walkway in the dimly lit warehouse, Djermay was unfortunately positioned to see the main floor. Ten, sixteen... there must be at least twenty people lurching around on the ground level. From how they moaned and stumbled, Djermay was sure they were sick. Which means this whole building was a plague risk. He tried to breathe shallowly, not really trusting the mask to keep him safe.

The scary rich person leaned on the railing while Djermay clambered to his feet, trying not to touch anything. Looking over the seething mass, she remarked offhandedly, "This reminds me of the last time I ran into that historian." She laughed a little, not bothering to explain. Thank Verdellen – Djermay was sure he didn't want to know.

The crowd of sick people kept bumping into each other, but they seemed to be trying to get closer to where Djermay and the scary rich person were standing. Djermay edged back toward the window. Every time the wind buffeted the walls and they rattled, the sick people would get distracted and turn towards the sound and movement. Creepy.

Frowning down at the sick people, the scary rich person hmmed. "This may take longer than anticipated to move supplies out, if we have to shift things out the window." She turned abruptly and stalked toward one of the erratically connecting branches of the walkway, peering down at the stacks of boxes that were piled below.

So. Djermay was in a plague house. The window was his way back out, but the crazy rich person would kill him if he left without permission. And as much as he wanted to stay near the exit, standing in front of the window also made him more visible to the sick people inside and any of those potentially patrolling guards outside. Djermay tried to sneak across the walkway, in the general direction of the crazy rich person without actually getting too close. Maybe Verdellen would cut him a break and the sick people would rather mob the crazy rich person than him. He tried to keep her between him and the crowd as he edged around the perimeter of the building.

The shambling group of sick people didn't quite move as a group — some of them were trying to follow the crazy rich person around as she strode across the walkways or even leaned over the railing to crack open boxes within reach that interested her, heedless of the creepy way the sick people moaned and swiped at her from below. Another group of the sick people fixated on Djermay, clumping together under whatever part of the walkway he was on, when he moved. But if he held as still as he could, some of them would go join the other group. Until Djermay moved again — because just waiting on a rickety walkway only a dozen or so feet over a bunch of sick people who acted like crazed animals was really disturbing and he couldn't stand it for very long.

Djermay was almost relieved when the scary rich person started ordering him to come pick up piles of stuff she'd plucked out of the tallest piles of storage crates. He took roundabout routes through the walkways, leading the sick people who were following him from below into bottlenecks. Djermay moved faster when they couldn't see him around a stack of boxes or support pillars or whatever. He did a loop through the darkest part of the warehouse, where the creepy sick people couldn't see him, and dumped the fourth armful of supplies by the window. Then he heard clattering from behind him. Spinning around, Djermay saw a shadow rising up from below — a head, followed by stooped shoulders, swaying erratically. Then another head bobbed up as the first figure staggered and bumped into the wall. There must be a staircase in that corner. And the sick people stumbled into it. This day just kept getting better.

Freezing in place, Djermay's eyes darted from the disorganized group amassing at the outer edge of the walkways to where the scary rich person was obliviously digging through a pile of something or other. He didn't want to move or make noise to draw their attention and if he tried to start climbing out the window, the scary rich person might kill him. Freezing would save him.

The next clatter from the sick people ricocheting off the walkway's railings – one mis-stepping and half-falling off the walkway, arms smacking against the metal with a sound that made Djermay wince – finally caught the crazy rich person's attention. Her head jerked up and she scowled at the group of people weaving their way towards her. They were trying to take straight paths, but happily the walkways mostly weren't that direct, so another couple coming for Djermay simply flipped right over the railway, falling smack onto the metal floor with more unpleasant crunching and squelching noises. They seemed to have survived, though, because Djermay could see at least one of them trying to get back up.

The crazy rich person huffed and darted back toward him, hopping over rails and across gaps between walkways, careless of the drop. She scooped up the piles of supplies by the window, dumping most of them into Djermay's arms. Three sick people bumbled onto the right path to reach Djermay and the crazy rich person. They looked really bad as they got closer – mottled, pale, with slack skin, like-they-were-dead bad.

The sick people groaned, almost howling, as they stumped down the walkway toward the window, the whole network of metal shuddering underfoot. Starting to hyperventilate, motion from the corner of his shrunken peripheral vision caught his attention. Djermay glanced down to see both of the sick people who'd fallen dragging themselves upright. Their arms and legs were jagged and wrong with broken bones sticking out; their faces were a sloppy mess of mushed flesh and oozing blood. One tipped a ruined face up toward him, moaning.

Djermay yelped "Monster!", his voice sounding muffled through the mask. He tried to drop everything and run, but the crazy rich person spat a curse and caught Djermay's collar again. Twisting it tightly and hauling him up, to the point where he was standing on his toes trying not to choke, scrabbling at his neck, she hissed "You will not drop these items again or I'll throw you to the 'monsters' myself."

Eyes darting from threat to threat, Djermay babbled agreement and grabbed onto whatever she shoved at him, sidling towards escape as he did so. As soon as the scary rich person turned her back, he lunged for the window. He tucked his chin down so the mask caught on the bundle and clamped his elbows in tight to keep his armload with him. He bruised his fingers on the lattice as he tried to catch at it, Djermay's feet slipping on the bars. His face bashed against the inside of the mask as he scraped and slid down the side of the building in fits and starts. A little over a meter from the ground, the whole structure thrashed out from under him and Djermay dropped the rest of the way, landing roughly and rolling awkwardly. The ground itself was bucking, the walls of the warehouse rattling and groaning.

Doing his own groaning, Djermay managed to get to his feet without dropping the stupid supplies the crazy rich person would kill him over. The crazy rich person who was still nimbly descending the side of the building, another bunch of tools and bits tucked under one arm. She let go of the lattice and landed lightly, frowning and raising her eyebrows at the trembling ground. She gestured abruptly for Djermay to follow her, then strode briskly off, barely affected by the unsteady footing.

As they headed back to the lab, the spasms shaking the district – all of Caelspyr? – increased in frequency. Grinding metal shrieks and moans of disturbed underground systems vibrated up from beneath. Passing close to the quarantine blockade, angry shouts could be heard. It was hard to tell if the sounds of breaking glass and clattering rubble came from the structural damage or rioting.

Scowling in the direction of the clamor, the scary rich person muttered to herself.

"It would be better to avoid crowds entirely, even with the risk of internal collapses. I can't risk these supplies, particularly with this upheaval."

The ground chose that point to heave up, sending Djermay sprawling. The scary rich person kept her balance. Djermay struggled to get back up again, not willing to relax his grip on a single item. *If I don't let go, she won't throw me off a dock. She cares about the stuff.* Still, he cringed when the scary rich person hauled him upright, then shoved him forward.

The return route was nightmarish – staggering through even darker tunnels, being dragged up shuddering ladders, bracing himself against complaining mechanisms that bucked and jerked as they juddered along their tracks. Djermay concentrated on just trying not to drop anything and keeping up with the crazy rich person.

After what felt like hours, the crazy rich person wrenched open a hatch, which swung into a familiar metal corridor. The lab was just around the corner. Djermay bit back a sob. The tremors were still evident and steady, but the lab was, comparatively, *safe*.

Slamming through the doors in her usual fashion, the crazy rich person strode into the room with a gusty sigh.

"That was the most ridiculous, frustrating- What are you doing?"

Master van Gremphe was hurriedly snatching tools and papers from the counters, jamming them into a satchel. He wore a simpler mask than the one he'd foisted on Djermay. His eyes were frantic and unfocused, when he glanced up at them.

"A messenger came. Jaff has already gone to the dock. There's been an outbreak. It's the plague. The actual plague. In the water district. It's in the *water*. And that's not even the worst part."

"We have private cisterns, we'll be fine-" The crazy rich person tried to interrupt Master van Gremphe's panicked ramble.

"They're dropping districts. From the city. Just – down. They've dropped the central water district. The sewage district next to it. Two machinists' districts on the other side. Another three districts on the starboard rim." Master van Gremphe slung the satchel over his shoulder, fumbling with the clasp. "The starboard hub railyard collapsed. The messenger said there was rioting in the royal district. Emperor Ashford said the districts were dropped to quell insurrection. As if not wanting to be dropped from a very great height is treason."

The crazy rich person hummed. "Well, that is a concern for supply chains, certainly, but still, we'll be untouched."

The room shuddered. The joists groaned in protest. A sharp crack reverberated through the wall, followed by hissing and crackling noises. Djermay's stomach dropped. The lab was in the district just aport of the royal district itself. They wouldn't be dropped. The crazy rich person was right. This was just... side effects.

Master van Gremphe scooped up another pack from the floor, lobbing it toward Djermay, who flinched. The pack landed with a soft thump. Djermay recognized one of his spare shirts, sticking out from the bag.

"No one will be untouched. There's not going to be enough of the city left to keep us up." Without looking back, Master van Gremphe bolted for the passageway to the dock.

Djermay's mask was making a high whistling noise. Oh, no – that was his own breathing. His eyes bounced between Master van Gremphe's retreating figure and the scary rich person. He didn't want to go to the docks. And definitely not with the scary rich person behind him. Or in front of him. Or just... anywhere. No.

The scary rich person pursed her lips and tapped her foot. She let out a big sigh, just as one of the cabinets rattled open, spilling instruments and jars of liquids that sizzled when the containers smashed open. Djermay flinched and cringed back from the spray of glass, but the scary rich person glided out of the way. He looked toward his cupboard. Probably not much safer – there were containers of liquids in there, too. Djermay jerked back as the scary rich person moved suddenly, grabbing some papers off of a counter, rolling them up quickly. She caught up a few more items, jerking supplies out of Djermay's grip and shoving other things at him. She said, in a testy voice, "Drop *those* and carry *these*," and shoved Djermay ahead of her down the corridor.

The corridor was mostly well lit but dark spots were bobbing in Djermay's vision. *No, no, no. I don't want to go to the dock. I don't want to get shoved off a dock. No, no, no.*

But the scary rich person was right behind. *Right. Behind.* There was no retreat and only open air ahead. They came out of the passageway onto the dock. Djermay pushed back against the doorway and let the scary rich person stalk past him. A zeppelin was waiting there, hatches battened, its engines fired up, and its vanes all arrayed – it was all but cast off. The big northern man stood at the entryway to the cabin, glaring at Master van Gremphe. When he saw the scary rich person, his face went back to expressionlessness. He stepped aside, making a sweeping gesture of welcome. Master van Gremphe huffed and disappeared inside.

Djermay was shaking. He couldn't quite look at the edge of the dock, where the sky fell away. It wouldn't take much of a push to make *him* fall away. The crazy rich person reached back towards him without turning her head, trying to drag him in the direction of the zeppelin, Toward the edge. NO.

With a scream, he just dropped everything and wrapped his arms around the nearest post.

"No. No. Not going, not going, not going. No."

Releasing him, the crazy rich person made an exasperated gesture with her free hand.

"Fine. As you please. Keep the lab in good order while we're out." She scooped up the items Djermay had dropped and strode into the zeppelin without a backwards glance. The big northern man looked after the crazy rich person, then back at Djermay. Djermay gripped the post tighter. *Not going.* The big man cleared his throat and gave Djermay a solemn nod, then hauled in the last rope tethering the vessel to the dock. He stepped backwards through the door and closed the hatch. Djermay finally started to realize that he was safe. He was staying. Not going.

The zeppelin hummed and wavered as it navigated clear of the dock, steering around the various protruding spikes and mechanisms that jutted out from the underside of the city. Djermay's breathing began to even out as he watched the zeppelin move away. His voice echoed weirdly from within the mask as he talked himself down, almost giddy now as the danger receded.

"I'll stay here. The lab is safe. The crazy rich person said so. I'll be fine. I'm not going. I won't fall."

The dock shook. He tightened his hold on the post. *Can't let go.* With a screeching noise, punctuated by heavy clunks that rumbled through him, the dock started to list, then lurched. Djermay clung even tighter, his eyes still on the zeppelin shrinking into the distance.

"If I don't let go, I won't fall."

Thunk. The wind picked up, whistling noises rippling around him. Gusts battered the dock brutally as the now tiny zeppelin zipped... up?

No. The zeppelin wasn't going up, the dock was going down. Debris pelted him as the chunk of city it occupied tore away from Calespyr. Djermay fell.

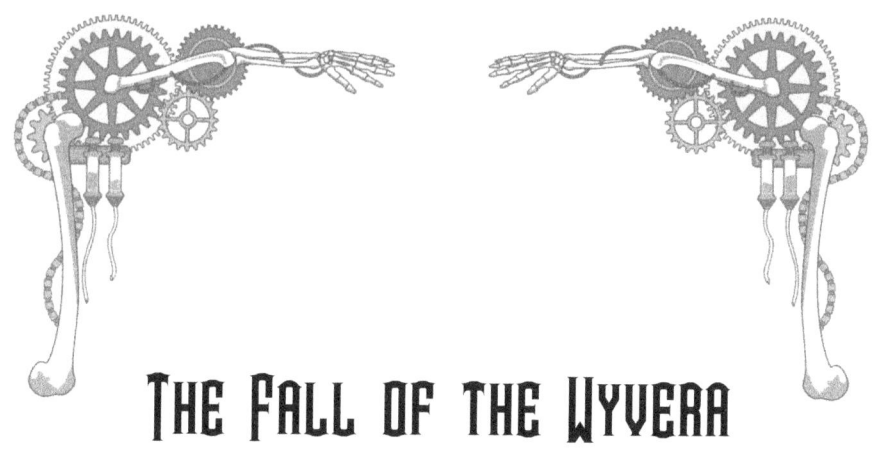

The Fall of the Wyvern

By Dex Greenbright

"Captain… Captain Zu!"

Zu shook off the memories that haunted him. He set down the bottle in his hand and grinned at his first mate.

"Henning! Got something to report, friend? Is that cargo of ours acting up again?"

"The prisoner's secure, but… we're losing altitude."

Zu adjusted the monogoggle that covered his left eye and scanned the sprawling landscape below. The mountains *did* seem larger than they were before.

"Have you found the leak?"

"No, sir. The outer shell is completely sealed, as well as the inner mechanics."

"If that were true, there wouldn't be a problem. Come on, let's have another look."

The mechanics passage was extremely narrow. Henning was by no means a wide man, but he still brushed against exposed gears and sensitive levers. By contrast, Zu glided past the equipment on all sides with room to spare. It was made for him, after all, before all that business with the plague.

They stopped every few paces to allow the captain to inspect a piece of machinery he found out of place. He would stoop down and stare at each part, carefully tuning the lenses of his monogoggle for a better look. Then he set the equipment back to his specifications.

Henning tapped his foot impatiently.

"None of this relates to our current condition, sir. Should we move on to the next hall?"

"No. All parts of the Wyvera are connected. Disturb one and you disturb them all. They may not be the problem, but they may have led to it. We'll get to the source soon."

Zu carefully inspected each section of his beloved ship until they arrived at a larger chamber filled with engine equipment. He arched an eyebrow at his first mate, who was failing to suppress a series of annoyed noises. The ship would stay aloft for hours yet, and if that's how long it took to inspect each room, then so be it.

He stopped suddenly, causing Henning to blunder into him. Zu placed a finger to his lips and glanced warily ahead. The engine chugged steadily. Gears groaned and clicked as they rotated. But, there was something else, too. He worked his way toward a row of pipes in the corner.

Henning frowned as he cupped his ear.

"There's nothing here, sir. Let's move on."

Zu glared at him, and Henning quickly covered his mouth. The first mate took on a determined expression and examined the different parts of the engine room.

Zu turned from his search to see Henning squinting and mouth in a firm pout. He smiled wide and nudged his first mate with his elbow.

"Calm yourself, friend. If you try any harder, your head will burst. I found the problem."

Henning released himself from concentration.

"You did?!"

"I just had to follow the whistling. It was faint, but the Wyvera always lets me know when she's hurt. Don't you, girl?"

Zu patted the pipes gently.

Henning leaned closer.

"So, what *is* the source of the leak, sir?"

The captain had already set to work, digging through a box of tools he kept handy in cases of emergency. He gestured with a wrench around the back of the pipes.

"There's a valve missing."

"It's broken? But we just did a thorough maintenance check before we left Dantus."

Zu pulled out a suitable replacement valve and fitted it to where the missing one should have been. Two slight turns and the whistling stopped.

"Not broken, no. It appears, Mr. Henning, that we have a saboteur aboard the Wyvera."

With the repairs completed, the captain strode down the main hallway with purpose. Somebody was intent on sinking the Wyvera out of the sky. Who was a more likely suspect than the prisoner they were transporting? Part of the cargo hold had been converted into a holding cell. It was sparsely furnished. There was a bench with a blanket for sleeping, a washbasin, and a pail for waste.

The prisoner sat on the bench, staring out the window. Her mane of dark hair reminded Zu of his wife. The thought stuck in his throat and he nearly choked on it. He quickly turned the cough into a clearing of his throat to grab her attention. She turned slowly until their eyes met. The illusion was ruined. The woman's eyes were bright blue, unlike his wife's sandy irises. That would make it easier to interrogate her. He hated interrogations.

"Comfortable?"

"Hmm, as much as I can be."

"It'll be much worse when we drop you off at the prison isle. The whole place hovers just above freezing every day of the year."

She pursed her lips and stayed silent.

Zu noticed her shiver slightly at the mention of the prison nicknamed the Iceberg.

"I imagine you would do anything to avoid that fate."

"Are you accusing me of something?"

"Not yet."

Zu crossed his arms and leaned against the back wall.

"May I ask you something?" The prisoner waved a hand dismissively and Zu continued. "I will take that as a yes. What exactly are your crimes?"

"I spoke my mind."

"Even the Emperor wouldn't send you to the Iceberg for that."

The woman flashed a crooked grin.

"Explosives speak louder than words. The people need to hear the crimes of the Empire. They've become complacent in their floating palaces while the world below rots to death."

"A dissident, then? You would have loved my father. Though he would disapprove of you. He advocated peace above all things. Back to the matter at hand. How eager are you to return to your work? Spreading the truth or whatever your mission is?"

"It's the most important thing in the world. Are you thinking of letting me out?"

"What do you know of mechanics?"

"Less than nothing. I've no interest in joining your crew, Nomad."

Zu stroked the single vertical line of his beard as he thought. She was suspicious, but not enough to be directly responsible. He smiled politely and exited the makeshift prison. He stopped by the crewman posted outside. Girtch was one of his employer's men. Between Girtch, Baako,

Moug, and Freddie, Mr. Everett had nearly doubled Zu's usual crew for this one mission. He wondered if the culprit were one of them, or if his crew, whom he considered family, had betrayed him.

"You're absolutely sure she hasn't made any attempt to escape? And she's never been out of your sight? Possibly exploring the ship?"

"Never, Mr. Zu! I been keepin' her under careful watch. No problems at all."

"Good. Keep it up, Girtch."

He patted the man on the shoulder, though he wasn't sure if the gesture was to reassure Girtch or himself. Back in the Wyvera's control room, Zu found Henning poring over maps. Owynn stood at the helm, the late afternoon light glinting off the navigator's glasses. He left the pair to their work and walked over to the large front windows. The peaks were nearly behind them now, giving way to rolling meadows full of untended crops. The plague and those damned Automazombs had made sure few were left to work the land.

He tucked his thumbs into his thick leather belt. What a waste these past years had been. Under his left hand, he felt the familiar cold metal of his flask. He smiled as an idea began to take shape in his mind. He swiveled around to face Henning.

"Tell the crew. We feast tonight!"

The airship's small dining area was really just an extension of the galley. With the crew being doubled, there was barely enough room to move. Still, the group had a grand evening. There was food, singing, contests of strength, and drink. The captain was locked in alcoholic combat with Moug. The heavily muscled man sported some equally heavy tattooing that covered his arms like sleeves. Zu and Moug each grabbed a glass from the table, downed the contents, and slammed the glass down. The tattooed man grinned wickedly, flashing a mouth full of metal teeth.

"You're already slowing, Zu! You slow more, I beat you easy!"

"Oh really? Time to put your rum where your mouth is!"

A few rounds later Moug was wobbling severely. The captain took another glass and stood up.

"I'll finish you off later, friend. I need to make a speech before anyone passes out."

Zu maneuvered through the crowded room. In the corner, he spotted Freddie with his arm around Lillian, whispering into her ear. He chuckled to himself at the thought of Lillian, with her vast collection of instruments of death, snuggling up with one of the new crew. Either the boy was even more naïve than he looked, or Lillian had gone soft. Only time would tell. He climbed up onto a counter of the galley. A hush fell over the room as Zu cleared his throat.

"I trust you are enjoying yourselves?"

The room filled with the clanging of glasses and enthusiastic yells. The captain smiled.

"I hope our newest crew members are enjoying the Wyvera's hospitality?"

Another round of cheering erupted.

"Excellent. Before the night goes on much longer, I have an important matter to discuss. The Wyvera has been losing altitude."

The crew all started talking at once, a mix of concern and pride-fueled denial.

"The issue has been fixed. We'll still make our destination. However, the question of why remains. I give you many freedoms aboard the Wyvera. So long as the work gets done, you can do as you please, go where you please. However, one of you has harmed our livelihood and home. I will lay no blame until the evidence is clear, but when it is, the Iceberg will be your last stop."

He looked around the room. Hopefully, one of the crew would reveal him or herself and that would be the end of it. Owynn was shuffling nervously, but he always did that. Lillian and Moug eyed each other with suspicious glares.

Zu slid off the counter and put himself between the two crewmembers.

"This isn't an issue of old or new crew. We're all in this together."

The room mulled over his words for a few long minutes. The sullen mood was finally broken when Girtch released a hull-shaking belch. The whole crew laughed. Soon everyone was back to their party, more raucous than ever. Despite the circumstances, Zu was glad to have a moment of pure revelry. They'd been far and few between these past years.

Guarded whispers filled the airship the next day. The old and new crews stayed mostly separate, each group blaming the other for jeopardizing the current job. Zu walked among them, making sure some actual duties were being performed while at the same time listening for any clues as to who the culprit may have been.

He made a quick stop in the galley storeroom. The darkness of the space didn't bother him. This was his home; he knew every inch. He popped the cork of a rum bottle and took a swig. He slumped to the floor, a nostalgic smile spreading across his lips. This was one of the Shunniran Gold bottles his wife had bought him as an anniversary gift. It was one of the few things he had left to remind himself of all he had lost.

He took another drink and pulled a tiny trinket out of his right vest pocket. The little lump of clay looked like a cross between a heart and a rabbit's head. His daughter had made it for him as a good luck charm when they first moved to Dantus. A delicate green ribbon wrapped around the base of the charm's long ears. Zu clutched the trinket to his chest.

Poor little Sylvia. Neither she nor her mother or brother stood any chance against the thieves that invaded their home. If only he had not been away working for Mr. Everett. If only they weren't forced to move to the cheaper Undercity district. If only their debts to Mr. Everett had not been so great. If they still owned the Wyvera together, his family might be with him now.

Tears started pooling in his monogoggle. He flipped a tiny valve to release them and wiped his cheek sullenly. As he sat with his regrets and his rum, Zu heard a pair of voices approaching. He took one last mouthful and listened from behind the counter.

"You don't think it was really s-sabotage, do you Lillian?"

"That's what the captain said."

"But what do *you* think?"

"Old parts rusted off? Oversight? I don't see why it has to be one of us."

"I'll bet it was the prisoner. She seems awful c-conniving."

"Shows you how much you know, Owynn. That woman's being sent away because she's trying to make this world better again. The Emperor's forgotten his people and left us to rot."

Owynn gleefully snickered to himself.

"That doesn't sound like you're usual r-rhetoric, Lil. Don't you have a portrait of the prince in your b-bunk?"

Zu could easily picture Lillian's signature scowl and folded arms. He heard the muted whack of Lillian's palm smacking the back of Owynn's head.

"Ow! See, there's the Lillian I know. Gentle and with a g-good sense of humor."

Lillian harrumphed.

"I still say she's not to blame. Captain Zu should never have taken this job. We should be helping, not shipping her to that awful prison."

"Mr. Everett didn't give the captain a ch-choice, Lil. Zu has to take every job or he can't buy the Wyvera back."

"Why does he even bother anymore? He always said he was doing it for his family. Now they're dead and he's taking more jobs than ever and drinking more than ever too. Face it, Owynn, the captain's gone off the deep end."

"Let's j-just get this stuff to the cargo room."

Zu sat until the two were well out of earshot. He stared at the bottle and reflected on Lillian's words. His weapons master was always quick to give harsh advice. Still, he didn't have time to worry about the subtleties of his motivations and memories. He had to think of something that would spur the saboteur into exposing himself. He had hoped his speech had done the trick, but in the midst of a party, the words inspired suspicion where Zu was hoping for panic.

He continued his rounds and collected some juicy, but useless, tidbits. Moug was saving up for a large new tattoo by the best artist in Dantus. Freddie had fallen for Lillian, unfortunately for him. Girtch was tired of listening to the prisoner yap at him all day about how innocent she was and was thinking of moving her cell to something smaller and less comfortable. Henning was crafting a love poem for the dancer he met on their last job. The twins, Aria and Yuri'ik, were learning an acrobatic fighting style used on the Shunniran island of Djimbuk from Baako.

To each group he saw, he would drop small hints that he knew who was responsible for trying to sink the Wyvera from the sky. He wanted to make sure the entire crew thought the official capture of the saboteur would be early the next morning. He even had Girtch construct a new cell next to their current prisoner. Zu's tactics were less subtle when he talked about how horrifying the Iceberg was and how the person who wished to harm the Wyvera would suffer every day for the rest of their life.

It wasn't usually in Zu's nature to frighten his crew, but it wasn't usually in his crew's nature to try to drop the whole airship onto the dead lands below. Hopefully his words would be enough this time to rouse some kind of brash reaction, one that had a weakness the captain could exploit in order to fix this mess of a job.

Captain Zu woke before dawn to find the air had changed. It was warmer, humid. He jumped out of bed and nearly toppled over. They were sinking again and this time much faster. Zu dashed past the crew's quarters, shouting as he tumbled down the increasing decline.

"Henning! Owynn! Somebody get out here!"

His head was spinning. He expected a reaction from the culprit, but not this severe. As he reached the control room he found Henning frantically pushing buttons and tugging levers in order to right the tilting airship.

"Henning, report!"

"Someone's cut our ballasts, sir! Backup engine's down, too! There's no way to gain altitude and we're still falling!"

Ahead of them, the meadows had given way to the dusty shanty towns of the Empire's plague refugees. The capital was rapidly approaching. If they were going to crash, Zu had to make sure it wasn't in the dead city. He stopped Henning, grabbing him firmly by both shoulders.

"Look... Hey! Look at me, friend. We'll survive this. I know we will. I'm going to go investigate. Anyone else comes in here, you give them the order to dump any and all unnecessary cargo. Got it?"

Henning nodded nervously. Zu slipped past Girtch, who had just stumbled in, bleary-eyed. The captain let his first mate handle the crew. The Wyvera needed him more right now. He raced off toward the mechanics passage. He would have to work fast to save the ship and their lives.

The main passage was in complete disarray. Steam billowed out of broken pipes. Knobs and gears were bent and broken. The backup engines wouldn't be able to save them this time, but they also weren't the biggest problem. The actual room housing the engines was more of the same. All of the machinery was dented or broken. He discovered a large wrench jammed into the secondary engine. Zu yanked the tool out and continued his search. Even louder than venting steam, the captain could hear the roar of the winds outside.

"D'alor, no."

Only he and Henning had keys to the hatch that led to the balloon outside, but the lock had been smashed off. Zu's brow furrowed. Whoever was hurting the Wyvera was going to pay dearly. He gripped the wrench and kicked the broken hatch.

The winds howled as he climbed the metal and rope frame. From here he could see that one of the front balloon compartments had been deflating rapidly. He turned the lens of his monogoggle for a better view and spotted a short figure violently attacking another compartment. Z clambered up the frame and approached the airship's attacker from behind.

His grip on the wrench tightened when he saw who was responsible.

"What in the name of the Grandmother of Gods are you doing?!"

Lillian paused her fierce attack on the balloon's thick shell and turned cautiously toward her captain. She pointed her curved dagger at Zu and chided him through gritted teeth.

"I'm doing what's right! That woman doesn't deserve to rot up in the Iceberg. It's the Emperor and his cronies that should be imprisoned. I don't know how you even agreed to this job!"

Zu sighed.

"The job, the politics, it's more complicated than that and you know it. Help me fix this and I promise you won't be punished for this mutiny."

"Free the prisoner and promise us all safety."

"This job is my only chance to free the Wyvera, our home, from Mr. Everett. You know I can't free that criminal… wait, 'all?'"

Lillian shifted her gaze, glancing over Zu's shoulder. The captain noticed the subtle change and ducked just as Moug's fist flew past his face. Zu laughed as he jumped away from subsequent swings.

"To be honest, I expected you might be a part of this, Moug."

"Stop hopping about, rabbit man. I will smash your face good."

Lillian returned to stabbing wildly at the balloon's surface. She finally ripped a tiny hole in the compartment. It emitted a slight hissing noise. As she ripped the hole wider, the gas escaped faster and with more force.

Zu abandoned the wrench: Moug's superior strength gave him no opening to use it. Agility was the only thing keeping Zu alive. He had to detain Moug quickly, before Lillian was able to do any more damage.

The deflated compartment had loosened the ropes and left the metal framing exposed. The balloon's thick and sturdy fabric clung feebly to its skeleton like a giant starving beast. Zu made his attacker chase him up the metal frame. He lured Moug onto the Wyvera's external metal ribs. Then, the captain jumped down onto the balloon, grabbing a loose rope while he slid. He would be able to climb back to safety quickly, leaving Moug to carefully retrace his steps down the solid frame. Nobody that heavy would be foolish enough to attempt his trick.

Zu looked back as he climbed the rope up the other side. Moug was hesitantly studying the balloon and the metal frame. The captain focused on the task of stopping Lillian from doing any more harm. He was almost within arm's reach of a metal frame to pull himself up when what felt like an earthquake nearly shook him off the airship entirely.

He stared in shock as Moug slid down the deflated compartment. The tattooed man gracelessly tumbled down, grasping desperately at the ropes as he passed. Zu could only watch helplessly as Moug's limbs got increasingly tangled in loose rigging. Zu felt a violent tugging at the rope he was on, and quickly clambered up onto the metal frame.

The force of Moug's struggling against the ropes was shaking the entire ship. Lillian was knocked back, her dagger slipping slowly down the side. She fumbled and rolled toward it. Just as she was got close, Zu stood between her and the blade. His tall, lean frame towered over her.

He kicked the dagger away.

"I won't let you destroy us."

"Oh, by Ahmetz the Just! You'll find another ship, you fool!"

"You still don't get it, do you? Where are you planning on crashing this thing? The zomb-spawn are the only things here. We'll all die."

Lillian gaped down at the landscape. The dead gray of the refugee camps mixed with the crumbling stone of the city towers. Already the Wyvera was low enough to see the shuffling corpses wandering aimlessly. It wouldn't be long before the spawn of the Automazombs would notice the faint smell of meat above their heads. They would follow the smell to the crash site, groaning their call to others, indicating a feast was at hand.

Lillian looked back at Zu fearfully.

"I…"

"Help me fix this. Before it's too late."

Lillian nodded in silent defeat. Zu directed her to hold the ship's wound closed. He grabbed a tube of chemical glue from his belt and pasted it quickly onto the fabric. The balloon sizzled as the fibers fused together. The hissing noise of escaping gas was quieted. He wiped the remaining glue on a nearby frame. It had the wonderful effect of only fusing cloth, but it was still rather sticky on one's hands. That task complete, Zu and Lillian turned their attentions to Moug. The man was still trapped in the ropes that once provided a support frame for the deflated compartment. He had managed to wriggle his way toward the rear compartment where they stood, which made it easier to reach him.

"Moug, we're going to pull you up. Don't resist."

"Lillian? You switch sides now? Fine! Once I free the prisoner, maybe she give me your cut." He held up Lillian's dagger. "Also, thank you for giving me way to finish the job! Ha!"

Moug stabbed violently at the inflated compartment. There was a great ripping noise, and his giant arm nearly disappeared into the fabric.

Zu and Lillian shouted at him in vain.

"No!"

"You don't understand! The zombspawn are down there!"

Their words were drowned out by the wind. The ship shook violently. Their work with the chemical glue was undone in an instant. The compartment was ruptured.

Using Lillian's dagger, Moug slashed at the ropes binding the rest of his body. One by one the ropes surrounding him frayed and snapped. Zu and Lillian rushed down the ladder to safety. The tangled mess of rope and man jerked lower and lower.

Zu helped Lillian down to the catwalk. When he looked over to Moug, he saw the man sawing through a large rope that constricted his chest.

"Stop! That one-"

The rope snapped. Moug dropped well below the catwalk level, dangling by a single knot around his leg. He screamed. Zu leaned over the rail. He called out to Moug, but the man was fixated on the swarming masses of the dead. They moaned and snarled as they sensed the presence of living flesh above them. The spawn of the Automazombs were on the move. Moug shouted angrily as he struggled to climb to safety.

Far above, Zu grabbed Lillian by the arm and dragged her inside the engine room.

"If we stop to pull him up, the Wyvera sinks and we all die. Help the others lighten our load. There are three compartments left. Hopefully it'll be enough to keep us afloat. Now, tell me, how many of the crew are involved in this?"

"It was just me, Moug, the prisoner, and-"

Zu's path was blocked by the youngest member of the new crew.

"Hello Freddie."

Freddie gave Lillian a nervous smile and pulled a revolver from under his coat. Shakily, he pointed it at Zu.

"I came to help but I see you already caught the captain?"

"We can't go through with it, Freddie."

"But... it's not right. That's what you said. We had to stop it because it's not right."

"There's too much as risk. Now, help us make this aircraft lighter or get out of the way."

"No! I mean... you said we could run away together with the money the prisoner offered. What... what about love?"

Zu suppressed a laugh.

Lillian rubbed her eyes and heaved a frustrated sigh.

"Okay, so maybe I lied to get you to help. We needed a mechanic."

Freddie shook his head in disbelief. His index finger twitched precariously over the trigger.

"But... I..."

Zu was tired of this little distraction. He grabbed the gun from the young man's hand and instructed Lillian to take him to the cargo cells. They didn't have the time for personal drama right now.

They emerged from the mechanics passage to find the entire crew mobilized into dumping everything overboard. While losing the largest balloon compartments was sinking them quickly, at least the dangerous tilt had been corrected. The twins burst through the door from the galley, awkwardly carrying a barrel between them.

The captain yelped quietly.

"That's mine."

Henning rushed past him with a box full of unopened bottles. Zu grabbed one and chased after the first mate.

"Why?"

"Sorry, sir. Alcohol is a luxury! Everything unnecessary goes over. Those were your orders."

Zu saved a few more bottles from their cruel fate and went to help some others in throwing a table out the back hatch. Anything that wasn't bolted down or food was eventually thrown. Even some of the floorboards took the plunge. They were still cutting it close. The Wyvera's decent had slowed considerably, but they were now forced to maneuver around the former capital city's multi-story buildings.

Yuri'ik shoved a box of engine parts that had been destroyed by the saboteurs out the hatch. It landed on the heads of the zombspawn below, slowing a few of the monsters down.

"Cap'n! The whole city's following us. They're trying to grab our ropes."

Girtch popped his head out to have a look.

"Moug?"

The whole crew, aside from Lillian and Zu, clambered to the portholes to see the oncoming horde and Moug trying to fight them off with Lillian's dagger. Everyone shouted concerns and speculations of their impending doom. Zu, eager to maintain control of the situation, ordered Girtch, Henning, and Baako to stay put and keep trying to lighten the Wyvera from the inside. Zu took the twins and Lillian back through the mechanics passage.

Zu could forgive Lillian: she'd been part of the crew for years. The other two could rot or freeze or both up in the Iceberg for all he cared.

Still, he wasn't a monster. He couldn't leave Moug to die at the hands of the dead.

Even with four people pulling, the tug of war lasted several minutes. The dead weren't willing to give up their prey. They grabbed at the rope and the collar of Moug's shirt, desperate for a better handle on the meat they craved. They very nearly had him, too. He landed a few good punches, but the dead took advantage of the man's outstretched arms. Moug fought frantically as they crowded around, sustaining only a few scratches from the wretched spawn of the Automazombs.

Moug shouted encouragement to the crew above, and punched another zombspawn in the face. It fell back, knocking a few others to the ground as well. Little by little, he rose above the crowd of shambling horrors. He gave one final indignant gesture as he was hoisted to safety.

When Moug was a few short meters below the broken hatch, the team stopped pulling. Zu leaned out and tapped the man on the bottom of his boot to get his attention.

Moug writhed, trying to get upright.

"Why you stop? Pull me up!"

"Were you bitten by the dead?"

"What?"

"Did they bite you? Their bite, it's infectious."

"No. No bites!"

"Good. Now, you have a choice. Spend time on the prison isle until Mr. Everett himself goes to retrieve you--"

"You crazy, thinking I choose that."

"*Or!* Or you die here and now. A feast for the dead as punishment for mutiny and sabotage."

Moug looked down at the thousands of gray faces, filled with gnashing teeth, hungry for flesh.

"Iceberg! I choose the Iceberg."

He grumbled as they dragged him into the Wyvera. He nearly pushed Girtch out the hatch as he stumbled and clawed his way upright again. Moug was escorted to the cargo hold, where the second prison cell was waiting for him.

Zu tossed Moug into the makeshift brig where Freddie grumbled to himself.

"Madam, you nearly got everyone aboard killed today. Yourself included. Nobody can side with your views if they're dead. You two... for your sakes I hope Mr. Everett finds you useful enough to send for. If not, may the lady of destiny look on you kindly."

Over the next few days, the crew performed their duties solemnly. Lillian was trusted with few tasks, and spoken to even less. Any talk was of how astounded everyone was that they had survived. The Wyvera was still passing dangerously low, but the mountains were behind them. Captain Zu monitored the dread enemy's progress through a spyglass. Most had given up the chase and merely wandered the foothills in search of a live meal, but a few seemed determined to catch the Wyvera. The zombspawn were not known for their brilliant strategies. They would likely fall over the icy cliffs when the zeppelin reached the northern shore.

Zu and Baako had taken on the task of repairing the mechanics and the engines. Many parts were beyond repair and had to be thrown overboard. They did manage to return some limited steering functionality to the airship, much to Henning's delight. The rest, however, proved to be nearly impossible to fix.

Baako stood over the captain, gripping a spanner with both hands.

"Mr. Zu, sir."

"What's on your mind, friend?"

"I have something important that you must hear."

Zu plucked out a screw that had been wedged between two gears.

"Is it about my drinking? Honestly, I get enough grief from Henning. If a Nomad cannot do as he pleases, what, by D'alor, is the point of living?"

"No, sir. It's about Moug and the ship, and Mr. Everett."

Zu stopped and turned to Baako. He studied the man's face, judged him sincere, and gestured that he should relate whatever news he felt he needed to share.

Beads of sweat coated Baako's forehead.

"I know you plan to leave Moug at the Iceberg, so perhaps that is enough. But you may change your mind when you know what he has done."

"And what might that be?"

"Mr. Everett did all he could to make you indebted to him. He wanted to keep you in his employ permanently. But you, your only wish was to fly away with your family. When he realized that, he schemed a way to keep you tethered to him."

"What are you saying?"

"It was Moug he sent… to murder your family."

Zu couldn't believe his ears. His eyes welled up at the painful memories. He could feel his knees about to give way and propped himself up against the wall. He knew Mr. Everett would lie and cheat his way through business dealings, but murder? Zu's hands curled into fists.

Baako frowned.

"But that didn't weaken your resolve, did it Mr. Zu?"

Zu shook his head silently. The loss of his family had only made his longing for freedom stronger. He was fairly sure he knew what was coming next.

The Djimbuk mechanic could no longer meet Zu's eyes.

"Mr. Everett enlisted us to sink this airship and kill you. The prisoner was to bait any of your crew with anti-Teraltian sentiments. I'm sorry, sir."

Zu glowered, drowning the sadness he carried for his family with hatred for Everett and his men. Taking on a man like Baako would probably be suicide. The fighters of Djimbuk were known for their

104

cunning and ferocity. Still, his life was all Zu had left in this world, he certainly wasn't going to give it up without a fight. His response was a low growl as he took a defensive stance.

"Well? I can only assume you told me this so you can finish the job."

Baako snapped to attention. He took a step back as he held his hands up in front of him.

"What? No! Girtch and I, we're with you Captain. We yearn for a life in the skies! Free to roam as we please, if you'll still have us?"

Zu relaxed slightly. His heart pounded and his mouth was dry. His heart would get over the initial anger and shock, but he felt his mouth could use some encouragement. He slipped by Baako on the way to the galley and patted the man's shoulder.

Baako flinched.

"You're not mad, sir? If I had spoken sooner-"

"Ohh, I'm livid. I'll be visiting Moug's cell before we hand him over. Also, there may not be a letter to Mr. Everett concerning any extra prisoners in the Iceberg. Still, I say finding two loyal new crewmembers is cause for a minor celebration. Come; let's drink to being alive."

Later in the evening, after Zu had numbed the pain and toasted his good fortune in finding allies among enemies, the captain paid a visit to his ever-expanding brig. A small lamp flickered where Yuri'ik was playing an old Northerner's card game. Every now and then he would glance up and make sure the prisoners weren't doing anything suspicious. He nodded to Zu and continued his game.

The political dissident sat on the small wooden bench, curled up against the porthole. The moonlight illuminated a tiny sliver of her face. She ignored the captain's presence and continued to stare outside. Zu felt a twinge of guilt, knowing that he could release her at any time, but it soon passed. By her own admission, she was willing to kill innocents in order to further her goals. The Iceberg was a harsh punishment, but it was better than setting her free.

Zu turned his attention to the shouting coming from the new cell.

Moug and Freddie were seconds away from a brawl.

"I rip your face off, you little rat!"

"Hey! I tried to save your life, you ungrateful bastard."

"You do a better job, maybe those ghouls never almost eat me."

"Captain! Mr. Zu, save me from this madman. He's gone off the rails!"

Zu stared at the two men. One had ripped away his love and the other tried to help in ripping away his life. His hand slipped into his pocket and caressed his daughter's little good luck charm. There was a spark in the captain's eye that made Freddie take a nervous step away from the cell door. The young man stumbled over a loose board and propped himself up against the wall. Zu's piercing gaze struck both of them dumb. The light and jovial captain his crew was used to was nowhere to be found.

Zu directed his focus on Moug.

"Front and center, you child-murdering snake." His anger grew with Moug's hesitation. "Now!"

Moug sneered and walked up to the door of the makeshift cell.

Zu turned toward Yuri'ik. The calm had returned to his voice, but a threatening undercurrent remained.

"Open the cell."

Moug grinned slyly, showing a mix of tooth and metal.

"I am pardoned! Smart man, Zu."

Captain Zu quietly wrapped his right hand with a long chain while Yuri'ik did as he was told. The door was barely open when Moug took his chance for freedom. He barreled into Yuri'ik and made a break for the exit past the captain. He only got a few steps out of his cell when Zu's chain-covered fist smashed into his jaw. One of Moug's few remaining original teeth went flying. He staggered back into the cell.

Moug growled, holding his jaw tenderly. He spat a large glob of blood onto the ground.

"You find out, huh? Girtch or Baako? I should know who to kill after I get out of thi--"

Zu landed another punch, this time crashing into the man's cheekbone. Moug stopped trying to talk and flew into a wild rage. Zu was much faster than the bulky Moug and ducked each swing easily. In the confined area of the brig, Moug's size was a disadvantage. Meanwhile, Zu had plenty of space to maneuver, even considering he had to avoid Freddie. The young man was cowering in the corner with Moug's blood splattered across his stunned face. The captain landed a few good blows to Moug's stomach and groin, effectively incapacitating him.

Moug crashed onto the wooden bench, nearly cracking it under his weight. The dazed Moug weakly grasped the air between himself and the captain.

"Hold still... I kill you... All of you."

Zu grabbed Moug's head and pressed his face into the porthole glass.

"Do you see the icy cliffs ahead? Before the sun rises tomorrow, you will be a resident of the most feared prison in the world."

"Mr. Everett... have me out in days."

"Not likely. Mutiny is messy business in a sky-oriented society. No, you'll both be stuck here for a long time. Maybe it'll give you time to think about all the lives you've destroyed."

"Your wife... and children... were weak. Boy didn't fight back. They deserved death."

Moug's skull made a sickening *whunk* as Zu knocked the man unconscious. The captain slowly turned to leave, dropping the chain to the ground. He signaled for Yuri'ik to lock the cell again. Freddie looked up at the captain, his face covered in a faint red mist.

Zu looked down on him with a small measure of pity.

"Wash yourself up. No telling where that mangy dog's been."

Zu sighed and trudged off to his quarters to clean up. The job was very nearly complete. After the prisoners were transferred, a decision would need to be made. Should he repair the Wyvera and fly with his loyal crew? Abandon everything and become a hermit? Take revenge on Mr. Everett?

After he had cleaned all of Moug's blood from his hands and shirt, Zu lay in his hammock, watching the dark sapphire sky. He was too weary to deal with the future right now. He would speak to the crew once they landed. This was as much their future as his.

The Wyvera anchored at the docks just outside the prison an hour before dawn. They were greeted by the warden and four guards, each wearing thick fur coats. More watched from the high stone wall and guard towers. At least a dozen guns were trained on the airship's cargo bay door.

All three prisoners were chained together at the wrist. Zu gave Moug a rough kick to get him walking, and off his ship for good. The man had gotten twitchy over the night, and looked pale.

The warden stepped forward and made a sweeping gesture at the Wyvera.

"Welcome, Captain. Had some trouble, I see?"

"It's been sorted out. As a result, you have two new guests."

The warden frowned at Moug.

"Bit sick, isn't he? Something to do with your bird's troubles?"

Moug was doubled over, coughing up blood and bile. Additional guards streamed out onto the dock to clean up and escort Moug through the prison yard toward the medical building.

Zu kept his face placid. The addition of two prisoners had turned easy payment into a negotiation. It was best not to worry the man over nothing.

"The man doesn't fly well."

"The medic'll patch him up. Though your bird might be hopeless."

Zu looked over his shoulder at the wounded Wyvera.

"We'll manage. We just need parts and balloon gas."

"Sure, sure. We can take it out of what we owe you for the prisoner. Nothing extra for these two though. Not part of the agreement."

"These are Mr. Everett of Dantus's men. I'm certain he would pay for their safe return."

The warden eyed Freddie, then nodded to Zu.

"I certainly cannot charge you for spare parts you find for yourselves around the docks. And if a gas pump were left unattended…"

Two more guards came to collect the political dissident. When she was behind the iron gate, the warden handed over payment for the woman's transfer. Normally, the entire sum would be delivered back to Mr. Everett; payments short of their promised amount were punished severely. But now Zu knew the full extent of his employer's treachery. The money would go to his crew to secure their future. Zu shook the warden's hand and turned to pass on news of the arrangement to the crew.

On the way, he passed Lillian and Freddie saying their goodbyes.

"Look… Freddie."

"Mmmh?"

Lillian leaned in and gave Freddie a passionate goodbye kiss. She lingered there a long while before releasing the young man once again.

"I used you, you used me, we were both used by Moug and that prisoner woman. Some other situation… maybe we could have gotten to know each other…"

"Grruuughhh…"

"Freddie?"

Freddie crumpled to the ground, becoming even more ill than Moug had. Lillian knelt down to try to comfort him. She shouted at Captain Zu.

"You beat up Freddie as well? How could you? Moug, that makes sense, but…"

"I did no such thing. What are you--"

A flurry of shouts and screams exploded from inside the prison walls. An alarm wailed, sending the entire island into a panic. Extra guards, toting large rifles, clambered up the towers to help quell the fighting. At the center of the violence, Zu saw the familiar, over-muscular shape of Moug.

The warden walked up to Zu with a placating gesture and a greasy smile.

"Nothing to fear. Riots happen every now and again. That Moug of yours will get solitary for this. The guards shoot to injure. I can't be paid for his return if he dies."

A pair of guards approached Freddie. Lillian helped prop the young man up. As soon as he was close to standing, he leaned toward Lillian.

She pushed his shoulder away.

"I'm not interested in another go. Not after you've been sick all over the ground here, not to mention on my boots."

Freddie's face twisted into a snarl. His skin was pale and his eyes took on a faint grayish-red hue. He lunged out and tackled Lillian, biting and scratching, mauling the woman before she could even think about drawing a weapon against him. The guards pulled Freddie off of his victim, leaving Lillian sputtering and in shock. Freddie quickly turned his attack to the guards, making quick work of them.

Zu held the warden back from assisting the guards.

"Stop! You'll only get killed too."

The warden emptied his pistol into Freddie until the young man fell.

"What in the Dark Lady's domain is going on?"

"We had a run-in with the zombspawn. We thought Moug was clean. But--"

Lillian was already showing signs, twitching oddly and vomiting blood. Zu quickly unholstered his pistol and aimed for his weapons expert's forehead. One shot and she was down for good.

The warden called out to the guards in the towers, shouting orders to kill any attackers. His voice was drowned out by the screams and alarms inside the prison walls. Zu raced toward his airship. They couldn't fly. Not without pumping more gas into the balloon compartments, and that took time. There was no way they would be able to make it far skirting so close to the icy ocean waves. He and his crew needed a different escape route.

Owynn emerged just as Zu made it to the rear bay.

"C-captain! What's going on? Where's L-lillian?"

"Zombspawn! This whole place is infected. Get the crew out here now!"

Owynn scrambled off to spread the news. The crew poured out onto the landing dock faster than Zu had dared to hope. If they acted quickly they might survive this. The warden had gone up to the nearest tower to give the kill order in person. Zu climbed up the ladder after him. The siren had been stopped so that the other guards could hear the new orders.

Zu grabbed the warden by his collar and spun him around.

"We're taking a boat. Don't chase us down to retrieve it."

"What? No you're not! First you need to pay for the chaos you've spilled here!"

"You're joking."

The warden broke away from Zu's grasp.

"I should arrest you for this! We haven't had any trouble with these Automazomb spawn until you came. Paying for the damages is the least--"

Zu grabbed a wad of Imperial bills from his pocket and threw it at the warden.

"Fine, keep the money! We need that boat!"

"Take a fishing boat. I doubt we need all of them after this disaster."

Zu slid down the tower's ladder and pointed in the direction of the pier for water vessels. He took one final look at his gorgeous Wyvera. The potential futures he and his crew could have planned were a hazy dream.

There was only one clear path now, and that led to the Iceberg's fishing boats.

As they raced along the docks, Zu caught a glimpse of the prison through barred windows. The dead were gaining the advantage in the prison riot. The alarms had brought more prisoners and guards into the large yard. There they met with Moug's rage.

Zu had never seen the zombspawn plague take hold so quickly before. This was the most dangerous strain he'd ever heard of. Guards screamed on the other side of the wall. More must have been turned. The screams traveled, as newly dead killed their way into the buildings, creating even more of the wretched zombspawn. By the time the tower guards realized they needed to shoot to kill, they were outnumbered.

Dead arms reached for Zu and his crew through barred windows. A handful of zombspawn burst through a wooden door ahead of them. The captain was able to take out a few with his pistol. Baako and Yuri'ik downed a few as well, but they were still blocked from their goal.

Aria sent her crowbar into the face of an ex-guard.

"What do we do, captain?!"

"I'll come up with something."

"Come up with it fast!"

Zombspawn shambled closer in ever greater numbers. They'd soon be hopelessly surrounded. Zu used his empty gun as a bludgeon. He guarded his crew as best he could. If he took enough out, the others might make it to safety. He swallowed his fear and braced himself for the fight.

Girtch's pushed his way in front of the captain.

"I'll buy you time, Mr. Zu."

Before Zu could protest, Girtch shouted a taunt and barreled into the zombies that blocked the crew's path. Zu and the rest of the crew raced past. Girtch's fist fight with the dead wouldn't stop them for long.

The fishing boats were just ahead.

Yuri'ik led the way, shouting back to Zu.

112

"Which one do we take?"

"Any of them! Just go!"

Owynn grabbed Zu's sleeve. He was near collapsing from exhaustion.

"W-wait! Take that one, to the right!"

"Are you sure?"

"You want someone who c-can actually helm one of these things, right? I've sailed one just like that b-before."

"Right. Yuri'ik! That tall one there."

He pointed urgently as his chief mechanic bounded up the gang plank. Yuri'ik went straight for the crank that would raise the anchor. Baako and the captain arrived next and began working on the ropes that held the craft up against the pier.

Aria and Owynn ran past Zu and scrambled aboard at the same time, away from the gaping maws of the zombspawn. Owynn's heavy steps shook the plank as they ascended, causing Aria to lose her balance and slip down. Her crowbar splashed into the ocean. Owynn reached out and caught her arm before Aria fell too. She screamed in surprise and pain, her feet dangling close the icy waves.

Henning picked up a loose board and was swinging it at any dead that came close while Zu finished untying the ropes. He cracked another ghoul in the head and sent it splashing into the frigid water.

Behind him, Zu called out.

"The boat's free. Come on!"

Zu and Baako ran to help pull Aira to safety. Once she was on the gangplank, they all ran to safety. Yuri'ik was nearly finished dredging up the anchor. Aria and Baako took directions from Owynn to get the vessel running.

As Henning turned to follow, one of the gray-faced dead bit down on his forearm. He let out an agonizing wail and bashed the culprit over the head until the monster's skull shattered.

Zu waved from the top of the gangplank, beckoning Henning aboard.

"Hurry, friend!"

Henning frowned and squeezed his bleeding arm. The zombspawn shuffled past him toward the ship, paying no mind to the infected first mate. One of them reached the gang plank and started slowly climbing. Henning rushed forward and kicked the thing into the water. More and more of the dead were pouring out of the prison onto the pier. Henning took down another pair of zomb-kin as the fishing boat slowly chugged forward.

"Captain, pull up the plank."

"What?! No! Get up here Henning. That's an order!"

Henning raised his bitten arm so that the captain could see. Zu cursed and slammed a fist against the boat's wooden rail. Henning had been with him from the very beginning. Ever since he discovered the lieutenant fending off a gang of desert raiders that had killed his squadron, they had been the closest of friends.

Zu sighed and lowered his gaze.

"Defying your captain's direct order, huh? That'll be two days in the brig."

The Wyvera's first mate smiled and saluted his friend.

"Yes, sir. Sorry, sir."

"Right then... you're dismissed."

"Thank you, captain."

Henning took out another pair of zombies and gave Zu a wry smirk. Among the spare nets and ropes that littered the pier were barrels of liquid fuel. He pried one open and spilled it out onto the dock. The shambling ghouls didn't even notice the liquid rushing past their feet. Another barrel was lifted over their heads and poured onto as many as possible. A third became Henning's podium for his last stand. He pulled out a small pipe he carried and a box of matches.

Zu and Yuri'ik shook off an dead attacker who grasped onto the gangplank as they pulled it in. The rest of the horde was sluggishly joining them, eager for a meal that was slowly drifting away. Henning lit his pipe and flicked the match onto the fuel at his feet.

The captain looked on sadly as Henning and any zombspawn within reach went up in flames. When the pier collapsed, Zu joined the others in adjusting the sails toward warmer waters.

That night they held a small memorial. Zu held up a bottle of Irenorn vodka he found aboard and addressed his surviving crew.

"Today we have lost friends and enemies. I pray that those whose bodies have succumbed to the ghoulish plague have souls resting with dark Ershk-gula. She will honor the heroic deeds of Girtch and Lt. James Henning, and guide them to their peaceful rest. In the end, we are left with many fine memories of their lives. They will all be sorely missed."

He lifted up his bottle and took a long draught. The others did the same with their own glasses. Beyond a few memories shared, the group was silent in their mourning. Eventually, Zu parted from the rest and took a walk out on the deck. The sun was just beginning to rise over the tall cliffs.

Zu gazed at the horizon. To his right, the ocean and sky merged into an endless swath of blue. To his right, waves crashed against the rocky shore. The crisp salty air filled him with a sense of adventure. How strange that a son of the Nomads would find himself the captain of a water vessel. His people wandered the deserts and mountains centuries before the old Haak Republic was a thought. Water was scarce and sacred. It was for drinking and bathing only; never for travel.

The ocean craft rocked steadily as it hit the waves, much like the Wyvera shifted in the air currents. The ocean spoke to his longing for freedom. His former employer could rot up in that floating city for all Zu cared, just like the undying dead decayed along the ground.

He wondered if anyone had ever bothered to sail out past the great continent. He'd never seen any charts or heard stories about anyone exploring the ocean before. Zu smiled and took another swig from the bottle in his hand. He was a new breed of Nomad, driven from his home by the kin of the Automazombs, ripped from all he knew and loved, and directed to a path of an extraordinary opportunity.

A tentative voice called from the doorway.

"Captain?"

"Yuri'ik, my friend, what can I do for you?"

"Owynn was wondering what course to set."

Zu flashed a crooked grin.

"Due south to Port Fenzir. And call the crew together. I have a proposal to make."

LAST GIRL STANDING

By Dex Greenbright

Evellyn Hawke lay on her stomach, carefully controlling each breath. She adjusted the focus on her telescoping goggles. In the valley below, the city of Luggermire writhed with shambling, bloodthirsty corpses.

That Automazomb has to be here. She'd already checked Wanniton and Aeromnica and the little unnamed farm villages that dotted the road between. Her list of known Zomb locations had never been this off before.

Every time she passed a still-occupied government building, library, or a chapter of the Inventors Guild, she asked for information on the mechanical helpers-turned-killers. Useful tidbits like locations and descriptions went on her list. The list had grown, shrunk, and grown again over the years as she personally hunted down the Guild's mistakes.

Many people were skeptical of her intentions. Government officials tended not to trust anyone wearing an engineer's pin. Evellyn knew she should take it off now that she was expelled from their ranks. But the pin was a part of her, like the green ribbon around her upper arm.

She touched the ribbon and closed her eyes. Gods damn those zomb-spawn. In Liridon's last letter, he was securing a zeppelin ticket for Caelspyr so he could speak with a Master Historian Subbek, who was apparently notorious for crackpot theories involving the Haak. The letter was dated a week before the crash of the floating city. Her chances of reuniting with her friend died when she felt what she later learned was the great tremor.

Liridon's letter confused her at first. He had been so doggedly pursuing the common people's experiences with the Automazombs and the plague, it seemed strange that he would start speaking of the Haak. She strongly suspected that she did not receive a key page or whole other letter that would have explained the shift in focus.

Whatever his current goal, it had to be Automazomb-related. It always was. She felt a pang of guilt. It was her advancements in mechanical limbs that provided a much-needed breakthrough for the project. Certain unscrupulous members of the Guild had twisted her invention and sent out woefully undertested machines, but all of those foolish and greedy men were dead. Which left the responsibility for fixing the horrible state of the world resting solely on her shoulders.

So now she scanned the city below for signs of a lumbering, mechanical killer. Liridon's death had strengthened her resolve. She would set things right.

The Automazomb she hunted today was reportedly fairly human-looking. No extra arms, no mechanical treads replacing its legs. This particular machine didn't even emit the tea-kettle whistle that over half of its brethren did. Those were easy to hunt down. Evellyn idly wished it was some sort of spider-like fiend, so she could pick it out of the dusty, gray crowd.

Hours drifted by like clouds. She shifted her leg to make sure her satchel was within reach. Its contents were her life. Beyond the food and change of clothes that one might expect from anyone traveling Eysan, she had her spare prosthetic arm, her favorite tools, a stack of old letters from Liridon, and an injector gun with accompanying vials. Ten of the vials lay empty. Only two vials still contained any concoction. *Focus, Evellyn. That's a problem for another day.*

The longer she watched the meandering zomb-spawn, the more she fidgeted. Unlike the original plague, the dead from this new plague decomposed. It was a slow process, but at least the new illness didn't leave immortal husks behind. Luggermire was filled with corpses missing ears and noses and even the occasional eye. Their hunting method was essentially stumbling forward until they found prey, then swarming.

Automazombs were much more dangerous. They could smell a living person. Their red eyes saw perfectly both day and night. If one was down there somewhere, Evellyn had a limited time to find it before it hunted her instead.

Hunger gnawed at her. The sun peeked out from under the clouds as it slowly sank into its bed. Every muscle in Evellyn's body tensed. No luck today. She had to retreat soon, find a safe place to bunker down for the night.

Two red points of light caught her eye. Evellyn leaned right and adjusted the goggles. There! Between two of the taller buildings: the Automazomb! She mentally noted its location in the city and the direction it was ambling. She had to move quickly to keep ahead of the night.

Evellyn crept in a wide arc around the dead and anything with a large enough shadow to hide them. *One, two*, she counted the streets she passed. *So far so good.* An eerie moan bubbled up from a block or two away. The hairs on the back of Evellyn's neck stood up. When no other dead responded to the call, she breathed a sigh of relief.

Five, six, echoes of mechanical whirrs and clanks whispered from the city center. Evellyn loaded her injector gun. Her second-to-last full vial clicked into the chamber. She rounded the corner cautiously. Three dead stood idly near an old storefront, facing the window. One began clawing the glass when Evellyn's reflection appeared in the window. It groaned softly. The others next to it joined the alarm and started shuffling toward the first. Evellyn kept them in the corner of her vision as she snuck by. The zomb-spawn remained focused on the window.

With the injector gun in one hand and the other, metal hand gripping the strap of her satchel, Evellyn crept toward the Automazomb. She used debris for cover as she circled the machine. The streets here were littered with rubble from the riots that followed Caelspyr's crash. Some of the brick and metal might even have been flung from the city itself, as the crash site was just a few days' walk away. The Zomb was digging through a pile of bricks littering the sidewalk. The metal claws grafted onto its hands were scuffed and dulled. As Evellyn made her way closer, she had to cover her nose. Bits of a dark green dress poked up from the debris. There was a body beneath the bricks.

A Zomb locked onto a meal was a creature of singular focus. Evellyn could stomp, or even shout, right now and would be in no more danger than if she were still up on the hill. She wouldn't, of course. The dead back down the street were still moaning to themselves and drawing more of their kind to the window. She wouldn't give them a reason to change direction.

She stopped behind a broken autocarriage and checked the injector gun one last time. Everything was in place. She took a deep breath, then climbed. From the roof of the autocarriage, she scanned the Zomb for the best injection point. Its head was completely covered in metal plates. The engine on its back billowed steam. Shoulders were bare, but not a good delivery method for the chemist's concoction. *Come on, you big brute, show me your neck.*

Evellyn didn't have to wait long. The Automazomb reached down into the brick pile and pulled an arm free with a squelch and a crack. The machine whirred louder as it prepared to feed. Slowly, jerkily, it stretched to its full height of nearly seven feet and turned to face Evellyn.

Her heart jumped into her throat.

"Oh gods."

The Automazomb glared at her with those glowing bulb eyes while it made quick work of the arm. It was evaluating her as food. But it also gave her the chance to see that yes, its neck was exposed, just as she suspected. She wished there was time to celebrate this fact, but she had precious few seconds before she was next on the menu.

Evellyn grinned. She ran along the roof of the autocarriage to get a little extra height in her jump over to the Zomb. But she didn't factor in the thin layer of dust on the roof. Her foot slipped. She fell to the ground at the Zomb's feet. Her injector gun landed next to one of the sturdy metal supports. The dread machine stomped the ground, gears and pistons working hard to help the beast find her again. Evellyn saved her injector before it was crushed.

As she got to her feet, she heard the gut-wrenching sound of glass shattering. She glanced at the injector. It was missing its vial! The

Automazomb growled. Greenish liquid dripped from its right foot. Evellyn cursed aloud as she dug through her satchel. *Empty. Empty.*

"Godsdamned empty vials!"

The Zomb took a lumbering step closer. Its mouth hung agape. Evellyn's hand touched a slightly heavier glass tube. *There it is!*

She deftly snapped the vial into her injector gun.

Then, she saw movement behind her quarry.

Zomb-spawn.

Evellyn didn't need a guess as to what had drawn them. Her mission relied on utter silence, and she'd gotten rattled. So many Automazombs she'd hunted, and she still was making mistakes like this? She cursed again, caring less what monsters might hear.

She was too short to reach the Zomb's neck now. And she wasn't equipped to fight the dead. She scanned the Automazomb for another injection point. Crook of the elbow? Thigh? No! She spotted a narrow gap between the reinforcing plates covering the chest.

The Automazomb reached for her. Evellyn ducked, then rushed forward. She slammed the injector against the Zomb's chest and squeezed the trigger. There was a soft *ki-shnt!* as the concoction was forced into the machine.

Zomb-spawn moaned from the gathering darkness. The Automazomb tried to grab her a second time. Evellyn used her prosthetic arm to push the thing's hand away. One of these days she swore she would build a weapon attachment for herself, but for now the functionality of fingers was too useful to lose in exchange for a sword or gun.

Evellyn could see two zomb-spawn stumbling toward her. More were surely behind them, or coming from the other side of the street. The Automazomb in front of her grumbled again. The concoction should have been working its way through the monster's muscles and gut.

The zomb-spawn groans built upon one another into a racket that made Evellyn shiver. She had to escape, but where? And how? She had no idea how many of them were out there in the dark. The closest zomb-spawn reached out an arm ragged from decay.

Evellyn punched the Automazomb square in the chest with her prosthetic arm.

"Hurry up!"

She swung her satchel at the first of the zomb-spawn. It stumbled sideways. That gave her an opening to at least clamber up onto the autocarriage again. She nearly made it when one of the dead grabbed her pantleg. She kicked at the zomb-spawn with her free foot.

The Automazomb clicked and whirred. It grabbed the zomb-spawn's arm with both hands and bit right through the bone. Evellyn scrambled the rest of the way up onto the autocarriage. She pried the dead fingers off her leg and threw the zomb-spawn's severed hand to the ground.

As night truly came for Luggermire, Evellyn made herself as small and unreachable as she could. The only light came from the Zomb's glowing eyes and the tiny points of stars high above. The only sounds were the dead meeting their end at the hands of the monster that created them.

By the time the sun rose the next day, Luggermire no longer belonged to the dead. The Zomb left no signs they had ever shambled through those streets. The Automazomb itself had gone, off to hunt new prey.

Evellyn lay on the roof of the autocarriage, exhausted and frustrated at the loss of a vial. She was done now. She lifted the flap of her satchel and scratched a new line into the leather. Fourteen Zombs total had been fixed through her efforts. There had been hundreds of the machines deployed. Some broke, some were destroyed by people, but there had to still be dozens more out in the world, spreading the new plague.

She sat up and sighed. The ruins of the floating city were barely visible on the horizon. She hadn't been this close to Caelspyr since it still roamed the skies over Teraltis. So much had been lost. For the world, for the Empire, for her. It hurt to think about.

After some time, she slid down and started walking. Evellyn checked her list. An Automazomb was supposed to be wandering the forests near Glaudston. Two or three days' walk, at most. She camped in an abandoned farmhouse that night. The family's zinc-battery bulb lantern gave her an idea on how she might avoid getting caught in the dark again. She repurposed the lantern and a few other found items into a glass-and-mirror-enhanced torch. She affixed it to her goggles.

The next day, she walked along the old roads. Not a single living soul traveled with or past her that day. She tried not to think about how few people she'd talked to in the past year. She also tried not to notice how close this road was taking her to the great scar, with the remains of Caelspyr at the head of it.

In fact, Glaudston lay half buried in dirt and metal. What had been the portmost outer rim of Caelspyr dug into the very forest Evellyn was meant to search. Its rusting metal skeleton towered over the canopy. She told herself she was only picking the next closest Automazomb on her list. Deep down, she wondered if that was true. Did she secretly want to see the ruins for herself? Or entertain the possibility of finding Liridon's remains, for closure?

And what if van Gremphe's laboratory was still standing? She could find his recipe for the concoction. From what she'd seen of the man, he was meticulous in his note-taking. She assumed this was out of necessity, since his employer was prone to grand fits of destruction. Lady Wyn herself didn't appear interested in posterity, or allowing others to attempt to replicate her experiments.

Before she knew it, Evellyn was climbing up a crooked ladder into the Undercity.

The Undercity, which she'd been told was capitalized as if it were a neighborhood name, was a maze of layered catwalks and buildings that housed the various machinery that had kept the city flying and functioning. Find the right door and one could find tiny homes, markets, bars, even temples nestled together among the machines. But the more occupied the space, the more mangled it was in the crash. Not to mention the stink of death and rot. Evellyn preferred to find paths outdoors.

It would have been a difficult enough feat while Caelspyr still flew, but the crash destroyed buildings and walkways alike. Evellyn wished she had a sturdy rope, or a grapple chain, in her satchel. A grapple hand attachment for her prosthetic arm would be perfect right now! *Which would require a workshop to create; all of those are inconveniently topside.* Evellyn pulled her

123

mouth to one side in frustration. She worked to convince herself that having any large attachments to the arm would risk severing the electranum connection that allowed her to use the metal fingers.

The only shining light in all of this was that no zomb-spawn prowled the catwalks and buildings she'd crept through. She was careful to keep quiet, since the dead could still be on the ground below and she didn't want to attract attention. But the tense burden of staying out of death's jaws slipped further away from her thoughts the longer she explored the Undercity.

Evellyn found that she only had two possibly upward options on her current path. The first was a chute that had become dislodged from its housing and now created a sort of tunnel ramp. It looked rickety at best. The second was a stuck door leading to a building whose roof, if any Undercity buildings could be considered to have roofs, connected all the way topside. She went for the door.

The door was not locked, but the crash had bent it out of shape. Evellyn took out her screwdriver and pliers and sat down to remove the hinges. If the door wouldn't swing open, it would come off. Four of six screws came out without issue. The last two screws were stuck tight. Evellyn sawed off the heads, then pushed, kicked, and yanked the door until, with one final grunt of effort, it came free. The heavy metal door tipped over the catwalk railing and crashed to the ground below.

Birds startled out of the trees. Evellyn leaned over the railing, nervously staring at the forest below. She could hear only the faintest of echoing groans. Somewhere, the dead had heard her. But she couldn't see any, so she turned her attention again to the building.

Evellyn pulled her goggles back down from her thick, kinky hair. She smiled. The torch she outfitted was already of use! She flipped the switch and waited for the torch bulb to warm up. The room smelled absolutely rank. The air was swampy. She spotted a row of cisterns, most of them cracked. The floor glistened yellow-green.

Her torch warmed to a decently bright, yellow glow. She made her way down the ramp as she searched for the best path up to the topside, preferably using a path that would keep her dry. A metal staircase in shambles along the left wall beckoned. The flickering light of the lamp made the long shadows appear as if they were stirring from a deep slumber. Then she heard the sloshing of dead feet in dirty water.

Evellyn sucked in a breath. She smacked the torch switch until it turned off.

"What was I thinking? Oh gods. *Ohhh gods.*"

A single, lengthy moan echoed.

She inched back to the open doorway. The uncloseable, unlockable doorway, thanks to her.

The first moan was answered with a higher pitch gurgling sound. Then a groan and another moan. Evellyn turned and ran.

Her foot slipped as she raced back to the rickety chute. She turned to see three dead shambling out of the building. They jostled on another in an effort to catch her. One looked like it might fall over the rail, but it maintained enough balance to stay on the catwalk. It even stumbled into an awkward jog.

The chute hung over the catwalk so that the opening was at Evellyn's eye level. She got two hands on the edge and put all her weight into pulling herself up and in. The chute dropped half a meter. The drop knocked her flat on her back.

"Oof!"

The trio of dead sped up at the sound of her voice. More were out on the catwalks now, loping closer and clicking their teeth as if to say "you will be chewed, you will be eaten." That made eight that Evellyn could see. She jumped to her feet and tried the chute again. The extra fall had settled it enough to feel stable this time.

She climbed inside. Behind and below, dead hands banged on the chute and reached inside the opening. Evellyn flicked the switch on her torch. The calls of the dead surrounded her. She winced as she ascended through the chute. *They're just echoes. The dead can't climb.*

The chute creaked and swayed. They didn't need to climb if they could bring her back down to their level. The chute angle grew ever steeper. With any luck, that meant she was getting near the top. Evellyn planted her feet against the sides of the chute to keep from slipping back. She gripped the seams with her fingertips.

When she came to a crosspath in the chute, she continued up. The other directions angled down and she had no intention of risking ending up any lower than where she began. After several more minutes of arduous climbing, the chute ended in a vent. Light streamed in through the slats. Evellyn punched with her metal hand until the vent broke open. She squeezed her way out and looked around to get her bearings.

Caelspyr's topside was a mess. The wreckage looked like an earthquake and several tornadoes had had their way with the city. Not much was left standing. What had been an upper noble district full of parks and gardens was now overgrown with opportunistic vines and weeds. Evellyn could barely make out the ruins of the palace at the center. She currently stood on the middle level, once the busiest center of business in all Eysan. The stone facades had been torn away by the crash. All that remained were the structures' warped, iron skeletons.

Not that any of these sights were unexpected, exactly, but seeing the once-great city still shook Evellyn. She used to have friends who lived here and family, coworkers, mentors. Her own city of Kibou was still flying, last she heard, but for how much longer? The world had lost confidence in the floating cities. They were supposed to keep people safe from the chaos of the ground.

Evellyn sighed.

"Just like the Zombs were *supposed* to save us from the plague."

Lady Wyneira's laboratory was palace aport, so far as Evellyn recalled. On Kibou, it would have been called tower aport: a little ways to the left of island center. She remembered a few street names and landmarks from her previous trip. *Verdellen, you've been with me so far. I'll find your temple and give an offering if you help me still.*

Evellyn climbed centerward through the streets, boggling that such a verb was required. The ground was buckled in so many places that simple walking was impossible. Occasionally, she spotted gatherings of zomb-spawn in the distance. They growled and gurgled, but couldn't follow her. The dead had almost as much trouble with hills as they did with chutes.

On her way, Evellyn thought she heard human voices. *Am I not alone in the city?* She abandoned the search for the lab to follow the sound. After walking in the wrong direction for a solid half hour, she found nothing but a flock of birds hassling a noisy coyote pup over a scrap of meat. Evellyn's hopes fell. She wiped away disappointed tears and returned to her search.

Late in the afternoon, she found a train station. A large sign proclaiming it as Taylor station lay at her feet. She wanted Samnovyr station in the noble district. A broken and half-burnt map clung to the wall. She plotted her route and began following the tracks.

When the sky grew too dark to see without the torch, Evellyn entered the most intact building she could find. Going up to the second floor would be enough to stop the few dead that might still be on her trail. Tomorrow, she would find Lady Wyn's lab, or its burnt remains. That woman did always have a shocking amount of explosives in her possession.

The next day, Evellyn had to find a new path. A whole section of Caelspyr had seemingly vanished, leaving a gaping sinkhole as big as five city blocks. Oddly enough, there were ropes dangling into the hole, reaching all the way to the true ground below. Evellyn spun around. She couldn't see or hear anyone. Whoever left these was probably long gone. She coiled one of the ropes around her satchel strap. It was heavy, but after her adventures in the Undercity, she didn't want to be without.

That evening, she thought she heard voices again. Loneliness gripped her. Even if it was just more animals, she had to see. As she drew closer, she saw a light. Not the glow of Automazomb eye-bulbs, either. Firelight.

On top of a collapsed building, five people sat around a fire. They all turned when Evellyn approached. She couldn't hide her smile. Real, living people. Did they used to live on Caelspyr? Were they here during the crash? She had so many questions!

She climbed the pile of rubble and up onto the flat surface that had been a wall. Two of the five stood up. One was a thin man with a rifle. He kept it aimed at the ground, but his expression was distrustful. The other was… moving oddly? His clothes were ragged, bloodstained. Most of him was in shadow, but his awkward movements put a knot in Evellyn's stomach. The man's feet and arms were chained, and his mouth was covered with cloth.

A woman wearing a black vest gestured for Evellyn to step closer to the fire.

"What brings you to Caelspyr's grave, traveler?"

Evellyn swallowed hard and cautiously stepped forward. Her eyes stayed on the chained man. She froze when she saw the grayish skin and open, bloodless wounds. This group kept a zomb-spawn with them? Her skin felt cold.

The woman in the vest waved her off.

"Ignore Theo. He's harmless. Come on over and sit. Tell me what brings you here."

"You have... It's a..." Evellyn took a deep breath. She didn't want to waste this opportunity to speak with real people for once. "I'm sorry to intrude. You're the first people I've seen in a long time."

"Sure, that's what made you climb up here, but why are you on Caelspyr's grave at all?"

"I'm looking for a friend's workspace. I'm an engineer, see?" She pointed to the pin. "His notes might not mean much to anyone else, but they're everything to me."

Another woman, who looked like she could lift Evellyn off the ground with one arm, pinched her brow.

"You need help, kiddo? It's a big city. Treacherous, too. Theo wasn't always like that, you know."

The man with the rifle frowned.

"Poor Theo. Still, now he can lead the dead away from us."

The last person around the campfire was a gray-haired man with brass-rimmed spectacles. He tilted his head sideways. Evellyn gripped the strap of her satchel and averted her gaze. The man's voice was gruff and sharp.

"Nice rope there."

Evellyn's hand went to the coil she'd lifted from the sinkhole. Her cheeks felt hot.

"I found it down by a large hole in the ground. Was it yours?"

"Damned right it's ours! A hole she calls it! They jettisoned whole neighborhoods, our homes, and now you come in to swipe the only belongings we have left?"

"I… I'm sorry! I didn't…"

The woman in the vest, who had to have been their leader, smacked the man in the sternum so hard he coughed, then she smiled sweetly at Evellyn.

"The rope is yours now. We have plenty. Now, have you eaten today?"

Evellyn admitted that she had not. She was handed a plate of beans and a few strips of jerky. The group shared some stories about how they met and became friends. They were intensely curious about Evellyn's wandering years. She wasn't sure how much she should tell these people, but they seemed nice enough. She spouted off a quick half-lie about her work in artificial limbs and the additional research notes she needed from Caelspyr to start her business. She showed them her prosthetic arm and told them how she cut her original arm off to save herself from turning into zomb-spawn. That was out in the Eastern Desert. She had been lucky to survive, and luckier still when a Nomad airship captain let her aboard and build her new arm out of parts in his workshop.

That impressed the growly old man. After that, he kept wanting to study her workmanship. The strong woman kept asking why she was out there at all, why her Guild friend hadn't mailed the notes, why she couldn't write new notes, why she hadn't fled the area, why this why that. Evellyn didn't have convenient answers for any of those questions. How could she trust people that didn't give out their names? She opted to yawn instead and insist that she must be going, before zomb-spawn spotted the fire and swarmed them.

The group's leader pouted.

"You should stay here. By the light. We'll bait up Theo in the morning and lure any dead off. We can even help you in your search, if you like?"

"You're all very kind, but I've been on my own for a long time. I would prefer it."

The man with the rifle looked to his leader, then to Evellyn.

"If you insist, at least let me escort you. More eyes and all that."

Evellyn bit her cheek. It was unsafe to walk at night. Even with her torch. She agreed to the escort. The man walked with her over a few blocks to a sturdy looking stone mound. Eyso's rounded temple was the only thing standing. Her loyal followers would surely take it as a sign, if any were around to witness. She bid the man goodnight, then went inside.

As soon as he was gone, she ran back out and over several blocks palace-ward. Her instincts had helped her stay alive this long, and now they were telling her not to stay. She caught the attention of a couple zomb-spawn, but was able to lose them before a full horde amassed. She ended up in a maintenance shed behind a university building.

She did not see the odd group the next day. Evellyn kept her guard up as she made her way up to the wall that separated the nobles from the neighborhoods dedicated to business and other "petty" things. Young trees sprouted between the stones. Other stones had fallen out entirely.

When she got over the wall, she saw a massive, man-made cliff rising to the sky. She had to hike around another sinkhole to reach it. *Another portion of the city they felt they should drop, probably when their situation got dire.* The cliff on the other side was constructed out of metal pipes and beams. Ornate bronze sculptures and wrought iron littered the ground near the cliff. Etched in marble, Evellyn found a plaque that read "Mudassme."

She shielded her eyes and tried to glimpse the buildings atop the cliff. It *could* be the Mudassme mansion up there. She hoped it was. If their home had been in one of the sections dropped, she might never find its final resting place.

This meant that somewhere inside that cliff was Lady Wyn's portion of the Undercity. Although Evellyn wondered if that term still applied. The Undercity housed the hundreds of workers and their families, while this area would have been completely off-limits to commoners. Nobles owned everything above and below their residences.

Evellyn tied a loop on the end of her rope and tossed it up. It caught on the jagged mouth of a hole leading into the cliff. She climbed in and switched her torch on. It flickered and she tapped a few times to get it to stay lit. There weren't any replacement power sources here. She didn't want to be fumbling around here in the dark. This was just one more thing that would be better once she reached the laboratory; she remembered the lab had a row of windows near the ceiling. Assuming they weren't blocked by debris, she would be able to see once she reached the lab itself.

The hole deposited her in a cavernous warehouse. Crates, and the heavy machinery used to move those crates, lay haphazardly against the wall. She checked the room for dead, then climbed down. Following the largest hallway out of the warehouse, Evellyn found another large storage space, then another. The narrow hallways and passages were just as labyrinthine as her first journey around the Undercity. She didn't need a reminder of how well that went.

She heard zomb-spawn moaning behind a chained door. Someone had the good sense to round them up and lock them away. That man Jaff, perhaps, or the servant of another family. It was very difficult to determine whose property she was on at any given time. The only indication seemed to be the décor in the hallways, which may as well have been a secret code to Evellyn's eyes.

As she passed another set of doors, cracked just above the lock, a gray arm reached out to swipe at her. Evellyn jumped away. The face of a zomb-spawn pressed against the door next; it was trying to bite its way out. Its loud gurgling moan inspired more of the dead, hidden behind doors all down the hall, to add their voices.

Evellyn ran. The light of her torch bounced with each step. No matter if those monsters were locked away, it only took one on the wrong side of the door to end her. And these halls were so narrow. Gods, what was she thinking coming to Caelspyr?

She blew out a breath. *Focus on the concoction.* She was the only one left who knew it existed, who could put right the mistakes of the Guild. In the name of all that she'd lost.

"For Liri--!"

Evellyn stopped. This wall was *familiar*. It bore a deep groove and a scorchmark from a, well she would have considered it a failure, but van Gremphe said his employer had been extraordinarily pleased by her experimental flight rig zooming off down the hall. Evellyn had found the lab!

The wooden double doors were open a crack. Evellyn took her spanner out of her satchel, in case she needed to bash in the skull of any dead. She scooted over, waggling the spanner ahead of her. No zomb-spawn took the bait. Evellyn peeked inside.

Several metal beams no longer supported the tall ceiling's back left corner and instead barred the door from opening more than a quarter of the way. The ceiling was partially collapsed there, but the rest of the room was remarkably well-preserved. At regular intervals, narrow ladders allowed access to more storage for larger items, jutting crookedly from hooks higher up on the walls. The windows near the ceiling were dingy and half were shattered. A few of Lady Wyn's unfinished projects had tumbled out of place on the slanted floor. If she hadn't known the city was in shambles, she would have guessed it was a typical bad day for the lab.

Evellyn squeezed inside and closed the door behind her. She was surprised how little mess there was. The workbenches were bolted down and the shelves were gridded by chains that kept most of the materials from jostling. Van Gremphe's attempts to save his work materials from his zianovallic employer had inadvertently saved the laboratory from complete destruction when the city fell. Cracked glass jugs dripped a clear liquid that trailed down and pooled at the opposite end of the room. It bore the faint odor of something very flammable.

Paperwork and small tools littered the wet floor. Evellyn glanced over them in her search for the instructions on how, precisely, to craft the concoction. She knew some of it, but chemistry was not the place for miscalculations. But very few of the papers regarded chemistry, or any of the sciences at all. More than half were missives to and from family members negotiating funds and social functions. Nobles were baffling. Evellyn's father had been noble, before the family disowned him because he joined the Inventors Guild. *Absolutely baffling.*

There were other letters, too. Requests for Lady Wyn's various connections across Eysan to provide her with materials or suitable designs.

Evellyn recognized her own handwriting on one of the letters. It was to van Gremphe, concerning safety measures that Wyniera was ignoring. The woman was determined to create an Automazomb of her own. No, not a Zomb. There was to be no human basis for the brain and musculature. Lady Wyn was building a full-mechanical. Entirely metal, with an electranum brain. Only a noble could afford the massive amount of precious metals required for such a task.

It was from Evellyn's correspondences with van Gremphe that she learned what to call Lady Wyn. Not that he told her. He usually referenced the woman as "my noble lunatic employer" or the like. But when he was discussing calculations or precautions, he used the term he called her to her face. Such as "Lady Wyn calculated that the latest version of her full-mechanical will be released south of Beskra. Don't die."

And there were letters from Liridon, too. He and Lady Wyn had crossed paths many times. From Liridon's perspective, she always seemed to show up when he'd gotten himself into a bind. It was as if she had an extra sense that told her where danger and adventure could be found. Evellyn had laughed at this. Liridon always leapt into situations headlong. He didn't realize he was telling Lady Wyn exactly what she needed to swoop in and collect whatever interested her at the time.

"And I shall be ignoring any and all correlation to my decision to enter Caelspyr."

Evellyn smiled at that. Doing what her friend would have done had worked out brilliantly. Instead of sulking, she was in the laboratory!

She took a step further and read another of Liridon's letters. The date at the top was...

"It couldn't be!"

Evellyn snatched up the soggy paper and brought it over to a patch of sunlight. It wasn't her eyes, and it wasn't a trick. The date was just the day before the crash.

Greetings Lady Wyniera,

First, may I say that Master Historian Subbek was an absolute treasure trove of interesting stories. Thank you again for suggesting we speak. I can see why the other Master Historians ignore him, however. What he claimed as concrete proof was really only rumor and myth. But, he did mention a place the Haak called, loosely translated, "the last refuge." I've heard that before, in my own travels. I'm taking off immediately for western Shunnira to check their libraries for the exact location. I know your friend Von Grumpy is occasionally in contact with my friend Evellyn Hawke. If you could, please, mention my whereabouts to him so that he can tell her? I worry about her.

Thank you again, and best of luck in your endeavors,

Adept Historian Liridon Maraukna

A breathy laugh escaped Evellyn's lips. He was alive? She blinked away a tear and sighed. Oh, sweet Alillia, he was alive! Western Shunnira? That was tremendously far without an airship, and who knew where he was two years on, but it was a start. Evellyn's heart felt light. And even if her search took another two years, there were still Automazombs in Shunnira that needed to be reprogrammed.

But first, she needed to make more of the concoction. Van Gremphe hadn't written the instructions for it on any of these papers. Instead of wasting more time, she decided to find the chemicals she did remember. It would need time to mix and heat and titrate; she could resume the search then.

There was a small wooden cabinet resting against a canvas tarp-covered project. It was a bit under a meter tall, half as wide, half again as deep, and was tightly wrapped in coils of rope. Van Gremphe wasn't subtle about what he cared for most. And that was his collection of chemicals. Being employed by a noble had certain monetary advantages.

First, she tipped the cabinet back upright. The glass and ceramic containers clinked as they settled. Then, she cut the rope with a rusty saw hung on the wall. While she worked on the rope, she listened for the dead. She could never let her guard down. But all she heard was the same low groaning she'd been hearing since she passed all those locked rooms.

The contents of the cabinet were a chemist's dream. Bottles, jars, and canisters filled with liquids and powders of all colors. She was concentrating so hard on reading the labels that she almost didn't see the sheet of paper glued inside the cabinet door.

Zomb-Correcting Solution. Makes roughly twenty doses. Inject within five years or effects will be partial. Don't let your determination get you killed, Evellyn. This is the last time I'll say it: the sins of the Guild are not your own. Trust me.

Evellyn grinned and started gathering up all the ingredients on the list. There was also a box with every test tube, flask, distiller, and tubing she would need, all carefully wrapped in cloth. Evellyn was beginning to suspect van Gremphe was planning on sending her this cabinet, but was prevented by the city falling from the sky. She whispered her thanks, then brought the box over to the workbench.

She set up the little burner and mixed the first couple of liquids into the large flask. Evellyn jumped when she heard a metallic thunk down the hall. She didn't remember brushing up against any precarious metal objects, even when she was running. *Focus. Then get out.*

Less than ten minutes later, just as Evellyn had gotten a sufficient amount distilled into the second flask, there was a sharp growl just outside the door. A rotting gray hand and tattered sleeve came into view.

Evellyn gasped. She had closed that door. Hadn't she? The dead weren't known for their ability with doorknobs. They bashed their bodies into surfaces until a door yielded or their prey got away. There was no time to think about how or why. The zomb-spawn had squeezed in after her. And another was behind it. Evellyn yanked a long crowbar off the wall and swung it at the first zomb-spawn.

Its head cracked open like a melon. The dead crumpled to the ground. The second one lunged at her. Evellyn stabbed it with the opposite, pointed end of the crowbar. She hit this one in the chest. Its arms continued to reach forward, trying to grab her. She kicked it back, off the crowbar, and swung around to hit it in the jaw. *Damn!*

The second zomb-spawn tripped backward over the fallen ceiling beams. When it landed, Evellyn stabbed it again. This time, directly into its neck and through the base of the skull. After that, the dead finally lay still. Evellyn dropped the crowbar, disgusted. She shook off her nausea. *The door. Have to close the door.*

She made sure it latched shut. But she had a feeling she needed a way to defend herself. The concoction was less than halfway done. She paced the lab, scanning for anything that would make a decent barrier or, better, a weapon against the dead.

Brass claws poked out from beneath one of the canvas tarps. Evellyn held her breath. Pulling down the tarp revealed a metal creature that had aspects of a human, a bear, and a steam train. It had fangs, for gods' sake. And claws, and funnels protruding from its barrel chest, and were those swords tucked into the arm? Lady Wyn's full-mechanical machine was a death machine.

Evellyn tipped her head sideways briefly. A death machine was exactly what she needed right now. She popped open the head casing and dug into the programmatic wiring. She knew nearly as much about the machine's inner workings as Lady Wyn herself. Evellyn had been consulted on numerous programming issues. Van Gremphe even sent her the schematics of an early prototype.

"She went with that? No wonder it flailed its arms so erratically." Evellyn lowered her goggles and soldered one of the wires down where it should have been. "Ugh! And this is utterly useless. That's one, two... five different controls for the right foot and only one for the left. Balance issues maybe?"

It felt good to build again. Chemistry was a chore. Hunting down Zombs felt wrong on multiple levels. But creating something with her hands? She would do this for eternity if she could.

Fixing up the full-mechanical - *Fullmech? Yes, that sounds pithy* - took time. She paused a few times to initiate the next directions for making the concoction. More of the dead were at the door, pounding on it. The door had a taken damage from the crash. It cracked more with each hit.

Evellyn's heart raced as she fixed up the fullmech. One of the planks in the door broke entirely. The zomb-spawn on the other side shouted in their guttural noises. They would get her. They would eat her. Evellyn hastily checked over her work. Everything looked like it was in place. She flipped the switch on and scooted out of the way.

The fullmech jerked upright. Its neck clicked as it looked left and right. The gears in its limbs creaked. When it faced the dead, the fullmech clacked its great, fanged jaw open and shut. It stomped with clawed feet over to the door. Evellyn went back to the workbench. If any of the dead came in, she was confident the fullmech would deal with them.

A second later, the fullmech punch its oversized fist through the door. It grabbed a zomb-span by the head and squeezed until it popped and cracked. Once the dead stopped squirming, the fullmech deposited the pieces of skull it had acquired into an oversized container atop its back. Its free hand grabbed another victim. Evellyn squeezed her eyes shut. *This is what it's programmed to do. The dead, they aren't people anymore. They're not.*

Evellyn chided herself. She'd been wandering abandoned cities and desolate countryside for years now. She'd avoided more of the dead lurking in fallow fields than any normal person had ever seen. And sometimes, yes, she destroyed them, too. Best to not let the unnerving method of disposal concern her and let the fullmech do its dirty work.

In the back of her mind, she was plotting her escape. The halls were clearly no longer an option. The dead came endlessly. When the Zombs malfunctioned, they spread their new plague to every place people lived. And the new plague spread so quickly and violently, a lot of citizens fought instead of running. A wise strategy for a human foe, but in this situation it merely gave the illness more hosts to twist into - Evellyn glanced briefly at the zomb-spawn the fullmech was currently tearing limb from limb - rotting slaves to the plague's hunger.

A loud bang broke Evellyn's concentration. A familiar voice boomed. It was the woman in the black vest.

"Dammit, what is that thing?"

The growly older man huffed.

"You promised me if we followed the girl, we would find something worth taking. What's a noble doing with a Zomb in her basement?"

"Less chatting, more shooting!"

Evellyn rushed to scoop the next ingredient. Half of it spilled on the workbench.

"Shit."

She heard the muscular woman next.

"Boss! I heard the kid. She's still alive in there!"

There was a sharp tsk, then gunfire. Evellyn bit her cheek. It sounded like she made the right call making herself scarce last night. She scrambled to sweep the spilled powder onto a sheet of paper and get it into the mixture. Then came stirring. Painfully slow stirring. But van Gremphe's directions clearly stated that she could not overstir at this stage or all her work would be lost. She wished the chemist were here to perform the work himself. She wished also that she hadn't been so starved of human attention that she apparently led a group of - what were they, bandits? - to Lady Wyn's lab.

A bullet smashed one of the glass jugs behind Evellyn. She jumped to shield her work from stray glass fragments or the flammalble liquid once contained in the jug.

The gang's leader scowled from the doorway while her team struggled to keep the fullmech and zomb-spawn at bay.

"You killed Theo!"

Evellyn thought one of the zomb-spawn she'd killed had looked familiar. But that meant... She snapped back to the woman.

"You sent your zomb-spawn pet after me! And those metal sounds makes sense now. You cut the locks. All of those dead are loose because of you!"

The woman pursed her lips.

"Gods, so much trouble and it's just a lab. Girl, you tell me where this noble stashed her wealth right now, or I shoot you and your monster Zomb here dead."

"Good luck with that. It was never alive."

Evellyn ducked as the bandit leader tried again to shoot her from across the room. The first bullet broke another jug. A second ricocheted off a chain link and struck a barrel. Against all odds, the barrel was not filled with explosives. Evellyn knew Lady Wyn had at least some black powder lying about.

"Stop shooting or you'll kill us all!"

The bandits' response was more gunfire. Evellyn wouldn't help even if she did know if or where the Mudassme family kept a treasure vault. These people had no idea what idiots they were being, shooting blindly into a madwoman's lab. She tapped her fingers on the edge of the workbench. The last flask was slowly turning from light green to a deep brackish brown. She plucked it from the surface and tilted the flask. The contents oozed. The color, the consistency, the smell were all spot on. Evellyn was back in the Zomb-fixing business.

Meanwhile, the fullmech was losing its fight against the bandits and from the sound of things, the bandits were losing their fight against the dead. One of the women screamed that she'd been bitten. A man cursed that they had let too many of the monsters out. Without their ex-friend Theo, they had no way to bait the dead away from them.

Evellyn stashed her concoction in her satchel, then climbed up a ladder to the storage level. The space was little more than scattered hooks and impressively anchored braces for wire shelving. Cloth and leather bolts, metal rods, old inventions, and varying thicknesses of rope were haphazardly displayed. Evellyn decided against using her rope. The broken window panes above her couldn't support her weight. She searched the storage level for a ladder. She thought she'd seen one, but it turned out to be the frame for glider wings. It seemed she had to settle for the more time-consuming task of repurposing the ladder currently supporting her.

While balancing on a sturdy bit of shelving, she reached into her satchel to produce her screwdriver. While she didn't want the bandits to die down there, she didn't want them following her either. They tried to kill her! Multiple times! If the bandits cared about their lives, they would escape down the maze of noble hallways. She secured her rope to the top of the ladder, then slowly unscrewed the ladder from the platform. It clanged against the support struts holding parts of the storage level up.

Below, the fight spilled into the lab. Only two bandits remained. They retreated to the lab and were holed up against a workbench shouting at one another. Their argument? Both of them claimed the other was bleeding because of the zomb-spawn. Then they would protest that it was the beastly Zomb that did it and they wouldn't, in fact, be turning into a gray husk bent on devouring living flesh.

More zomb-spawn stumbled into the room. One of them paused to let out a gurgling cry, calling more of its brethren to the feast.

Evellyn planted her feet as she dragged the ladder up.

The noise drew the attention of the bandits.

"Where are you going?"

"Don't leave us here to die!"

Evellyn propped the ladder against the wall. Those two were bleeding badly. She could tell by their twitchy movements they'd been infected. There was no time for amputation, no clean tools. The only people she'd met in months were doomed.

She closed her eyes.

"I'm sorry."

She climbed up to and out of the broken window. By the time she set foot in the overgrown garden on the other side of the window, the livid screams below had been cut short. Shambling dead or truly dead, Evellyn didn't know. She was afraid to look. Either way, it made her next task easier.

Evellyn pulled a matchbook from her bag. She set the whole thing alight and dropped it into the lab. The burning matchbook fell into the pool of flammable liquid. The room was engulfed instantly. Evellyn staggered away from the row of windows. The heat was intense. Then, something in the lab exploded. The ground shook. Evellyn raced in the opposite direction of the cliff. The Mudassme residence - and two other buildings neighboring theirs - crashed down the cliffside.

Once the ruins of Caelspyr settled again, Evellyn stopped running. She stood with her hands resting on her knees to catch her breath. A laugh sputtered out. She gently patted the flask in her satchel. Evellyn checked her list of Automazombs. There were three reportedly wandering the foothills of the Perregron Mountains. She squinted at the setting sun on the horizon. In the morning, she would head southwest. From there, once she'd fixed those Zombs, she would charter a flight to Shunnira and Liridon's last location.

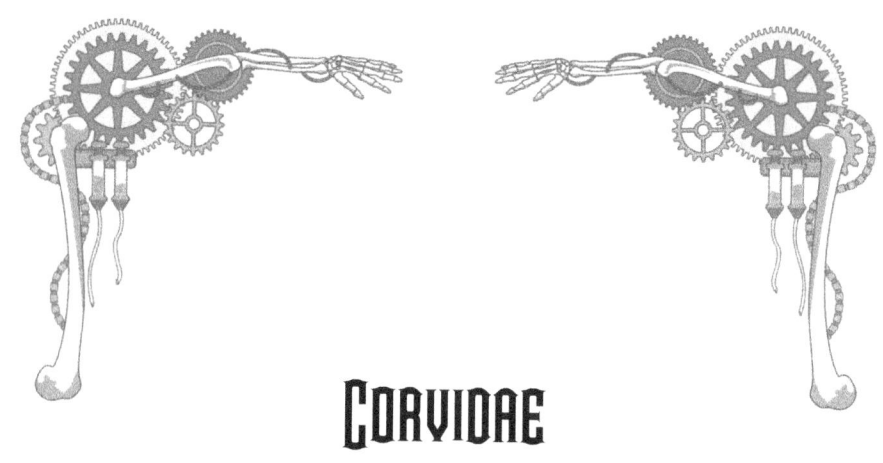

CORVIDAE

By Jessica L. Lim

There is such a thing as honor amongst thieves. At least, that is what Raven believed. He had to, otherwise, what sort of life was he living? He may have been expelled from the Teraltian Armed Forces, but he had accepted his fate with as much dignity as he could muster. He had faced the disillusionment of his precious officer candidacy and endured the label of "whistleblower". The uniform, the rank - Master Staff Sergeant - and eventually even his name had been stripped from him... but never his honor.

And for all his quiet disdain toward his new field of work, they were not precisely 'thieves'. In his more optimistic moments, Raven considered them a tactical team of ...variable quality. Raven knew his teammates, and maybe even his benefactor, regarded his retention of military standards with a certain amount of derision. Admittedly, Magpie was really the only one to voice as much, but he could sense times when Jay or Crow agreed with Magpie's objections or observations. He could only ever guess at what Rook thought. But such is the burden of being team leader. The difficult and unpopular decisions were Raven's to make and his alone.

Their mysterious benefactor, whom they only ever knew as "Sir", had commissioned them to locate and rescue the scion of some Teraltian high lord. "Names are not important right now," Kaspar, Sir's man, had explained. "All you need to know is that this boy is in the hands of the enemy."

"Understood," Raven replied.

Strangely, Kaspar had done much of the legwork for them. Raven had fully expected to go in blind but he was grateful to have some intelligence regarding the situation.

"The boy is being held in the disputed land between Teraltis and Aadobur. Sir hired an aircraft to take us there."

"What do we know of the guards?" Crow inquired.

"Probably mercenaries."

Rook laughed, "I wonder if they'll give us a challenge."

"Sir does not want us to cause a ruckus. This is supposed to be a quick in-and-out job."

"There's your challenge, Rook. It will be more fun this way, too," Jay enthused.

"Once we have the boy in our custody, we are to take him to the rendezvous point."

"And the payoff?" Magpie asked.

"Deposit upon delivery. Gear up. We are to meet the *Ka'le Hafa.*"

The aircraft Kaspar had hired on their behalf appeared to be a mid-size transport vessel. She was outfitted as a zeppelin, but she appeared to be as sleek as a military craft.

"Look at all those nacelles," Crow pointed out. "She's got lots of speed."

"She must make a lot of special deliveries."

"None more important than the one we are to deliver," Raven snapped. "Let us board."

They entered through the cargo bay, which was stocked with miscellaneous boxes and containers of various shapes and sizes, destined

Corvidae

for an assortment of ports, in both countries. This was the reason Kaspar hired *Ka'le Hafa*. Neither the Teraltian authority nor the Aadoburi would find anything suspicious about a transport vessel passing through the disputed area, as long as it didn't linger.

The skeleton crew seemed to be as diverse as the Corvidae, but they spoke in an odd mongrel dialect neither Raven nor his team could decipher.

The others stood around Raven as the crew prepared to leave port. According to Kaspar, one of the Teraltian lord's men, Denard, was to meet them on the ship.

"Do you reckon they understand us?" Jay questioned.

"They understand the job," a voice replied from somewhere above them. "They understand money. In that, they are not unlike yourselves."

The team instinctively looked up at the man dressed similarly to the crew, only his flightsuit looked too clean.

"Mr. Denard," Raven intoned.

"You recognize me?"

"Not exactly," Magpie replied. "But you're too good looking to be the captain or one of the crew."

Raven glared at her. She remained unapologetic. He sighed inwardly; another lecture about procedure seemed to be imminent.

Denard ignored Magpie's impertinence. In his hand, he held something shiny and silver. He flipped it open. It was a pocket chronometer. "We must make our way," he said. "Time is slipping through our fingers as we speak." He snapped the lid close, gestured to the ladder that led up to the catwalk, and turned away.

Magpie opened her mouth to comment, but the second reprimanding look she received from Raven silenced her.

The team reconvened with Denard in the galley. "You are familiar with our situation. My noble employer has been given instructions to deposit a rather large sum of money to an unmarked account that will undoubtedly be redistributed to various other accounts." He pulled out his chronometer once again and flipped open the lid. "Countdown started one hour ago. You have nine hours remaining to retrieve the boy." *Snap.*

"Let's call him Felix," Jay suggested. "It's easier than saying 'the boy' all the time."

Denard nodded. "Felix has not been moved since you were first briefed, at least, not that we could tell. It's possible there are underground tunnels leading back toward Aadobur."

"That would certainly make things interesting," Rook remarked. "I don't suppose you have a layout of the place. Kaspar only said that it was a ruin. "

"We didn't have access to a map," Denard answered. "I have but a rough sketch. It is Haak in origin."

"That's better than nothing."

The team and Denard pored over the sketch, once it was produced. "We believe Felix is being held here," Denard explained, pointing to one of the chambers furthest in to the ruin.

Crow squinted at the drawing. "This looks like a temple." He grabbed up the sketch and started turning it every which way excitedly. "*Yes!* It is! It's an ancient temple to Skirmante. Heh, that's kind of ironic. Because smart birds like corvids are sacred to Her and we're-" When he noticed everyone looking at him with various expressions of either amusement or disapproval, he cleared his throat and smoothed the paper back out on the table.

"There are a few chapters about this area in the history tomes. Temples dedicated to Skirmante are pretty straightforward: high altar, antechambers, alcoves for acolytes, the usual. But once war came to this land, the temple was used as a stronghold by both sides at one point or another. As you can tell, it became a ruin not simply because of time but because various parts of the structure were assaulted at one time or another. There were also traps set."

"That's old tech, right?" Jay asked. "So chances of those traps still working…"

"Are still good." Raven decided.

144

"Yeah, it's better to just assume they work. Teraltian and Aadoburi soldiers would have avoided them, or used and reset them. If we're lucky, the mercs don't know about them and we might be able to use them to our advantage."

"Provided you know what to look for," Rook observed.

Crow grinned. "You doubt me? I have just the thing to help us do a little recon."

Crow's solution turned out to be one of his inventions, a small clockwork bird. At first glance, it looked like a thrush. However, upon closer inspection, one would be able to see it was not a natural creature at all.

"Her eyes are picture lenses," Crow explained. "They'll relay what she sees to this selenium phototube receiver," he gestured to a clunky, handheld viewing screen. "We'll be seeing things through her eyes with only a slight delay."

Raven nodded. "She will serve us well." Turning to Denard, he said: "We will need to land somewhere to send this bird out and give us time to plan."

Denard retrieved his pocket chronometer once again. "How much time do you think you'll need?"

Crow did calculations in his head. "Give us a distance of about five kils. The usable areas in the ruin are not as numerous as they would have been when the place was a temple. I would estimate about an hour."

"Two hours have already elapsed. How much longer do you think it will take you to retrieve Felix?"

"We will get him out in time," Raven answered curtly.

"You just worry about paying us," Magpie added.

Denard said nothing as he *snapped* the pocket chronometer close. His gaze dropped back to the sketch of the ruin. Raven was about to remind him that more time was passing when the man spoke: "I shall make your request to the captain and inform my noble employer of our progress."

"'Request'?" Magpie echoed, once Denard had quit the room. "He does know we're calling the shots here, right? It's not like he can go swoop in and get the boy himself with this crew."

Raven ignored her. Normally, he would use this time to speak with her about protocol. However, there was something else on his mind. Something about Denard and this odd crew did not quite sit well. He'd always had a good sense of when he was being lied to; it was that sense that led to his whistleblowing and eventual dismissal. He got the same feeling now, that this Denard was a tangle of deceptions dressed up to look like a man.

Denard returned shortly. "The captain suggests this place should be sufficient for your needs." He gestured to an area of the map. "The Aadobur patrol balloons shouldn't make much of us."

"Good," Crow declared. "This little bird is designed to be quick about her course." He activated the creature. It hopped into his hand, pecking and chirping at him as if it were a real bird. In his other hand, he held the receiver, where a flickering, grainy picture was displayed. He gave the bird a gentle toss into the air and it started flitting around the room.

"That's pretty *bind'as*," Jay slipped into Low Aadoburi as she delightedly watched the bird land on her finger.

"It's not going to do that to the people she's supposed to be spying on, right?" Magpie questioned. She reached out her own finger to pet the metallic wings. "I'm pretty sure they're definitely going to notice this."

Crow laughed. "Again with the doubt. No, this little bird is being controlled by yours truly." He studied the screen on the receiver. "Here we go," he announced happily. "Just as I said." He held up the image to his companions. It was difficult to tell what the figure was, but the delayed and tinny voice of Jay could be heard as the grainy, gray images started to shift.

"How in the world can you even tell what any of that is?" Magpie asked, touching the receiver cautiously.

"It takes a trained eye," Crow replied.

Once *Ka'le Hafa* landed, the team and Denard returned to the cargo bay. The thrush was released and just as Crow had explained, flew straight

146

to the ruin on propeller wings. He slowed the creature's arrival once the temple came in to view on the receiver.

Jay and Rook perched behind Crow, watching the images on the screen. Denard disappeared to confer with the captain. Raven decided it was a good time to speak to Magpie. She did not seem as interested in Crow's invention as Jay did - of course, he wasn't sure if Rook had any interest either, but he was at least with the others.

Magpie had her "darling pretties" – as she often called her throwing knives – spread out on one of the containers, an oilcloth in hand. She regarded her weapons critically as Raven walked up to stand beside her. "I think I ought to pack more next time," she remarked.

"You probably will not need to use any of these at all," Raven returned.

Magpie just grinned, "You can never be too prepared. Isn't that what you and your kind always say?"

Raven bristled slightly. "It is true," he admitted stiffly. "However, this mission should not require any bloodshed at all." He forced himself to relax his stance. "Magpie, I wanted to talk to you about-- "

"My attitude, I'm sure," she huffed. Her smile was caustic. "What have I done this time?"

"You need to hold your tongue. Something is going on here. You don't know who might be listening, Magpie. I do not understand your need to make quips."

Magpie selected one of her blades and began running the oilcloth lovingly over the steel. "And I have never understood your need to make such a *sa'asya* about it all the time."

"You know why," Raven rejoined tersely. "It is my responsibility to ensure this unit does its job and does so with military precision."

"I think you're wrong in that." Magpie twirled the knife in her hand expertly, testing the balance. "Not about the making sure we do our job bit, of course. I mean the military precision." She threw the knife at one of the nearby containers where it penetrated with a solid *thunk*. "I do the job I'm supposed to. I mouth off because I can. I was never in any army like you, but I know what I'm doing."

"You are a street rat." The moment the words were off his lips, he winced internally. Raven did not like using that information against Magpie, or Jay for that matter. Not that Jay ever gave him reason.

Magpie glared at him. He fully expected her to slap him, and he could not really begrudge her that. Instead, she smiled her caustic smile. "I may have lived on the streets for a time, but I *lived*. I didn't curl up and die like other street rats." She nodded over to Jay; "I kept her alive, too." She looked him in the eye once again. "I know what I'm doing."

"That was unkind of me," Raven agreed. "You have certainly come a long way. But I want you to remember that Sir chose me to lead this team. I need my people to follow my orders."

"Have I ever not?"

"Follow without question," he amended.

"I'm not one of your soldiers. You know why I'm here. You know why I'm part of this team, the same as every one of others. I've never done anything to jeopardize this unit and I never will. That's the best I can offer you." She picked up another blade, tossing it lightly in one hand before adding, "You may be Raven, but you're not *my* Raven."

Raven knew there was nothing he could say to counter her. He had joined the Corvidae years after Magpie and Jay had been recruited by the previous holder of his Corvidae name. He knew he could never take the place of the Raven who had saved Magpie and Jay from the streets of Aadobur, in terms of earning their regard. Raven disapproved of Magpie's approach to things, but he could not do anything about it. Sir never complained about her performance. He simply nodded to her then turned on his heel to check the progress of their little bird.

* * *

Ka'le Hafa resumed her course once the Corvidae had sufficient information from Crow's invention. While the team prepped their equipment, Denard quietly slipped over to Raven.

148

"My noble employer has every confidence that you will succeed," he whispered. "You shall be rewarded accordingly."

Raven regarded him suspiciously. "Your noble employer is very kind," he replied cautiously. Denard's demeanor disquieted him. From their first meeting, the man had been aloof. What did Denard presume he would gain now, to made him try to ingratiate himself?

Raven was saved having to converse with the man further when Crow hailed him. The young inventor held up one of the harnesses of their gliders. Raven nodded curtly to Denard and walked over to Crow.

"Now, I made some modifications," he explained, securing the apparatus around Raven's torso. "It's more sensitive to pressure, so be careful not to lean too far one way or another like in the past otherwise you might spin out."

"You could not have told me about this earlier? We could have at least had some time to practice."

Crow shrugged. "I only thought of it last night."

"Crow!"

"Trust me. It will work."

Denard gestured to the crewman standing by to open the hatch. "Fair winds," he called to the team, as they readied their jump.

Raven had drilled his team on this type of procedure many times. Jay was the first to fly. She had a penchant for the more daring of their tasks. She unfurled her "wings" expertly. Once she was a good distance from the aircraft, Rook followed, and so on until Raven brought up the rear.

Raven lived for moments like this, hurtling toward the ground with the wind whistling all around him. When he spread his wings, he truly felt like he lived up to his namesake. He closed his eyes briefly to soak in the sensation of flying.

The winds were not as turbulent as he presumed the desert gusts would be. Raven discovered what Crow's modifications meant when he spied Jay spinning. He heard her muffled whoop of joy, so he was not overly concerned. Crow demonstrated other capabilities of the gliders by diving with greater ease and precision. Raven could see how he contorted his arms and thus followed suit.

The team landed much more gracefully than they had in the past. "That was so *bind'as!*" Jay cried.

Crow beamed. "I told you it would work."

"Definitely an improvement," Raven agreed. He pulled on the straps to retract the wings and concentrated on refocusing his team. "We will have to practice some movements later. Right now, we have more pressing matters."

From the bird's observations, they could tell that the mercenaries did not have too many guards on the perimeter. "I guess this will be easy," Rook commented.

Jay volunteered to take point on this leg of the mission. What the youngest team member lacked in stature she made up for in stealth. She scouted ahead nimbly; the others trailed behind, more cautiously.

The ruins loomed ahead of them. Acacia trees clustered around the structure provided some additional cover. "They have some folk walking around the entrances," Jay reported once the rest of the team caught up with her. "But their eyes are not as sharp as they ought to be."

The mechanical thrush had observed that patrols were every half hour or so. There were not so many men guarding Felix that the team was overly concerned, but they also had to account for the old traps Crow had warned them about.

"Rook, Crow." The two teammates surged forward to the entrance. When they saw no one approaching, they motioned the others to follow. The corridor would take them to another antechamber adjacent to where they presumed Felix was being held.

Rook and Crow remained in the lead, with Magpie bringing up the rear. It was a standard formation for the team. The sandstone walls were crumbling in places, allowing shafts of sunlight to stream through the cracks. The team padded down the corridor as quietly as possible.

As they came to a T-section, Crow threw up his fist to call a halt; then he held up two fingers. Rook positioned himself closer to the young inventor.

Raven tensed. He was confident his two teammates could dispose of whatever threat unwittingly approached, but he could not undo his military training. If there was anything he learned from his dead comrades it was that they were dead because someone was not ready. Whether it was the commander or the soldier, Ershk-gula ensnared the unprepared. Such was the way of combat.

This time, the Corvidae were the Dark Lady's instrument. No sooner had the patrol turned the corner than Crow and Rook had snapped their necks. They laid the dead men on the ground as softly as if they were laying down sleeping babes. "Ershk-gula keep you," Raven murmured as he passed.

The team's next obstacle came in the form of one of the old traps Crow had warned them about. They found themselves at the base of a stairwell. The walls were not as dilapidated here, but there was still evidence of damage. Nature had found its way into the temple and the walls now sported some overgrowth.

"We need to find another way," Crow explained. "The bird didn't see this detail."

"What d'ya mean?" Magpie asked.

"The pattern of the stones on the stairs," Crow pointed out. "It's a rather specific dance. This was set by the high clerics and I don't know all the steps without the scrolls."

"Back the way we came then," Raven said brusquely.

Crow caught the leader's arm. "I think this means the mercs aren't as clueless as we thought," he observed.

Raven nodded grimly. "On point," was all he said.

Crow returned to the head of the flock. Raven had hoped the team would be able to follow Sir's orders of a quick in-and-out and no bloodshed, but it seemed that the Lady of Fate was inclined to be fickle.

The team found the next stairwell easily. This one was in a more obvious state of disrepair; half the steps were crumbled and it looked like one would have to skirt along the sides to find any kind of purchase as they ascended.

"The only reason these stairs would kill you is because you tripped," Jay noted cheerfully.

The Corvidae filed behind Crow as best they could. Unfortunately for Jay as she topped the landing, she triggered something. She let out a soft squeak as she was swept up into a net. A spear would have ended her if Magpie had not been quick to notice the weapon discharge from its wall mount. With a flash, one of her knives threw the spear off its trajectory.

Magpie assisted in freeing Jay from the net. Once she determined the youngest team member was well, Magpie whirled on Crow. "Nice warning," she growled.

Crow could only shrug. "I didn't know."

"Sorry," Jay said sheepishly. "I guess I tripped."

Magpie glared at Crow. "Everyone is in one piece," Raven intervened. "We have a job to finish."

"This trap was set recently." The others turned to Rook as he examined where Jay had tripped the net. "They know."

Raven did the calculation in his head. That first patrol must have missed a check-in by now. If he were in the mercenaries' place, and with the number of men they had at hand, he would probably have them surrounding Felix.

"This just got interesting." Rook's smile chilled Raven.

Raven could not dispute him. He reached for his sidearm. There was no sense in walking softly now. "Plan B," he said simply. This changed the Corvidae formation. Magpie and Jay now took point. Both women were quick on their feet and elusive; Magpie's skill with her "darling pretties" was often more effective than any bullet. Jay was a little less accurate, but she would not need to be with the smoke pellets she would discharge. Crow would be on her tail since she was in charge of reaching Felix first, leaving Rook and Raven to take care of whomever else stood in their way.

According to the bird, they would find Felix in one of the antechambers south of the worship hall. It was likely that the whole mercenary team would be surrounding the boy now. The odds were not particularly in the Corvidae's favor, but Raven whispered a quick prayer to Verdellen and Skirmante, asking Them to side with the team.

Once they found the entrance, the team waited for Raven's signal. He would have liked eyes in the room before rushing in, but it did not seem likely. His gaze found Magpie's: *do not screw this up.*

She nodded. They might have their differences, but Raven knew she would execute her role efficiently.

"Go."

Magpie and Jay flew into the room like their namesakes, followed quickly by the rest. From the point-of-view of the mercenaries, it would be like bats flying out from their cave.

As Raven surged forward behind his team and noticed the bewildered expressions on the faces of the mercenaries, he could not help but wonder how they did not see this coming. Then again, they had probably anticipated a larger team. They probably thought the traps would have been enough defense.

In all his years of combat, Raven thought the experience of engagement would change over time. He heard some comrades and veterans describe it as slow motion; like watching things happen through water. Especially when there were fatalities in the unit. But Raven could not recall any time where a military engagement was anything more than a blink of his eye.

This rescue operation was no different. One second, he was firing off his first shot… and then his weapon was empty. Lady Fortune favored the Corvidae once again; had she been a fickle goddess, the team might have been put in a trickier situation. As it turned out, the team's lighting strike was enough to dispatch the mercenaries.

"Report," Raven barked. He was still on high alert and quickly reloaded his sidearm. The mist from Jay's smoke pellets was beginning to dissipate, revealing fifteen fallen mercenaries.

"All of theirs are down," Rook's voice answered from somewhere amidst the fog, "none of ours."

Raven surveyed the antechamber. It was not really an ideal room to have holed up in. It was far too open, with only a few crumbling columns for cover. Much like the first corridor, the room was illuminated by murky light from the deteriorating walls; the only difference was the gap in the ceiling — most likely the remains of a skylight — casting a distinct shaft of light over Skirmante's seal on the floor. Along the walls, he noticed the torches had all been doused. Raven nodded to himself. If he had been in command of the mercenaries, he would have made the same call: blind the room. Unfortunately for the mercenaries, Raven's team was more effective with the tactic.

Why would the mercenaries have kept the boy in such a room? Knowing the general layout, he would have kept the hostage in one of the smaller alcoves or at least transformed the antechamber into a more suitable holding cell.

"Status?"

Now that the immediate danger had been dealt with, Raven and his team relaxed slightly. They were still guarded, of course, but they were not nearly as tense as they had been before charging in to the antechamber.

"Through-and-through in the shoulder," Rook declared, "and a graze on the leg."

"Grazes on us, too," Crow added, "Jay and me both."

Raven looked over to Magpie, who looked a little disheveled but seemed otherwise unharmed. "And the boy?" He scanned the room for Jay and Crow since they were the first two in and were tasked with locating Felix.

"They threw him down here," Jay announced. She was flat on her stomach a few paces from where Raven stood, Crow and Magpie hovering over. As Raven and Rook approached, the team leader realized the youngest Corvidae had thrown herself over the grated trapdoor to shield Felix from stray bullets.

Magpie helped Jay to her feet, revealing the face of a boy around twelve years of age peering up at them through the rusting grate. The hole

154

had enough space for a single body to stand erect, but little else. It was not very deep either; the grate was only a few feet over his head.

"Boy, we are here to rescue you," Raven explained. "Are you all right?"

Felix gulped. "Y-yeah," he answered. "Did my father send you?"

Raven nodded. He knelt down to examine the grate. It looked simple enough to just pull up, but his instincts insisted on caution. "Bear with us a little while longer."

"Something wrong, boss?" Magpie queried, as Raven stood.

Raven shook his head, not as a response, but in an effort to clear his head. The more he thought about the situation the team now found themselves in, the more unsettled he became. He stepped away from the grate; his team took the hint and followed suit.

"What is wrong with this picture?"

The others looked to one another for guidance. "What do we know about these mercenaries?" Raven pressed.

"They're sloppy," Magpie noted.

"Their traps were rudimentary," Crow added. "If they had Felix for as long as Denard claims, I would have expected more sophisticated defenses."

"This formation was desperate," Rook said.

"Exactly."

"Maybe they're just not very good mercs," Jay suggested.

"They were good enough to kidnap a boy from a well-trained security team."

"You lot might want to take a look at this," Rook called. He had slipped away from the others and now crouched beside the corpse of one of the mercenaries.

"What did you find?" Crow queried.

"I wasn't really paying attention to them when I was shooting at them," Rook remarked. "Let's see just who these nice folks are." He pulled off the mask the dead man had been wearing to reveal an Aadoburi with a streak of lightning tattooed on the left side of his face.

"*Vish'lekai*," Magpie murmured.

The *Vish'lekai* were Aadoburi renowned for their any-means-necessary tactics, which often included suicide missions. They were also proficient at making bombs and explosives.

What had clicked for Raven was beginning to sink in for his team. They all looked back to the grate.

"Crow," Raven said tersely.

The younger man stepped forward and began to examine the grate more closely. At first, he found nothing. Crow prostrated himself in attempt to look at the fixings at eye level. Despite the murky light, he could see very thin strands of some kind of wire, as fine as gossamer. "*Yel'na*," he muttered.

"What? What's wrong?" Felix demanded, uncertainty and fear creeping into his voice. "Why aren't you getting me out of here?

Crow smiled down at the youngster. "Just need a moment, lad," – he tried to sound reassuring – "This grate is sealed tightly. We gotta make sure we have the right tool to open it." He righted himself and returned to the group. "It's rigged all right," he reported.

"Any guesses?" Rook asked.

"If what we know of the *Vish'lekai* is accurate, it will explode," Raven pointed out. "Now the question is how?"

"No," said Magpie, "the question is can we make it out of here alive, and if so, will we make it with the boy?"

"Can you disarm it?"

Crow considered the question. "It depends on if we can find the explosives. Cutting the wire without knowing the full picture could set them off."

"Maybe we should have kept one of them alive," Jay lamented, nudging the nearest corpse with her foot.

Raven ignored her. He checked his timepiece. Approximately an hour had passed since the team had jumped from the *Ka'le Hafa*. "We have to assume whatever they rigged is set to take the whole place down. We do not have time to dismantle this."

"If we don't disarm it, we'll have to outrun it. Depending on the firepower, once the trigger is set off, we won't have much time for an escape. It could all come down in anywhere from a moment to two minutes," Crow noted.

"Let us see if we can find the device," Raven suggested. "Maybe it is not as bad as we think."

Magpie scoffed. "They may have been crappy guards, but have you ever heard of the *Vish'lekai* doing a half-assed job with explosives?"

"We have to be sure," Crow interjected, staving off another argument between Magpie and Raven. "The wires take some finding, but I think we can trace them back to their source."

Magpie did not argue any further and fell in line with the rest of the team to examine the grate once again.

When he heard the team finally approach again, Felix called up: "Did you get the tools you needed to get me out of here?"

Jay peered down at the boy and grinned. "Just about, Felix," she answered.

"F-Felix?" he echoed. "My name's--"

"You're Felix to us, lad," Jay interrupted. "It's just easier that way."

"What do I call you?"

"Jay," she replied. "How long have you been down there?"

While Jay kept Felix distracted, the others followed Crow as he used his lantern to expose the thread. "Wow," he breathed, "I take back my remark about their rudimentary traps. I can't believe they embedded the wires into the cracks! That takes time and effort. It's probably why..."

"Crow," Raven growled.

The younger man flushed, "Sorry."

The team ended up exiting the antechamber. The wires led them to exactly what they expected: an elaborate latticework of explosives.

"Yeah, I don't think we're dismantling this," Magpie remarked.

Raven clenched his jaw. Their in-and-out mission had just become that much more complicated.

Crow continued to examine the mechanism, despite the apparent hopelessness. He shifted his lantern to the left and right of the contraption and even followed the nearly invisible wires around the corner. He returned a few moments later. "Okay, this isn't the only array—"

"Shocking," Magpie interjected.

"—but on the bright side, it appears they're rigged to detonate from the outside in."

Raven nodded grimly. "So that buys us a little time," he noted.

"What now, boss?" Magpie asked.

"We get creative," he answered tersely. Raven turned on his heel and returned to the antechamber. Jay was still chattering with Felix; she looked up at him questioningly when he entered, but still maintained the flow of conversation. He shook his head slightly and turned his attention back to the chamber.

Crow and Rook appeared beside him while Magpie subtly filled Jay in on the situation.

"The second we pull up the grate, we trigger the explosives?" Raven asked. He knew the answer but needed confirmation.

"Magpie was right," Rook said, "*Vish'lekai* are not known for doing things half way."

Raven snorted, "Maybe we should tell Sir to recruit a few of them to replace us if we do not all make it out of this."

Rook and Crow eyed him curiously. It was rare for Raven to make caustic remarks – that was usually Magpie's role. Raven ignored them and walked toward the shaft of light illuminating the room. He remembered the source had been a hole in the ceiling.

"Crow, how much time would you say we will have once the first explosive is triggered before we would be crushed?"

"That's a tough estimation to make," Crow said slowly. Raven looked at him expectantly. "With all of Lady Fortune's favor on our side, I'd give us three minutes, and that's only if the foundation is as sturdy as I think it is."

"The temple has stood for this long," Rook noted. "I say we take what we can get."

Raven called Magpie and Jay over to them before fully explaining his plan. "We will have to ascend out through that skylight. Everyone but Jay will go out first. She will get Felix and we will be able to pull up the pair of them because they are the lightest."

Jay grinned at the prospect but Magpie scowled. "Are you sure everything won't just come down on top of us all?"

"No," Raven said honestly, "but this is the best plan we have."

It was clear that Magpie disapproved of this idea but, surprisingly, she argued no further.

While the others prepared their grappling hooks, Crow advised Jay on the best and fastest way to lift the grate and get the boy out. "We'll fire your hook off," he explained, "so once you make it to the stock, just grab hold and hang on for both your lives."

She nodded. Crow clapped her affectionately on the shoulder then went to join the others. Jay walked back over to the grate. "Hey there, Felix," she called down to him.

"Are you getting me out now?" he asked.

"We sure are, but you've gotta help me out a bit, okay?" He nodded uncertainly. "So I'm gonna pull up this grate and set it aside. The moment

I hold out my arms to you you've gotta jump up as high as you can and grab hold. Do you think you can do that for me?"

"Why are you the only one helping me?" Felix asked. "Isn't that first fellow stronger? Should he be the one to pull me up?"

"You're a clever lad," Jay declared. "It's true that one of the others might be stronger, but I'm faster on my feet and we have to make a rather speedy exit through the hole in the ceiling. Our weight combined will be easier for the rest to pull us out. I know this all sounds a bit scary, but I need you to be really brave, okay?"

Felix's eyes widened at this new piece of information. "I can do it," he gulped.

Jay smiled, then looked over her shoulder to check on her teammates; only Magpie lingered in the chamber. Jay couldn't see her face, but she was certain the older girl was watching her anxiously. Jay rolled her eyes and waved Magpie off. She couldn't move the grate until everyone else had ascended.

Finally, the floor was clear. Jay peered down on Felix, "You ready?"

At his nod, Jay slipped her fingers through the grating, took a deep breath, and pulled.

Immediately, the concussive force of the explosions reverberated around the chamber. Jay threw the grate aside and reached for the boy. He jumped and held fast as she hauled him up. The walls and bits of ceiling were beginning to crack and crumble around them.

"We have to fly now," Jay shouted as she and Felix scrambled to their feet. She ended up pulling the boy along as more explosives detonated closer to the chamber, causing them both to stumble towards the dangling grappling gun. She whispered a prayer to all the gods she'd ever known, asking for everything to remain stable long enough for her and Felix to make their escape.

Above them, Magpie peered down from the skylight and tracked their progress, muttering a litany of her own: "Make it, make it, make it, make it, make it…"

"Climb on to my back, Felix," Jay instructed. Once she felt the boy was secure, she grabbed hold of the gun and activated the retract button. The ascent was much slower than she would have liked, especially as the chamber began to collapse. "Hang on tight, kiddo!" Hand-over-hand, Jay started to climb up the rope. When she and Felix were close enough to the opening, Magpie and Crow aided in pulling them up completely.

"Go!" Raven shouted to his team.

The temple continued to fragment as the Corvidae and the boy raced over the remains of the roof.

As they neared the edge, Rook took hold of Felix. "Grab hold of my neck, boy." He spread his wings and leapt before Felix could completely process what was happening. Felix gripped tightly once he realized they were airborne.

The team landed a considerable distance away from the destruction.

"Somehow, I don't think that's what Sir had in mind when he said he didn't want to cause a ruckus," Magpie noted dryly.

"It's a good thing the temple was already ruined," Jay chimed in.

Raven glowered at them. "Crow, radio the *Ka'le Hafa* and let them know we have the boy."

* * *

"See, this is why we should never trust hired wings," Magpie remarked.

The team found themselves standing in the cargo bay of the *Ka'le Hafa* at gunpoint. Once they rendezvoused with the airship and took to the sky, Denard revealed his duplicity and ordered the mongrel crew to detain the Corvidae while he checked with Felix's father as to how to dispose of them.

"Please know that it grieves me to betray you like this," Denard said solicitously. "You certainly live up to your reputation. My noble employer wishes me to express his gratitude, of course, but he does not wish to part with money if he doesn't have to."

"Glad we could be of service," Raven replied darkly.

Denard consulted his pocket chronometer once again. "Were it up to me, I would give you a more honorable death than this, but alas, I am not at liberty to be so kind." He smiled apologetically and, with an inclination of his head, uttered a command in the coarse language of the crew, who opened fire.

As soon as he opened his mouth, each member reacted as best they could. Magpie and Jay dropped to the floor faster than the gunmen could fire - Magpie flicked out the throwing knives she had hidden up her sleeves and Jay threw smoke pellets to screen their movements. Raven, Rook, and Crow ducked behind whatever cover they could find, drawing their own guns as they did so. The Corvidae were only at a slight disadvantage in that they were not as readily armed as their captors. They still managed to hold their own with minimal damage to themselves.

Denard shook his head and chuckled to himself. He shouted for reinforcements as he moved a safe distance away from the firefight. He consulted his chronometer, then stalked off in the direction his men had taken the boy.

Raven noticed the movement. The team could not afford to lose their eyes on Denard. As far as Raven was concerned, their mission was not complete. They needed the boy still and Denard would most likely lead them to Felix.

"Crow, flash bomb," Raven ordered.

The younger man nodded and pulled the requested item from one of his pouches. "We'll have to remember to pack more of these next time," he remarked, rolling the device out onto the deck. The other team members turned away just in time for the bomb to affect everyone else.

Raven used the distraction to fly up onto the catwalk where he had last seen Denard. He had to trust that the rest of the Corvidae would react accordingly.

The *Ka'le Hafe* was not an overly large airship, so there were not many places Denard could go. However, Raven was unfamiliar with the layout of the vessel and one could never be too cautious. He knew of a ship or two with more than one hidden compartment where someone or something could wait to take a man unawares.

Turning one of the corners, he encountered two of the mongrel crew. They seemed surprised to see him alive - their hesitation was his advantage. He needed to conserve his ammunition, so he rushed at them. One of them tried to get a shot off but his aim was thrown off by how quickly Raven closed the distance between them.

Raven winced as the bullet struck the wall near his head. He took it as a sign from Verdellen to take care of this quickly or else Her favor would go elsewhere. He ducked underneath the shooter's arm and threw him into his companion. Raven pulled the gun out of the mongrel's hand and shot both of them in the head.

He took the dead men's guns. There had been a time in his life when taking the weapon of the fallen had been taboo. Now that he was Corvidae, such things were no longer sacred. It was far more important to have the upper hand in situations such as this.

The next corner he turned brought him to his quarry.

Snap. Denard stood alone in the corridor, chronometer in hand. "I did try to tell my noble employer that contracting the Corvidae was not like contracting just any other crew." He put his chronometer away, "You were much faster than even I anticipated."

"Where is the boy?"

Denard smiled, "On the ship. Somewhere. You'll need me to negotia--"

Raven silenced him with a bullet to the brain. He was no longer interested in discussing business with a man like Denard. Raven may not have had the education that Crow had, but he was clever enough to figure Felix was probably in one of the rooms in that corridor.

"Felix!" he called out, "Felix, lad, I need you to come out here!" Raven hoped that this tactic worked; he did not have to time to knock down every door.

When a few moments passed, he readied himself to kick in the first door when the one at the end of the hallway slowly opened and Felix hesitantly stepped out. His stance was both unsure and defiant as he first regarded Denard's body and then Raven. His gaze dropped back to the corpse once he found his voice. "You killed him," he observed quietly.

"Yes," Raven kept his stolen weapon at the ready but he did not have it trained on the boy.

"He was my father's man," Felix continued, all the while keeping his eyes on Denard. "He was a good man."

"He followed orders," Raven conceded; he could not speak on whether Denard was anything more than a man who did his job. "Now I need you to follow orders, Felix. You must come with me."

"Will you take me to my father?"

"We will take you to safety," Raven answered carefully.

Felix finally looked up again. "Why should I trust you when you just shot Denard?"

"How old are you, boy?"

"Ten," he replied, lifting his chin proudly and meeting Raven's eyes directly.

"Ten is old enough to make difficult decisions," Raven explained. "You trusted me and my team enough to get you out of that hole; you trusted us enough to get you onto this boat; and now you must trust us again to do what is right."

Felix considered carefully. He nodded once.

Raven did not think the boy was overly convinced, but he did not have the time or the right words to win him over completely. He gestured for Felix to follow him. "Stay close," he advised.

They picked their way back towards the cargo bay. The *Ka'le Hafa* was still flying; that either meant the vessel was fixed on a straight course, or the captain was still alive. Either way, Raven did not trust that hired wings were the best way to return to headquarters. There were still bursts of gunfire every so often; fortunately for both Raven and Felix, they did not seem to encounter any of the danger.

Magpie was the first team member they came across. Her mouth lifted in a half smile when she saw them. "So far, so good," she commented.

"Status?" Raven barked.

"Most folk we came across tried to shoot us," she said. "We shot back a bit more accurately than they did."

"The others?"

"Cleaning up, I believe. Crow is probably pilfering some useful gadgets. Last I saw him, he was heading toward the cockpit."

"Back to the cargo bay," Raven ordered. He tapped a device on his belt that began to blink green. It was a signaling device Crow invented; the details of how it functioned eluded Raven when the younger man tried to explain it. All Raven knew was that it was useful for when the team was spread out while on a job and needed to rendezvous.

Raven, Magpie, and Felix did not have long to wait once they made it to their destination.

"Nice to see you again, Felix," Jay said cheerfully. The boy only offered a weak smile in return; there was some blood staining the front of her shirt and with the way she was standing and smiling it was unlikely any of it was hers.

"Is everything taken care of?"

"We might have a problem," Crow started sheepishly. "When I was in the cockpit, the pilot opened fire. Sometime during the firefight, one of the bullets struck the control panel. There's damage to the navigation and steering."

"I guess using the ship to get back to base is no longer an option," Magpie remarked.

"What now?" Rook questioned.

"Fly away," Raven replied.

"Come with me, Felix," Rook ordered. The boy gulped but complied quickly.

Crow opened the hatch; a blast of wind blew against them, almost knocking Jay and Felix off their feet.

The jump from the *Ka'le Hafa* was a bit more dangerous than the one from the collapsing temple. For one, they were much higher up in the sky and the winds were far more unforgiving. The team had little choice, however, as the vessel lurched suddenly and a klaxon blared throughout the ship.

It was not one of Raven's most graceful dives. Once again, he found himself glad of Crow's adjustments to their gliders. Raven contorted his arms closer to his body to increase his speed and put distance between himself and the rapidly descending aircraft. The wind blew them all a bit off course, but it could have been much worse.

Raven found himself tumbling and rolling once he hit the ground. He was lucky. Jay managed to get herself stuck in a tree, but other than that the team was relatively unscathed.

Raven surveyed the surroundings while the others helped Jay. Judging by the wooded landscape, they were somewhere in central Teraltis. He guessed they had been on the *Ka'le Hafa* long enough to get them past the Itu Range.

"What do we do now?" Rook questioned.

"There are still some cities and villages inhabited here," Raven noted. "We had best try our luck there."

"Seems to me Verdellen holds us in Her hands quite a bit this time around."

Raven regarded the other man darkly. He was not particularly eager to find out what would happen once their luck ran out and he did not appreciate it being pointed out to him.

"Crow is likely to have a map," Rook continued mildly. "Either that or his Scholarly brain remembers this area from one of his scrolls."

The two men rejoined their team. "Are you all right, Jay?" Raven asked.

Her smile lacked its usual cheer. "A little twisted up, but I'll be fine."

"Perhaps we should make camp here," Crow suggested, "get our bearings and sort out a plan."

"We need to move," Raven objected. "I would rather we find a town or a village and contact Sir."

"Even if we find one, what makes you think they'll have working anything we can use?" Magpie demanded.

"We should stay here," Felix offered timidly. "My father will be looking for us now that the ship's crashed. He'll send others."

Raven thought about that as well. If the boy's father sent a search party or recovery crew, there was a chance the Corvidae would be outnumbered. He tried a different tactic. "We at least need to make camp where there is water."

No one could find fault with that argument.

Crow did have a map with him. He estimated they were at least a two days' walk from the nearest town. "There's no telling if it still exists," he noted, "but this is the most recent map." Every month, the Imperial Survey Team took a census of the remaining citizens of Teraltis. "At the very least, there's a stream a few miles northwest of here."

The team and their captive headed out. Felix stayed by Jay, since she was the least threatening of the group. Raven frowned slightly as he observed how she favored her left side as she walked. He glanced over at Rook, who had also been injured back at the temple; he seemed to be faring well, but one never could tell with Rook.

Crow was on point with Magpie close on his tail. The concerned looks she threw over her shoulder did not go unnoticed. Raven did not want to run his team ragged, but he did not want them to be sitting ducks either. The more time they spent on the ground, the more danger they were in, and not just from the possibility of Felix's father sending out a search party. All they needed now was to be found out by-

"Hold!" Crow did not shout, but his voice cut clearly through the silent surroundings. The Corvidae instinctively froze in their tracks, each assuming a fighting stance. Since Jay was closest to Felix, she pushed the lad to the ground, crouching over him protectively. Crow produced a spyglass from his pack. The younger man had upgraded the contraption, of course. Raven wondered what Crow's enhanced vision spied.

He had his answer as soon as he had thought it. "Infected, three."

"Threat?" asked Raven.

Crow snapped the spyglass shut. "We should be fine if we maintain our present course."

Magpie rolled her eyes. "Doesn't mean they're not a threat," she observed. "They'll smell us sooner or later. We ought to dispose of them now."

"No," Raven said crisply. "I do not want to waste the time or the energy."

Raven could see the girl wanted to argue; she already had one of her daggers drawn. The moment passed, however, and the tension between them evaporated as quickly as it had manifested.

They moved on. Infected were certainly a danger, but Raven was confident the creatures would not be a problem at their current distance. During his first mission as Raven, the team had dispatched a small horde of the ghouls harassing a town.

Felix however... he looked as if he was about to soil himself when he heard the word "Infected". Raven could not blame the lad; he was a privileged boy who probably spent his whole life amongst the clouds.

The stream Crow had spoken of was beside a copse of trees. "Isn't it just *darling*," Magpie remarked. Raven had to admit it looked like a drawing he'd seen once in a storybook... there had been something about a picnic.

He nodded to Crow, who needed no other prompting. He produced another one of his inventions from his pack; this one's purpose was to test water for drinkability. "Mid-grade," he reported.

Each member collected some water in his or her canteen and then added a few drops of solution to purify it further. Jay offered some of hers to Felix.

"We will make camp here," Raven declared. He would have still rather have made it to the town, but the sun was beginning to wester and he knew better than to wander around in the dark.

"And then what?" Rook queried.

"We'll need to figure out what to do with the boy," Magpie noted.

"There is nothing to 'figure out'," Raven rejoined. "Sir will tell us what to do next."

"How?"

"He is bound to find out we have been betrayed. He will make a decision."

"I say we make an example of him so others will know what happens to those that break contract with the Corvidae."

Felix gasped while Jay tsked.

"We are not murderers," Raven said harshly.

"I think the people we just killed on the *Ka'le Hafa* would beg to differ. And those in the ruin."

"Casualties of war."

Magpie laughed derisively. "And what's one more then? At least this one would benefit us."

"*No.*"

"And if Sir orders us to kill him?"

"He will not."

"Won't he?"

He could feel the weight of all the team members' – and Felix's – expectant stares.

"He will not." Raven huffed out a breath. "*We* won't."

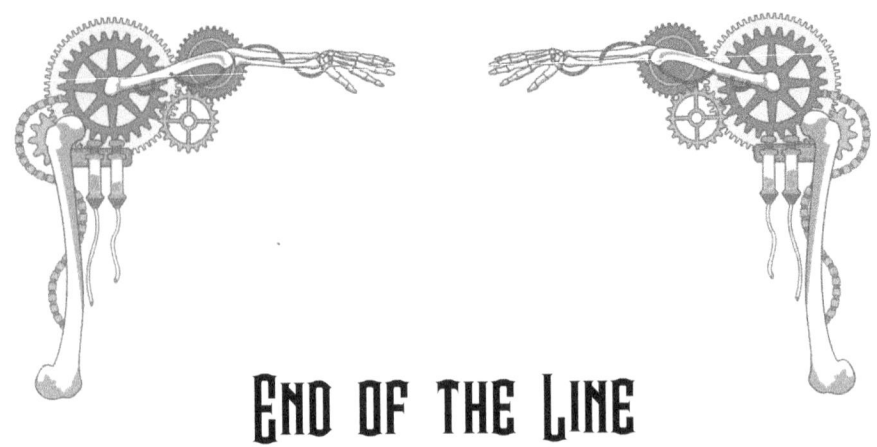

END OF THE LINE

By Dex Greenbright

Captain Zu shielded his eyes from the rain as he scanned the horizon. The downpour meant the raft might hit shore without his ever seeing it. He glanced down at the compass on the back of his leather cuff. Saltwater had stained the cuff badly. At least they were still headed south, thank the Lady of Fate.

Another gust of wind caused Zu to retreat beneath the stern's crude shelter. He sat on the makeshift bench next to Baako and took the oar from Yuri'ik's exhausted hands.

"Go, Yuri, check the nets. Then rest."

Owynn huffed from the bench behind theirs.

"How much l-longer, Captain?"

"Who can tell? But we're going in the proper direction. We'll keep rowing."

They would already be in Shunnira if they had been flying. The rusty, old fishing boat they had started out on had been torn apart by their first storm at sea. Baako nearly lost his life that night. It took a week to cobble together enough flotsam to make a raft, with an additional day to make the benches and shelter. All the while living off of fish and the last of the boat's vodka stores.

Zu chuckled to himself; a lifetime could pass before he ate another of those slimy water creatures and it would be too soon.

Behind him, Aria paused to wipe the sweat from her brow.

"I call next break. Nets, repairs, lookout, anything beyond this oar."

Zu shook his head and pointed to Owynn.

"We go in order, friend. Our navigator has been at this since waking."

"And if he gets stabbed and needs a medic? Then we'll both get a break."

Owynn scowled and pushed his oar hard against the waves.

"Don't go g-getting ideas!"

Zu laughed.

"Nobody will be cutting anyone. Just keep your focus on the airship we'll be flying once we reach port. A glimmering beauty with three-layer wings and engines ten times that of the Wyvera."

That quieted the crew. As with their ill-fated last mission, it was agreed that this trial would soon be past and belonged behind them.

In the mid-afternoon, while Baako took his break, their luck changed.

"It's land! Shunnira, straight ahead!"

Zu jumped up so fast he hit his head against the shelter's metal roof.

"Are you sure?"

"It's not rocky. Those are smooth sands, Captain. We've made it."

171

Zu squinted ahead. Through the wall of gray rain, he could see it; patches of pale land dotted the horizon. In the middle, he saw towers that looked manmade. He couldn't think of a lovelier sight.

He ordered Baako back to the bench. Captain Zu coordinated their movements into the marina. More from the left. Yuri'ik, slow down. Aria, you can do this! Nearly there!

Zu stretched out and lashed the derelict raft to a pier. One by one, they climbed up the ladder and ran toward the waterlogged town. The first light they saw was over the sign for an inn and bar named Verdellen's Favor. They ducked inside, looking like a horde of soaked rats.

The room inside was dark, lit by only a few lanterns along the wall. A small band of seedy Teraltian patrons sat in one of three wooden booths: a short, grouchy man with a metal arm, a greasy woman whose sneer gleamed with gold, and a somber brute. All of them sported monstrous tattoos that marked them as pirates. The driftwood bartop looked like a more hospitable place to gather, but it couldn't seat the whole crew. An ebony Djimbuka man with a white beard already sat at one end, while a dusty Aadoburi Historian took up the other.

Zu waved the crew over to an empty booth while he approached the bar.

A thick woman with braided hair locked eyes with him.

"You look like you swam here, stranger."

"We rowed."

"You're either brave, or stupid. Welcome to Port Fenzir."

"Thanks. We had a lack of options. I need rooms and information."

He dug through his coin pouch and produced two gold pieces. The only money to survive their time at sea.

The barmaid studied the coins, then him.

"Two Teraltian D'alis all you have? Two rooms for one night. After that, you either work or leave. Fair?"

172

"Perfectly. We're in the market for an airship. Does Port Fenzir have a field?"

"Up on Crow Hill, but…" She leaned over the bar to whisper the rest. "Near all of the airships are owned by…"

He followed the barmaid's eyes to the other bar patrons.

The largest pirate scowled back.

With their money expended, Captain Zu bartered away his copper belt buckle in exchange for two bottles of cheap rum. He joined his crew at the large corner table.

Owynn pressed his hands against the wooden surface.

"Do they have any airships?"

"Our future begins at a place called 'Crow Hill.' We can go tomorrow. After this rain clears."

Yuri'ik smirked as he stretched his arms over his head.

"I hope it's a pile of scrap. I need a challenge."

"That r-raft wasn't hard enough?"

Zu laughed as he opened the first bottle.

"You may get your wish. We don't even have money for parts, let alone a ship."

The trio of pirates sauntered over. The woman bent at the waist until her face was level with Zu's. She chewed the end of a processed herb, which stained the few teeth not replaced with metal. Her breath was a foul mix of the drug and day-old fish.

"Look what we have! A Djimbuka that wants to be a bird."

Owynn thrust out his chin.

"C-can't tell a Nomad when you see one? Zu's the best airship captain in--"

She shoved the navigator away with the palm of her hand.

"You can't fly, birdies. We own every ship in port."

The shorter man flicked his metal hand in the air.

"Now, now. The birdies could always give up their freedom to work for us."

The larger man grunted behind his companions.

"Always wanted a pet."

The woman tousled Zu's hair.

"What do you say? Servitude's a better fate than being eaten by the zomb-kin."

Zu leaned back and crossed his legs. He patted the curved blade strapped to his calf.

"We've fought the dead and survived. We would survive a tangle with you as well."

Baako picked up the cue and placed his revolver on the table.

"By pirate rules, killing your captain would give us your ship."

The metal-armed man growled.

"That only applies to pirates, fool. Try it, you'd only get a bullet in your eye!"

Yuri'ik scoffed.

"Have you smelled these guys? I'd rather make a new airship out of outhouse walls than step one foot on their vessel."

In an instant, the gold-toothed woman's sword went from sheathed to slicing a deep groove into the table.

"Enough, you scum! You'll die before even seeing another airship!"

At that, the barmaid roared.

"If you bloody up my bar, I'll have the Corvidae end you!"

The pirates spun on their heels. A dread silence fell over the bar. Zu kept his hand on his knife, just in case the pirates didn't fear these Corvidae. The barmaid's stern glare eventually won the standoff. The pirate woman spat on the ground next to Zu's boot. She gathered her crewmates and slunk away. They stopped by their old booth to down the last of their drinks, then departed into the rainy night.

Now that peace had been restored, Zu and his crew discussed their employment options. They all had useful skills, though none wanted to become too comfortable. The unknown reaches called to them. The topic of what the ocean held piqued everyone's interest.

Then the Historian came over and placed a jug on the table.

"I come bearing marsh wine. A local specialty."

Zu picked it up, inspected the light green liquid, and nodded his thanks. The Historian looked as though he would walk away. He took a step, paused, and turned back again several times before finding the words he was looking for.

"I... I hope it's not rude, but I overheard your conversation. You want to see what lies beyond the ocean."

"If anything does. It's not called the endless water for nothing."

"Lucky for you, there is something beyond. I have proof!"

Owynn eyed the man.

"N-nobody in all of history has returned from the ocean. How can there be proof?"

The Historian fidgeted with the end of his tunic.

"Ah. Yes, well, I meant that I've been searching for proof. That's why I'm at Port Fenzir, and why I'm talking with you. I think I've finally narrowed down the location of the right set of Haak ruins. But I won't risk those pirates looting the place. I need skilled people to help me get to the ruins."

Zu poured the marsh wine into his glass.

"Why not ask these mysterious Corvidae for assistance?"

"I've asked. They never take on more than one contract at a time. Port Fenzir hired them as Zomb-killers, but the mayor doesn't want them acting against the pirates. He says the zomb-spawn and pirates will kill each other and keep his Corvidae bill low. I wonder at times if the mayor isn't getting paid by the pirates as well. They loot the abandoned places and there is no shortage of those in western Shunnira."

Baako cleared his throat.

"We seem to be getting a bit sidetracked here. Are you offering payment, Mr. ...?"

The man beamed.

"Call me Liridon. As a Historian, it's my duty to preserve the history of the world. I've catalogued effects of the plague, the creation of the Automazombs, their mutation, and their horrid kin. I once thought that knowledge would help society recover. But when tragedy of this magnitude strikes, people have no attention for study. Their only thoughts are of survival."

"And now?"

"I sent my notebooks to the Grand Library. Hopefully some historian of the future can learn from it all. But there's little left for me here on Eysan. I've begun to set my sights on what lies across the ocean. Our goals are similar. If I can recover what lies within the ruins, I would like to travel with you. If you accept, I will fund your new airship, including all necessary supplies."

The crew sat dumbfounded at the odd Historian. Captain Zu stroked his goatee. This new benefactor looked harmless enough. Liridon's weathered skin and close-shaven hair gave him the appearance of a much older man. Only his eyes betrayed his youth: joyful and eager in the pursuit of knowledge.

Zu flashed a wide smile.

"We'll join you on this expedition. If we find one another agreeable, we can discuss further adventures. If not, you will pay us in a month's worth of provisions and lodging."

"Fantastic!"

Liridon pulled up a chair. He lifted his glass to toast the future.

* * *

They set out two days later. It was the first sunny day in a week, and Zu took it as a good sign. South of Port Fenzir lay a patchwork of marsh, jungle, and rocky outcroppings. There was no sign of pirates, zomb-kin, or the Corvidae along the main road.

Their new employer regaled them with stories of the people who made the ruins they would be visiting.

"The local legend says that during the time of the Haakon Republic, a man came from the water. There is no end of debate over his appearance. The traveler claimed his lineage was that of a long-dead civilization. A people before the Haak that had left Eysan to explore the oceans. Of course, the first Haak emperor had all records of previous settlements burned. There was no way to verify the man's claim, so everyone assumed – erroneously – that he had come from Homanoah."

Then, Liridon stopped and pointed to a trail branching off to the right. The path was grown over with wide, waxy leaves and strangling ivy. Zu gave a nod to Baako, who readied his blade as he led the group down this new trail.

Aria tapped Liridon on the shoulder.

"What makes you think he *wasn't* from Homanoah?"

"While I've read - and heard - a multitude of ideas on the man's skin tone, eyes, height, and whether or not his ears were pointed, everyone agreed on what he wore. The style and fabric was strange. A pendant around his neck held a unique gemstone that simply isn't found in the three countries or Homanoah."

A monkey howled from the canopy. The group paused for a moment to listen for incoming danger. When the forest quieted down, they continued their hike. Liridon took the opportunity to continue his story.

"Many Haak cities were razed by the Teraltian Alliance. They wiped out the upper nobles, but the merchants and lesser nobles went into hiding. Some built a new home in a series of caverns. It's those ruins I'm looking for. The man from across the ocean settled down and had a family. A Haak family. Some of his relatives went into hiding here in western Shunnira. Others hid in a library as Archivists. A Master Historian I spoke to befriended the descendants of those Archivists. They claimed that the family who hid in the caverns owned a map and whoever unearthed it could find land on the other side of the ocean. But nobody had ever been able to locate it, and anyway Teraltians are always obsessed with D'alor's domain, completely ignoring the waters whenever possible."

Zu adjusted the glass he wore over his left eye. There was nothing but greenery as far as he could see.

"How far are these caverns?"

"Six miles, I think. I had to work off of three different folk maps from various eras to cobble together the truth. But we all know they're not strictly accurate, distance-wise. I have my creation here if you'd like a look?"

Owynn eagerly came forward. Liridon handed over the parchment to Zu's navigator. There was a long period of silence as they waited to hear how long they might be walking.

"We should r-reach the end of these trees by dusk. The caverns should be in the hills beyond."

Liridon's expression brightened.

"Fantastic!"

"But, we're headed in the wrong direction."

The man's shoulders slumped, until Zu clapped him on the back.

"Not to worry, friend. That's why you hired us."

The deeper they went into the woods, the darker and wetter it became. Soon, they were forced to hop between mangrove roots. Biting insects buzzed around their heads. The murky water writhed with life below them.

Zu slipped as he helped Aria make a particularly long jump. He grasped a young branch to break his fall. He laughed as he worked to right himself.

"I'm not surprised that we haven't seen the zomb-kin. This path is treacherous."

Liridon scowled at the forest ahead.

"Don't underestimate the zomb-spawn. I've seen them cross rivers by walking along the bottom. The dead aren't bothered by anything."

A shot rang out in the distance.

The crew pulled their weapons. Zu signaled for the group to stay quiet. Baako was sent to scout the area. When he disappeared into the shadows, everyone listened. The forest was full of noise, but there were no voices or footsteps, or the beastly zomb-kin moans.

They waited a few minutes longer, before Zu ushered the group to resume their trek through the mangroves. Any danger must have been far ahead, if Baako had not yet returned or called out.

A second gunshot sent the area birds flying in a panic.

Zu adjusted his eyepiece. The Corvidae would probably leave them be, but the pirates would be especially dangerous so far away from the town.

Liridon stared up at the canopy.

Zu had a feeling the beads of sweat at the man's temple weren't only because of the heat. He kept his voice to a whisper.

"What worries you, friend?"

"My messenger falcon. I let him go on a solitary hunt a few days ago and he has yet to return. You don't think the pirates...?"

"If the locals have abandoned their hunting grounds and farms, I'm sure the pirates have found other, easier prey."

"That bird's been with me almost every step of my journey. I can't imagine traveling without him."

The third time they heard gunfire, it sounded much closer. It echoed, which could only mean one thing – they were nearing the rocky hills. But, once again, nothing came of it. Zu ordered the crew to move carefully from here on out.

Bugsong filled the air. As they walked, the canopy thinned, letting in the light of an orange sunset. The ground, too, became dry enough to walk again. They paused beside a waterfall to fill their canteens and eat dinner. Yuri'ik had bought fresh bread, fruit, and salted pork with the supply budget Liridon had given them. Zu grumbled at the lack of drink choices, but he was pleased to not be eating fish.

Halfway through, Liridon dropped his plate. He jumped up, pointing out a broken stone statue on a distant hillside.

"We're there! The caves must be right below our feet!"

He dashed off. It was surprising how quick someone so obviously bookish could become when excited. Zu stuffed the last of a roll in his mouth before racing to catch up with their employer.

Liridon was nearing a crest of the small, first hill before Zu got close. As he ran, Zu thought it strange that the hum of insects was louder here. But there was something strange about the noise. It was deeper – angrier – like the throaty growls of the dead.

One hand went to his gun, while the other reached for Liridon. Zu grabbed the Historian by his tunic and pulled him back. Both men fell to the ground. Liridon let out a shocked cry.

"What are you-?"

"Shh!"

Zu crawled forward on his elbows. From the hill's crest, he could see movement around a dark patch in the earth. Several figures moved through the underbrush. The one in the lead carried a massive gun. But, he didn't point it at the zomb-kin on his tail. When he reached the edge of the dark area, he aimed into the trees. A grappling anchor and length of rope shot out of the gun. The pirate swung across to safety. The dead behind him stumbled and fell. Their bodies crunched and splashed as they reached the bottom of a deep pit.

More of the mindless ravagers moaned in the distance. The man who had swung across waited on the far side of the hole. The gold-toothed woman from the bar appeared from the trees with a spyglass in one hand. With the other, she urged her companion to follow her away.

The man didn't budge. He hollered back to the woman.

"There's at least a dozen more wandering the hills. You want those rotters to find the camp? Besides, the more we trap, the sooner we can act."

"That many dead means the Corvidae will come nosing around. That would ruin everything. Cap'n will kill us if that happens. Now go!"

The pirates disappeared around the far side of the next hill to the west.

Zu pulled himself up to a crouch.

"I thought you said those bounty hunters ignored the pirates."

Liridon nodded.

"Unless it interferes with the affairs of the townspeople."

"It would appear the pirates plan on overstepping their bounds."

Zu was able to convince Liridon to return with him until they could make a plan. They found the crew making camp not far from the waterfall. Baako was with them. His expression was grim.

"Captain, this area is infested with pirates and the dead."

"We knew that when we embarked on this journey. The question is how do we avoid them."

"Too late for that. They had a twiggy girl following us. I almost didn't see her, but when I did, she leapt into the trees and vanished."

"Then they're smarter than we gave them credit for. They'll be more direct next time we meet."

Liridon unpacked the torches and lit the first of them.

"If we explore the ruins tonight, we could get the map before the pirates find us. I'd rather not meet them again, if it's all the same."

Zu took the lit torch.

"I like it; we act while their scout is sending her report."

The crew took down their unused tents with little argument. Liridon led them around and down the north side of the hill. They fanned out to better look for the entrance to the ruins. Everyone kept quiet and held their torches low.

Not long into their search, Zu came upon a stone obelisk. He beckoned the others over.

A mad grin spread across Liridon's face.

"A tombstone of the old Republic!" He tore off clumps of vine and moss, revealing etchings in the surface. He ran his fingers over the letters. "Lord Endis. High-ranking military official, even higher noble class. It's a memorial to his bravery in sheltering a group of merchants from the traitorous families of the northern reach."

Owynn adjusted his glasses.

"Does that mean they moved on?"

The Historian crouched down and continued cleaning up around the base of the statue. Beneath the tall point, four flat stones lay in a rough line.

"In memorials from Haakon, the stones always pointed toward the capital. This one does not. It's my guess..."

Liridon traced an invisible line from the obelisk to an overgrown rockface. He hurried over to a tangle of vines and tore them away from the boulders they covered. A small crevice split the rock.

"Yes! This is the entry we've been searching for!"

Baako raised an eyebrow at Zu.

"Were the Haakonese a tiny people?"

Liridon waved at him dismissively over his shoulder.

"*The Haak* were of an average size. They would have ferried in their larger companions by another doorway. Equally hidden."

Zu inspected the crevice by torchlight. The room beyond the initial tiny doorway was large enough that he would be able to stand up straight.

The crevice itself looked natural at first, but seeing it up close, he could tell it was manmade. He knew of at least two of his crew that wouldn't fit. Baako's broad shoulders and Owynn's girth would prevent both of them from entering the cavern. He took them aside.

"The pirates are up to something. Something they don't want the Corvidae to find out about. They've been keeping tabs on us; we should return the favor. Find their camp and learn what you can."

Owynn grabbed one of the gear bags. He fished around inside, until his hand came back holding a spyglass. Baako's preparations were more of the military sort. He took as many guns and knives as he could strap to his belts. They clasped hands with Zu, then hiked away in the direction Zu indicated.

Zu slipped through the opening in the rock. The walls were covered with inscriptions. Liridon had out a piece of red wax and was making a rubbed copy of the words. When the Historian finished, they entered the tunnel at the back of the room.

As they walked, the cave began to look more and more like mining tunnels Zu had read about. Metal support beams held up long sections of dirt between the rocky areas. Nooks were carved into the walls. Small ones held jars that Liridon suspected were vessels for food and drink. Larger rooms were nearly as big as one of the crew bunks aboard the Wyvera. Enough for a cot and a trunk, but not an extra inch to spare.

The rooms got larger as they went the deeper. A communal bath, a temple to Q'ua and Raucilla – complete with shrines to the more familiar deities, a dining hall, and even a small park. Instead of plants, the park was full of bioluminescent mushrooms. There were several colors, and Liridon suggested they might have been cultivated for food.

Then came the junction. The hallway that before had been straight, aside from short juts to either side, now branched into three long corridors. Two of them bore metal beams, while the third was natural and jagged.

Zu pointed his torch down the narrower of the carved tunnels.

"Do we split up?"

Aria shrank into her shoulders.

"Do we have to?"

Yuri'ik wrapped an arm around his sister.

"There's nobody here. What are you afraid of?"

"Pirates, zomb-kin, ghosts, beasts, cave-ins, booby traps, slipping and falling to my death in one of these caverns, what is there *not* to fear?"

Zu laughed.

"I'm sure Yuri'ik can keep you safe from any ghosts. As for the rest, we haven't seen any--"

A deep, gargling moan cut him off midsentence.

The twins both yelped.

"The dead are here!?"

Zu shushed them. He cocked his head toward each tunnel. The moans of the zomb-kin echoed and amplified through the chambers, obscuring which path was the source of the sound.

"It seems the sinkhole and the cave are connected. New plan: don't stray out of sight. We'll go through systematically." He pointed to Liridon. "If we see any shamblers, aim for the head. It's the best way to rebury the dead, and you can put that down in your books."

Zu led the way down the widest tunnel first, in case they needed to run back to the surface. The hall was lined with ancient torches. Zu lit them as the group passed. The extra torches illuminated paintings of robed figures on the walls. Even when on the run, the Haak refugees kept their nobility in their hearts. He felt for them; his own heart was Nomad, no matter how distantly he wandered away from Lobhi.

The tunnel ended in a series of wide openings, all leading to the same room. It was the largest chamber they'd come to yet. Most of the space was natural cavern, with sweeping stalactite formations, but the rest was carefully carved out into stadium benches.

Liridon abandoned the group in order to study the room. Zu hoped that meant the map would be hidden here. They'd spent too long underground already. But as the Historian climbed onto the stage, Zu realized something entirely different had caught the man's attention. He ran down after Liridon, but it was too late. The Historian belted out a verse from some long-forgotten opera.

Zu dropped his torch as he jumped on stage. He clamped his hand over Liridon's mouth.

"What are you doing?!"

Liridon took a step back. His expression was sheepish.

"To stand in a place of great history... I might never get the chance again."

"Not if you get us eaten you won't. Will we find the map here?"

"It wouldn't seem likely. No, my guess is it was buried with the man in question."

Zu nudged his torch with his boot. It was half its original size, and had snuffed out when it hit the ground.

"So, we need to find a catacombs, then. Did they follow the Dark Lady's rituals?"

"Why yes! They were the ones that invented the chemical baths that we use to this very day. Perfected now, of course."

"Are there any other clues we should look for? We risk death with each stray minute."

"Perhaps we can find a clue in the artwork, traces of the traveler's influence?"

Zu gestured for silence. Something wasn't right. He pulled his pistol. Shadows fell over the hallway. Scuffling footsteps echoed near the auditorium. Aria followed the captain's lead and drew her own weapon. Yuri'ik unholstered his revolver, but hesitated. With his other hand, he grabbed the spanner from the loop on his belt and brandished it like a club.

A pair of lanky forms appeared in the doorway. The crew opened fire. The first figure cried out, before crumpling to the ground. The second fired a few shots of her own before she darted away. Zu cursed under his breath as he ran up to the one they had felled.

Zu peered around the doorway and into the hall. The pirate's next shot struck the stone wall next to his head. He ducked and returned fire blindly around the corner. When he checked again, she was gone. He had to guess this was the girl from Baako's warning.

Zu grabbed one of the ancient torches from its place on the wall.

"Keep your weapons out. It seems our freebooting friends have caught up with us."

* * *

Baako and Owynn trudged through the drenched jungle. It had been three hours since they split off from the others. Purple-white lightning lit the forest every few minutes, giving them a chance to scour the area for campfire smoke.

Captain Zu's crew didn't have any sort of command structure, not like Mr. Everett, or the pirates. Baako had to catch himself from simply following the lead of the more senior Owynn. The way Zu put it, his crewmembers all had their own expertise and he relied on each of them to take charge if they had the most knowledge in a given situation. Right now, that meant Owynn and his maps would find the most likely spot for a pirate camp. Then, Baako would step up.

He never thought he would have to tell the captain about the darker part of his history. He kept his tattoos well hidden. But now? He still hoped it wouldn't come to that. The Corvidae were legends; they would be able to handle the pirates.

Baako paused from hacking through the strangler vines in their path so they could confirm their path. He stood over Owynn to help protect the map from the rain. He stretched over Owynn's shoulder to point to a spot south and west of the pictures of hills.

"We're headed this way?"

"Yes. I gather they should be, well, close by th-this valley."

"Do you think I could borrow your maps sometime? I'm not terribly fond of being lost."

"Me either. Can you imagine being in those cave tunnels with the captain? And he sent away his cartographer! Madness."

Baako smiled at that. Being hired to kill Zu was the best thing that ever happened to him. For the first time since he was a boy, he had friends. Thunder rumbled above them and, strangely, grew louder by the second. He cupped a hand to his ear.

"Motors. It's an airship!"

Owynn squinted up, shielding his eyes from the rain with his hand.

"It sounds b-big."

"There!"

A massive black ship slid over the treetops. It was twice the size of the old Wyvera. Lightning illuminated the row of cannons along the gondola. Two sets of wings spread out from wooden struts along the massive ballast compartments. It was heading southwest.

The two set off after the airship. Baako ran out in front, slashing his machete at whatever lay ahead. This wasn't the direction of any towns they knew; it had to be flying toward the pirate encampment. They crashed through the underbrush, keeping an eye and an ear on the ship above.

Damn the stealth mission. They needed to find the camp and get back to the cave before whatever had Captain Zu worried came to pass. Between the pirates and the dead, there was a real chance they could get left behind... or killed. Baako stumbled forward when the thick leaves gave way to open air. He tumbled down onto a rough, overgrown road.

Owynn gasped as he fell after Baako. The navigator's glasses clattered away as he landed face down on the patchy, worn cobblestone.

As Baako pulled himself up, he heard shouting and the thud of barrels being stacked. The pirates were just beyond the trees on the opposite side of the road. He shoved Owynn's glasses into his grasping hand and prodded him in the arm, motioning ahead. They hadn't been seen yet, or else they'd already be in manacles.

They snuck forward, cautious to make no sound. The pirates must have been operating out of Port Fenzir for months. They had built a series of wooden structures among their tents. The airship the crewmen had followed was anchored to a rickety watchtower. Barrels were being lowered from the still-floating ship and placed beneath a grass-roofed shelter. The need for dryness meant it was either food, or…

"Follow me. We need to see what's in those barrels."

The pirates were gathered around the airship's cargo bay, leaving the northern outskirts of the camp unguarded. Baako ducked behind tents and trees as he led the way around. When they reached the shelter, there was a loud cheer among the pirates.

Baako dared to peer out from his hiding place. A man with a black and silver coat strode out from the airship, onto the lift platform. He tugged a rope behind him. The other end was tied to a limping and very frightened man. His leg was purple below the knee.

The captain grabbed the man's shirt and pulled him to the edge of the platform.

"This one thought himself clever! Spying on us was the last mistake he'll ever make."

There was a chorus of gruff jeers. One pirate threw a mug of beer at the captive.

The captain gestured for silence before he continued.

"Now, those loose lips who gave us away, they will be dealt with separately. This poor sot… He will ensure the zomb-kin will continue to hunger for villager flesh!"

Baako snuck over to the barrels as the pirate captain continued his tirade against the town that refused the pirates during the plague times, but now profited from pirate activity in the marshes.

He jabbed his machete under the lid of an unstacked barrel, then pried up. The barrel was filled with black powder.

Owynn slammed the barrel shut and hissed.

"B-blasting powder?"

Baako's brow furrowed. The pirates meant to unleash the zomb-kin on Port Fenzir. How better to widen the door, and call the monsters forward, than an explosion?

"We need to return to Captain Zu immediately."

They crept back to the edge of the pirate camp just as the captain disappeared back into his ship. Part of the crew continued unloading blasting powder and other material. The rest of them dispersed to ready themselves for the coming raid.

As they slipped into the forest, it felt as if there were eyes upon them. Baako gripped his revolver, flicking open the holster with his thumb.

A branch snapped behind them. The two men spun around with their weapons drawn. The same slender girl Baako had seen before was now squatting on a branch just above the trail. She held a broken branch in her hand, and a crooked smirk on her face.

Owynn grabbed Baako's shoulder, stopping him before he could fire a shot.

"We c-can't draw attention, or the whole pirate army will be on us!"

Baako sneered at the girl, but took the navigator's lead and turned to run. The pirate girl dropped the stick and brandished a pair of pistols. She fired two shots into the air. Baako pushed Owynn forward with one hand and shot at the girl with the other.

"So much for that quiet escape. Move!"

They bolted through the underbrush. The rain came down harder than ever. Pirate lanterns cast wavering shadows through the trees. From the angry bellows, it sounded as if the entire crew had taken part in the hunt.

There was another light ahead. Baako shielded his eyes from the rain, just to see if it was an illusion. A pirate trap, perhaps? No, a trap would not advertise itself. If there was another traveler out here, they needed to be warned about the pirates. He pointed out the light to Owynn, and took off in that new direction.

When he approached the light, Baako waved his arms wide.

"Hail, friend!"

A multitude of voices responded.

"Who's that?"

"Some idiot villager who got lost, I bet."

"They have been getting lost a lot lately."

"Hush, Crow."

Baako and Owynn emerged into a small clearing, where a group of three men and two women gathered around a dying fire. A wagon sat at the clearing's edge, piled with weapons and other supplies.

One of the men stood up to greet them. He had a hard face, one that had seen more than its share of battles. He held up a hand to stop them from barging in further.

"Who are you?"

Owynn bent over, resting his hands on his knees as he struggled to catch his breath.

"Pirates… town… in danger…"

The older of the women jumped to her feet.

"I knew it! Those bastards have been plotting something."

"Magpie."

"But Raven-!"

Raven barely shifted toward Magpie, but it had an immediate effect on her. She dropped back down on a log and scowled. He again addressed Baako and Owynn.

"I ask again. Who are you?"

190

Baako glanced over his shoulder. The light of the pirates' lamps was growing brighter, closer.

"We are honest crew of the Nomad pilot Zu. Pirates are hunting us. I thought to warn you, but you must be…"

"The Corvidae." Raven raised a brow as he looked at the lantern light in the forest. "You best come this way."

The oldest of the men, A Teraltian whose wheat brown hair was peppered with gray, lifted the canvas cover of the wagon. Without a word, he directed the two to crawl inside. Baako questioned how well this plan would work as he wedged between a glider harness and a crate labeled as poison.

The old Teraltian shoved the canvas down as the first pirates entered the clearing. Baako kept perfectly still. He listened carefully to the voices; none of them sounded like they belonged to the sneaky pirate girl. That was a small blessing in itself.

Raven kept his voice low.

"Straying a bit far from your airship, aren't you?"

The pirates erupted in a chorus of worried cursing. A man's booming voice rose above the din.

"We're hunting."

"Oh? What's your quarry? Hopefully not boar. Only one we found became our dinner."

"Vermin monkeys looking to steal our supplies. You seen any like that?"

"Not a one. I suggest you search the deeper forests. This area's too close to the marshes for a monkey."

The pirates discussed among themselves, just quietly enough that Baako couldn't hear. Whatever they said, they weren't leaving. Magpie spoke up from her seat at the fire.

"Why don't you move along pirates, or don't you know what we could do to you?"

191

A second pirate with a higher voice than the first shouted back at her.

"How many Corvidae are there? You think you stand any chance against us? Your days are numbered."

The first pirate must have restrained the second, because anything else he said came out as a muffled mumble. Baako heard the sound of guns cocking, then the Corvidae leader spoke.

"Enough. Leave now, or never leave again. Your choice."

Wet leaves rustled as the pirates retreated. A minute later, Raven gave the order for the Corvidae called Jay to scout the area. A shadow darted past the wagon. Baako and Owynn tried to leave, but the canvas was still held closed. The Corvidae chatted about Crow's new invention and how Jackdaw was getting along in his training. When the others could be heard welcoming Jay's return, Raven gave the order to let Baako and Owynn back into the open.

Raven greeted them as they stepped back into the rain.

"We don't often see the pirates, let alone have need to speak with them. They've grown bold these past weeks. Now, you say they have a plot against the town?"

Baako nodded.

"We saw them luring zomb-kin into a trap. They're feeding men and women to these monsters. We think they intend to set the dead loose on the town."

"That would explain the sharp decrease in zomb-spawn in the area. We've done well, but there should be more."

Crow, who had apparently been fixing a small machine inside his tent, stepped out to join the conversation.

"And that would explain the missing vil... Baako?"

Baako squinted in the rain. Crow was a big fellow, wide around the waist, but tall enough to make it still seem healthy. Anyone from Eastern Shunnira would have that tan skin and dark hair, but he knew the man instantly from that cocky grin.

"En-!"

"Tch! Call me Crow, please. I left my name back in Beskra."

The two friends shared a brief embrace. Baako laughed as he clapped Crow on the shoulders.

"What paths we two have taken, hmm? I thought that glider looked familiar. Always the tinkerer, even after all this time."

Crow turned to his leader.

"Raven, this is an old schoolmate of mine. I studied Djimbuka machinery for two years before even considering the Scholars. It's how I designed the gliders at all."

Raven folded his arms and sighed.

"If the pirates are going after Port Fenzir, we'll have to step in. I was hoping fear was enough to keep them in line. We've got skill on our side, but they have numbers."

Owynn wiped the rain from his glasses.

"If we kill the zomb-kin before they're released, the pirates won't have a plan at all."

Baako pointed in the direction of where Captain Zu had seen the zomb-kin.

"They lured the monsters into a sinkhole."

Crow rubbed his chin thoughtfully.

"A few of my iron bomblets should fix that problem right up."

Raven ordered the remains of the fire covered. The wagon was emptied as the weapons were dispersed. They left for the sinkhole shortly after, with Baako in the lead.

* * *

Zu held his torch up to the narrow opening. This path was left in its natural state, and each new offshoot was smaller than the last. Liridon insisted that this was still part of the Haak encampment. The Historian made a rubbing of each etching he found. There were so many, his notebook was filled and he had started copying the old texts onto his tunic with charcoal from the torches.

"I'm fairly certain this way leads to the catacombs."

Aria whimpered as she peered down the new path.

"The zomb-kin disease... It doesn't change the ancient dead, does it?"

Zu exhaled a laugh.

"We'll find out soon."

Beyond the narrow entry, the refugees had dug deep niches into the stone. Each niche held a deeply violet, mummified corpse. There were dozens of niches, stacked three high in some areas. Labyrinthine hallways led in all directions. Clearly the refugees were many, and had taken their noble brethren with them for a proper burial. Zu wondered if there might not be hundreds down here. If the zomb-spawn *could* infect the long dead, he and his crew had no chance of survival. He interrupted Liridon's inspection of an emerald ring on a noblewoman's index finger.

"We should focus on the map. It's too dangerous to stay here long."

Liridon slipped the ring off the mummy and into his pocket.

"Of course. I'll take a few artifacts and leave the analysis for after our adventure."

Zu held the torch high above his head to illuminate far down the path. They hadn't heard so much as a grumble from the dead. The pirates, too, stayed out of sight. He urged the group forward, getting every pair of eyes to help in the search.

As they ventured deeper into the catacombs, Zu got the distinct feeling he should have packed a ball of twine to mark their path.

"How long were these refugees living in the caves?"

"Nearly fifty years. Ah, look! The markings are cruder here. These are children of the original refugees. By the years marked on some of the niches, this the right era we're looking for."

The group fanned out, searching each one. Zu was loathe to touch the dried purple skin, partly out of disgust, and partly from cultural taboos he would never shake. He wondered what an ancient map would look like, and if the paper would even survive all that time. He scanned the back of a young man's niche when he heard Aria's excited shouts.

"I think I found it!"

Liridon was at her side immediately. He and Yuri'ik pulled the body out of its niche. Gnarled hands the color of Aadobur wine clutched a scroll to the man's chest. The Historian cautiously slid the tan parchment out. He flattened it against the stone floor, and urged the torches closer.

"Remarkable."

Zu tilted his head for a better angle. The paper was made of thick woven fibers that had frayed and torn, but the image was still intact. A large oval was inked in the middle. On the right, he saw the familiar – if a bit rough – map of Eysan. Water waves surrounded it on the left and right. The frozen reaches above rising to the top of the page. But, amazingly, there was more to see. The left side contained two whole continents, only slightly smaller than Eysan.

"I've often wondered if there was more beyond the ocean, but I would have never imagined such a place actually existed."

Yuri'ik waved a finger at the left side of the map.

"Probably a fiction; a fancy drawing for children's stories! Two additional continents? Someone would have found it, or they would have found us."

Liridon rolled up the map and tucked it into his bag carefully.

"We have a chance now to verify the claim. We can be the first ambassadors of the three countries to these other places."

There was a sound like thunder. Loose stones clattered to the tunnel floor around them. Zu lifted his torch toward the exit.

195

"Assuming we get out of this cave at all. That's some storm."

The noise had riled up the dead as well. Zu cautioned his crew to only use weapons that didn't make much sound. The cacophony of groaning calls reached a crescendo. Zu glanced back at his crew and Liridon. If this was truly the end, at least he had lived a life to be proud of.

A lone zomb-kin stumbled down the tunnel. Zu holstered his weapon. No sense in alerting more. He unsheathed the curved sword at his hip and drove it through the creature's eye. The zomb-kin opened its mouth, revealing green-brown teeth and a decaying tongue. One last grumble escaped that body before it slumped to the ground.

Two pirate men emerged from the darkness behind the zomb-kin. They looked disappointed. One of them was the same metal-armed bar patron they met earlier. He sneered at Liridon.

"Cap'n told me Historians were treasure bloodhounds. Hand over the bag, before I shoot you."

The pirates had three guns between them, all of which now pointed at Zu's current employer and his crew. While he quickly plotted out the best move to keep his people safe, Yuri'ik pushed past him and fired his revolver. The bullet ricocheted off the metal arm. Zu yanked Liridon out of the way as the pirates opened fire. They would be dealing with the dead soon now. Zu drew and fired his pistol, grazing a pirate's leg. Aria shot the gun right out of the second pirate's hand.

The pirates turned and ran.

"We'll come back for the bag. After the dead do their job."

Zu snatched up the fallen gun and waved for the rest of the group.

"No time to linger. And don't let the dead touch you."

They followed the fleeing pirates through the labyrinthine cave tunnels. They took down the few zomb-kin they saw. But, Zu expected more. Many more. When they came to the man junction, he saw a row of wooden shields that blocked every tunnel aside from the exit. His gut twisted in a knot. The zomb-kin had been lured outside.

Zu pressed his crew harder. Whatever the pirates had planned, they couldn't let it happen. They raced up through the carved halls. Two shots rang out ahead of them. Zu gripped the wooden handle of his pistol.

There was light ahead. A lantern. The pirates had blown open the narrow, hidden entrance to the cavern ruins. It was now wide enough for a skimmer to glide straight through. Several figures gathered at the entrance. Zu stopped to take aim.

One of the shapes cupped its hand above its eyes.

"Captain, is that you?"

The winds of relief enveloped Zu.

"Baako!"

Baako turned toward the other shadowy outlines.

"It's him! Is everyone alive?"

Aria ran for the entrance in a huff.

"So far. You wouldn't believe it! Pirates, the dead, the very very long dead, ghosts, everyone in there wanted to shoot or eat us."

Zu exited more warily. There were more than just Baako and Owynn waiting for them. Only the tone of Baako's voice kept him somewhat at ease. When he reached the surface, he saw the bodies of the pirates from the tunnels.

"Who must I thank for this?"

Baako gestured with his open palm.

"May I introduce Raven and his Corvidae. When Owynn and I uncovered the pirates' plan to use the dead as part of their raiding party, they discovered us and would have killed us if not for the Corvidae's help."

Zu acknowledged Raven, then faced his own crew.

"It looks like that plan's already in action. I've had all I can take of the dead. I intend to stop them, for those we've lost."

There were murmurs of agreement, Yuri'ik loudest among them.

"We're with you."

"It will be dangerous. We only made it out of Irenorn by blood sacrifice."

Aria started trudging in the direction of town.

"I owe them a collective kick in the head for that. Keep, up, Captain."

One of the Corvidae, a woman only barely out of her teens, grinned.

"I like her style."

But there was one more thing to take care of before Zu could set out.

"Liridon, I trust you'll still pay whoever of my crew remains after this?"

Liridon gripped his bag tight. His eyes were full of worry, but he kept his composure well.

"I have no love for those thieving scoundrels or their zomb-spawn. Port Fenzir has been my home for almost a year now. I'll pay you extra for the trouble if you let me join you in saving the town."

Zu smiled at that.

"Let's get moving, then. They've got the lead on us. At least the rain finally ended. Corvidae, are you in?"

Raven turned to his own group and started barking orders.

"Delta routine. Rook, take point. There's no time to waste. We will defend the town to our last breath."

Zu almost laughed. This Raven was so like his lost friends Henning and Telford; once and always a member of the Imperial Army.

The Corvidae and the crew traveled together back to town. Owynn plotted out the most direct and fastest course. They didn't know how far ahead the zomb-kin and pirates had gotten, so Magpie was sent ahead to scout. She met back up with them a little while later with little to say except "They're fast."

198

Zu noticed his crew had sunk into a grim silence. Yes, they had chosen this fight, but not a one of them wanted to address what they were going to find. Irenorn Prison loomed over the lot of them. Their time on the waves had been much of the same. The crew had busied themselves with the task of survival and the promise of a future.

Now, once again, the wretched dead threatened to destroy that future. But they wouldn't succeed. Not with his crew, and the Corvidae, and even the good townsfolk fighting. Shunnira had welcomed so many refugees over the years that surviving could be their new national motto. Zu couldn't be prouder of the selflessness of his crew, his family, for joining this fight. Those pirates wouldn't know what hit them.

He took a deep breath. What his crew needed now was the same confidence in themselves that he had in them. He belted out a storm shanty.

"Blow the wind."

Owynn and Aria jumped, responding by instinct.

"Blow the wind!"

"Fierce the rain."

This time, Yuri and Baako added their voices.

"Fierce the rain."

Zu grinned and ran faster down the path.

"Fly straight through."

"Currents be true."

Then all together, they sang the most important line.

"By D'alor's grace, we'll ne'er be slain!"

Raven gave Zu an odd look. Zu knew his mind: silence was the superior strategy. Lt. Henning warned him against song often, too. But silence didn't improve morale. He ran his crew through more verses. So many, he started making them up. It was a simple tune. The only rule being that the last line was always "we'll ne'er be slain."

199

Liridon jogged alongside Zu, sneaking the song's history in between Zu's verses.

"Did you know... This was sung by... The Nomad division of the... Aadoburi Forces during... the Aadoburi-Teraltian War?"

Zu nodded. Before his people were, the kind term was "taken in," by Teraltis, they had sided with Aadobur. They sang a version of this very song, fighting like a hurricane gale until the last of the ballast warriors was struck down.

"Doomed histories are... SLAM DOWN LIKE HAIL! ...best kept to yourself, friend."

Liridon snapped his mouth shut and looked at Zu's crewmembers. It seemed the message was received. Any further singing was interrupted by a series of explosions rocked the forest.

Boom-Brrumm-BOOM!

The Corvidae dashed off in the direction of the blast. Zu was about to follow, when someone grabbed his shoulder.

Baako pointed toward the main gate.

"They've split their attack; we need to as well."

Zu agreed and let Baako lead the way. The crew raced at top speeds down the road. The dead moaned in the distance. He brandished the curved sword, musing that this was what it was made for. It was a gift from his grandfather, who had been one of the personal guards for his tribe's matriarch. Up until the creation of the Automazombs and their kin, Zu had used it mainly for cutting ropes.

Just outside the town gate, wooden shields were driven into the sandy ground forming a row. A cluster of dead tore into the rough cuts of meat lashed to the front. With the way they focused on the shields, it was not something so innocent as boar or goat.

Over the rooftops, Zu spotted a huge rukh airship. It was painted all black. Black flags adorned with menacing skulls fluttered from the ropes. He'd hadn't seen a rukh since he was very young. He would have given his left leg for the chance to fly such machine. They used the same gas that the floating cities did and were typically armed from masthead to rudder.

Owynn pressed his back against Zu's. He held a revolver in one hand and a knife in the other.

"It's a nice ship, Captain, but can we ogle later?"

One of the zomb-spawn was rushing toward them. Its arms were outstretched and its jaw hung open. It stared hungrily through one glazed eye. The thing's hands were gnarled and the fingertips were worn to the bone, giving the impression of claws. It groaned loudly, calling more of its kind.

Zu put all his strength into swinging the sword and beheaded the monster.

"I have an idea on how to be rid of the pirates. But it's going to destroy something beautiful."

* * *

Liridon raced through the main gate into Port Fenzir. Before the threat of the dead, Liridon hadn't considered himself much of a fighter. Now, through necessity, he could hold his own. But he still didn't know why Captain Zu had trusted him with such an integral part of his plan.

The townspeople were in a frenzy. Nearly a hundred enemies were descending upon them. The streets were filled with those fighting and those attempting to flee. The small peacekeeping force did all they could to aid and protect the people from enemies both living and dead.

The pirates were heavily armored. They were fully prepared for their three or four dozen pet zomb-spawn to turn on them. The dead weren't loyal to any living soul; they only followed their hunger.

A distinct whistle and engine rumble rose above the rooftops. Liridon skidded to a halt and lifted his head to listen. *No. Not here. Not now!* There hadn't been any Automazombs when he left to find the Haak ruins. Now he heard not one, but two Zombs rumbling about. As if the poor townspeople hadn't enough to worry about. The dead were relentless hunters, but the Zombs that survived this long had done so because they were nearly indestructible.

Liridon made his way to the Port Fenzir library. It was a small temple with only a single statue to Wise Ontaakh in a circular room lines with books. He had read every one of them since his quest brought him into town. The library was run by a single archivist who lived behind the temple. The woman had welcomed Liridon in and set up a space for him to sleep in the attic. It was a fine space, once the clumsily stored artifacts had been organized or sent to larger libraries. Liridon had set up a cot, a little writing desk, and an artificial branch near the window for his falcon to sleep.

He raced up the narrow, stone steps. He carefully slid the bag of Haak artifacts under his bed, then pulled his falconer's glove on. The bird wasn't indoors, so Liridon went to the open window.

"Haric!" *Oh, please be there.* He whistled for the falcon. "Haric, return!"

Wings flapped. The falcon landed on Liridon's arm with a friendly screech. Liridon paused to brush the back of his fingers against the bird's cheek. Haric looked like an old soldier with scars from beak to tail. He hadn't named his friend after Ro'ag's war sword for nothing.

"Come friend, we're needed."

As Liridon hurried back outside, an unarmed man ran past the library door. A pirate brute covered in metal plates from helmet to boots chased after him, waving a machete over his head. Liridon pulled on his plague mask, then whispered to his falcon and stuck his arm out the doorway.

Haric swooped after the pirate. The bird grabbed the helmet right of the man's head. The pirate shouted angrily. He turned and tried to snatch his helmet back. The falcon flew higher and higher, then dropped the helmet. It hit the pirate squarely in his stunned face.

Liridon used the commotion to grab the machete. Haric dove and clawed at the pirate's face. The man yelled for help. None arrived. With the pirate dazed and distracted, Liridon swung the blade with all his might. The pirate cried out as he fell. The blade buried deep in his back.

The pirate's intended victim still ran blindly toward what might have appeared, in his fear-driven mind, to be fellow townsfolk. They were, in fact, a pack of zomb-spawn. Liridon retrieved the machete and whistled for Haric to fly ahead. It was a command to frighten, not attack, this time. He couldn't risk his winged friend spreading the new plague by touching the dead. Haric instead got between the scared man and the zomb-spawn and beat his wings threateningly. The man nearly fell backwards as he changed directions. Liridon ran straight for the dead with the machete.

The blade came down on the shoulder of the nearest of the zomb-spawn. The monster turned to face him, moaning. It was a recent infection. Those bloodshot eyes had yet to completely glaze over. It had been a woman not two days ago. Her guts dangled out through a clawed hole in her torso. Liridon yanked the machete free and swung again, this time hitting the woman in the back of the neck. She stumbled and fell.

One down, five to go. The attack had drawn the attention of the other dead who were with the former woman. Liridon extended his arm and wildly slashed the machete back and forth, hoping to hit one or any of the dead. Haric circled above him, crying angrily.

Liridon frowned as he backed away from the zomb-spawn. He gave a low whistle to warn Haric back.

His falcon shrieked in protest, but didn't engage.

The zomb-spawn stumbled toward Liridon. Their groans developed an edge as they closed on him, gathering into a many-throated roar. Liridon turned and ran. While he was grateful he could help the villager, he was really needed elsewhere.

When Zu asked him if he knew of any reliable sources of flame that could be thrown or shot high into the air, Liridon had laughed. His strangest acquaintance, Lady Wyniera Mudassme, had left several instruments of fiery destruction in his care. She had escaped Caelspyr before it fell, just as he had, and used his last correspondence to track him down. Apparently, she was setting up a new workshop to construct and test a mysterious new machine. He'd asked many times what it was, but she would only ever smirk and promise that he would recognize it when he saw it. Which was… worrying.

Regardless, this new invention took up as much workshop space as it did Lady Wyn's attention. She decided that she would keep several of her prototypes in Liridon's care. The care instructions were short: the only acceptable reason for any of the prototypes to not be returned was if they had exploded. This, naturally, worried Liridon. He wasn't about to keep possibly combustible machines above a library. Instead, he had rented a storage shed away from as many buildings as possible.

Liridon raced through the streets. Haric drove off any human attackers, while Liridon cut down or avoided any dead in his path. One large zomb-spawn nearly caught him. Liridon had to hastily shed his green overcoat before the dead used it to pull him in. He loved that coat. If he survived, he would try to locate and disinfect it after Port Fenzir was safe.

The falcon stood watch while Liridon threw open the shed door and hunted for the right tool to take down a pirate airship. A hyper-flammable liquid could coat an arrow, but where would he find a bow? The flame-gun, a sort of modified musket with a tank of the same flammable liquid was probably the more thorough way to down a craft, but there was a serious risk of death for the user. Liridon settled on grenades. They were much like blasting sticks, but with heads that would send hot metal shrapnel spraying at the target.

If Lady Wyn was religious, Liridon had no doubt she worshipped Zianovalla and that she was, in turn, the goddess's favorite mortal.

He filled his bag with five of the grenades and ran back toward Captain Zu. The pirates he had bypassed or attacked on the way to the storage shed were gathered on the main road. Liridon saw them blocking the way and pointing weapons in his direction. Gunfire and smoke filled the air, but they'd aimed too wide. That time.

Liridon heard the voices of the Corvidae and the howling of the dead, and veered right, ducking between buildings to join the mercenaries.

Ahead, he saw the Corvidae pinned atop a pile of rubble from the ruined wall. Twenty of the dead pressed in on them on one side of the rocky hill. An Automazomb was climbing up the other side. A couple of pirates were stationed on a roof nearby with rifles, cheering on the dead and taunting the Corvidae. Any time they found an escape route, the pirates drove them back with gunfire. The Corvidae were trapped between the dead and the threat of crippling shots.

The youngest Corvidae member struggled with his weapons. His elders shouted for the boy, Jackdaw, to stay calm and to keep his mind focused. A zomb-spawn grabbed his leg. He screamed in terror. Raven grabbed the boy's arm, but the dead had a solid grip on him. They dragged young Jackdaw far enough down that they were able to tear into his leg with nails and teeth. Raven averted his eyes, his grip loosened and the boy slipped farther.

Jackdaw begged and grabbed at his leader.

"Help! Raven, Magpie, Jay, help me!"

The younger of the women, Jay if Liridon wasn't mistaken, knelt forward to try to help pull her friend to higher ground. Raven and the other Corvidae yelled when she did. Liridon cursed that he was not in a position to stop the deaths. But once bitten, a person only had scant minutes to cut off the infection. Jackdaw was lost to them. His cries were cut short when a zomb-spawn ripped out his throat.

Jay spun around to argue with her leader.

"You could have stopped this! You could have-!"

Dead hands clawed her clothing. She shrieked. The others tried to pull her away before it was too late. But a zomb-spawn that had been crawling up the pile of debris made its move and bit her on the wrist. The pirates on the roof whooped and hollered. Magpie aimed her gun down, seemingly in retaliation for the death of her friend. But when she pulled the trigger, it was not the zomb-kin that fell, but Jay.

Liridon was shocked. He always heard the two women were close.

He needed to get the surviving Corvidae an opening. Haric was soaring high above the town, much too far to quietly give the order to attack the pirates. He would have to whistle and hope for the best. His shrill orders for the falcon drew the attention of both pirates. One of them stayed trained on the Corvidae. The other targeted Liridon instead. Haric descended on that pirate, talons forward. But this pirate was much keener than some of her fellows. She followed Liridon's gaze above to her right. She had just enough time to dodge Haric's attack. The rifleshot struck the building behind Liridon.

The pirate and falcon fought on the rooftop. Haric was beaten away when the pirate used the rifle like a club. He drew back and flew higher, preparing to dive again. But his wing was injured.

Liridon whistled and yelled to his friend, terrified.

"Return to me! Break off! Stop!"

But the falcon didn't hear, or didn't obey. Liridon couldn't bear to watch. The pirate fired once, twice. Haric screamed. Liridon covered his ears. His friend. His dear friend was gone. He knew there would be casualties, but Haric?

Liridon raised his head, ready to swear vengeance upon the pirate. Then, he noticed someone jumping to the roof. Small in frame, with untamed brown hair and a metal arm. Liridon's heart flew higher than Haric had ever soared.

His voice dropped to an awed whisper.

"Evellyn?"

Evellyn touched her metal hand to the pirate woman's back. Liridon saw smoke and the pirate convulsed. He felt a moment's vindication that Haric's death was avenged, overwhelmed by relief that Evellyn was alive. The second pirate on the roof pivoted and shot at Evellyn. The bullet glanced off her metal arm, knocking her back a step. A support rod was dented, but the arm was not broken. Evellyn recovered and rushed the pirate. He tumbled backwards over the edge of the roof, while Evellyn managed to catch herself before her momentum drove her after him.

The events on the nearby roof hadn't gone unnoticed by the Corvidae. Raven shouted for his team to move, taking out some of the dead in their path during the retreat.

Evellyn shouted down from the roof.

"Leave the Automazomb for me!"

She looped a rope around the building's metal chimney and slid to the ground.

The Automazomb wasn't as done with the Corvidae as they were with it. The creature was four-armed but legless, having had those replaced with machine treads. To add to its grotesque appearance, its inventor had fashioned the steam exhaust to look something like the spines of some evil iguana. It rumbled forward on spiked, metal treads. Raven hung back, making sure his team got away safely. The Zomb swiped its meat-and-steel hands at him greedily.

206

Raven growled for Evellyn to hurry.

"If I'm not allowed to shoot it, how in the fresh hell am I supposed to keep it from killing us?"

Evellyn dashed forward, grabbing something out of the satchel strapped across her chest.

"I need an injection opening. If you want to help, find me one: stomach, neck, thigh."

Raven and Crow worked together to pin the Zomb's arms behind it. Each burly limb was a thick as a tree trunk. They used weapons and ropes and anything they could find to restrain the monster. It wrenched its obstructed arms and bit the air in front of the Corvidae. Liridon joined Magpie and Rook in keeping the zomb-spawn at bay while this went on. Devouring two of the Corvidae had only whet their palates for more. The monsters groaned hungrily. Liridon hacked away with the machete. Magpie preferred wielding both a knife and a small gun. Rook's attacks were much less refined, blasting the zomb-spawn with a blunderbuss.

Liridon heard a pained shout and spun around. The Zomb had freed one of its arms and was holding Raven by his neck. The man gasped and scratched at the dark gray arm. The monster's red eyes flashed. It drew him closer and chomped down on the man's face. Liridon looked away when he heard bone crunching.

Raven placed the barrel of his gun under his chin. His team looked on in horror as their leader pulled the trigger.

Liridon's jaw dropped.

"He... He killed himself."

Rook's stony glare intensified as he obliterated another zomb-spawn.

"Danger is part of our job, Historian. We must ensure we don't become what we fight."

The Automazomb did not care one way or the other if the man in its hands was alive or dead, infected or clean. The gears in its augmented jaw whirred. It began to feed.

Evellyn loaded a glass, liquid-filled vial into a gun with a long needle on the end.

"That man's death will have meant nothing if we don't fix this Zomb's chemical components."

Rook scrabbled up the rubble to help Crow hold the monster's limbs back. He encouraged Evellyn to do whatever it was she was going to, before they lost anyone else.

Evellyn jabbed the needle into the Automazomb's neck and squeezed the trigger. There was a soft *ki-shnt!* and she pulled away.

"Everyone get back!"

Liridon and Magpie joined the rest in running a good distance back from both Zomb and spawn.

The Automazomb sputtered and twitched. It suddenly dropped Raven's body to the ground. Its mouth drooped open to let any meat it had been eating fall out. Then, it just sort of *waited*. Everyone froze while it scanned the area. Liridon marveled; he had heard about Evellyn's exploits, but he'd never seen it in person. He truly believed her work would save all of Eysan. One day. Assuming vultures like those pirates didn't destroy everything first. The Corvidae kept their weapons drawn. It wasn't until the Zomb started hunting one of the dead that the team relaxed.

Rook holstered his pistol and gave Evellyn an approving nod.

"Your gun, it makes the machines fight for us."

Evellyn loaded up another vial.

"Yes, although it won't do anything about pirates."

Liridon gently patted his satchel.

"Ah, speaking of pirates, I have a delivery for Captain Zu. Would any of you care to take your fight to the pirate captain?"

Rook shook his head.

"Pirates aren't our concern."

"Even after they attacked the town? I thought-"

Magpie cut down one of the zomb-spawn. When she spoke, her voice was as sharp as her knife.

"The *pirates* won't turn half of Port Fenzir into more pirates. We'll follow the Automazomb and take out the dead it finds."

Liridon exhaled. It was a fair assessment.

"There is another Zomb. I heard its whistle."

Evellyn cupped an ear in effort to hear it.

"It seems my work isn't quite ended here, then." Her eyes locked with Liridon's. "Don't you go leaving, or dying, before we meet again. Got it?"

Liridon nodded. Then, Evellyn leaned over and kissed him on the cheek. Filthy as he was from cave exploring and battling the dead. He giggled like a child. She *kissed* him!

He felt a sharp shove behind his right shoulder. He turned to see Crow impatiently holding off one of the dead.

"If you're going to go, do it! Drag those pirates before the Dark Lady."

Liridon raced toward the dark black shape on the horizon. Zu would be following the pirate captain's ship. He caught one more glimpse of Evellyn slipping off down a side street. They shared a brief smile before they ran in opposite directions.

* * *

Three skimmer craft flew in a tight formation around the rukh. They flew low enough for Zu to appraise them. The central craft held a pilot facing forward and a gunner protecting the rear. The other two were guns-forward; they would have a single passenger who worked both positions. The skimmers had been modified to gain lift through a sleek ballast on each wing, instead of being glorified gliders. More like these protected the pirate fleet.

Zu noticed a few different pirate flag emblems on the various airships flying around Port Fenzir. This was some sort of multi-crew pirate syndicate. He kept his crew fighting in the shadows and behind buildings. He couldn't risk exposing any of them to the pirate gunships.

He saw a familiar man lugging an overstuffed bag across his chest. Liridon had returned! Zu had to laugh aloud. He thought he'd sent the historian on a roadrunner chase, requesting impossible weapons. And now here he was with, well, clearly something. He sent Yuri, the fastest of the crew, to fetch the man before he got himself shot.

Liridon breathed heavily, bracing himself on his knees when he finally arrived. He took off the bag. Its contents clinked together as it landed on the dusty ground. Zu lifted the flap with the toe of his boot. Inside were several metal tubes with flanged heads. The hairs on the back of his neck stood on end.

Zu lowered the flap.

"So, Liridon, what did you find?"

"She calls them grenades. They're quite safe, until you pull that peg under the head. Then you have precious few seconds to run for your life."

"And their firepower?"

"Sufficient for anything you have planned"

Baako's brow furrowed.

"Captain? Why do you need these?"

Zu's eyes landed on the rukh in the distance.

"Taking out the captain's ship, and as many more as we can, should make the pirates think twice about their attack."

"But, Captain, there's another way. I can take the ship. We need something to fly across the ocean, why not the rukh?"

"I don't follow."

Baako hesitated, then pulled his shirt collar down. There on his breast was a tattoo of a skull impaled on the dual swords of the god of war.

"I was a pirate. By the law of the black flag, I can commandeer that ship."

Aria hissed at Baako angrily.

"Unless they *kill* you. Don't be an idiot. You only just joined our little family and you're going to throw your life away on the off chance a pack of wolves will listen to how you want to be their leader?"

Zu let his crew argue over potential suicide missions while he thought. He would need a distraction in order for his plan to work. And these grenades sounded perfect for his attack. Baako wasn't wrong about their need for an airship, but a rukh was unwieldy. Especially for such a small crew. He had planned on shooting down a few medium-sized zeppelins, from which they could craft an appropriate ship.

With the details of his plan falling into place, Zu cleared his throat.

"Baako, you may try your luck at commandeering, but be ready to run if you see any skimmers flying against formation. The twins and Liridon will cover you. Be safe, all of you. Owynn, you're with me."

Liridon protested as Zu went for the bag filled with grenades.

"I would rather not part with these until I need to. Lady Wyn is very-"

"Can you fly a skimmer?"

"Er, no."

"Then grab anything that isn't an explosive and stay here."

Liridon rescued a few notebooks, pens, and personal items out of the bag, then handed it over. Aria argued loudly with nobody in particular. Zu wished them all luck, then led Owynn down a side street.

Skimmers, even fitted with ballasts, couldn't fly indefinitely. They had small engines that needed fuel, guns that needed bullets, and pilots who would have to attend to bodily needs. But Zu hadn't seen any skimmers landing in the cargo bays of pirate airships. That meant they were setting down somewhere else. He guessed it was the airfield which the pirates had boasted that they all but owned.

His suspicions were proved correct by the telltale buzzing of skimmer engines. From the cover of a building, Zu peered toward the airfield. A handful of pirates tended to their airships. There was a row of three zeppelins about the size of Zu's old Wyvera - may she soar again in the beyond - and five or so skimmers scattered about.

A contingency of six more pirates fended off the dead while their cohorts worked. They wore old airship parts as armor that protected them from bites and scratches. The dead were not being shot, but merely pushed back, repeatedly. Pirates threw chunks of human flesh to try and lure them away from the airfield. Zu nearly threw up at the sight of the bloody vats of butchered limbs waiting to be flung like treats for the dead. How many in the surrounding villages had been murdered in order to make this raid possible?

Owynn blew out a breath.

"What's your p-plan, Captain? Beyond flying skimmers."

"Shoot everything we see, then deliver Liridon's present to the rukh."

"Sounds downright simple the way you say it. Pirates and the zomb-kin will try to stop us before we get anywhere near the airfield."

"What if we were zomb-kin?"

Zu raised his arms and groaned. Their clothes were filthy from their little trip in the caverns and fighting their way through the dead to reach Port Fenzir. Owynn gestured that Zu should tilt his head slightly. Zu limped closer to Owynn and let his head flop to the side. Owynn sighed and followed Zu's lead.

There was a good chance this little charade would fall apart instantly. The pirates might be fooled by appearances, but it seemed the dead were able to smell living blood. Zu made ready to draw his gun on anyone or thing that got too close. Just as he had hoped, the pirates didn't fire upon them. Every step was one they wouldn't have to make while under fire. A quarter of distance, a third, half: Zu was beginning to wonder if they might come right up next to the pirates before shooting the lot of them.

One of the dead turned to face Zu. It raised its head awkwardly. Zu nudged Owynn to try a different path. The swarm of zomb-kin was on the north side of the field. They would try the west side. A trail of zomb-kin followed far behind them. The zomb-kin moaned. Zu responded with what he hoped sounded the same. The pirates shouted for one of their fighters to move to intercept.

A pirate threw an arm. Zu watched it fly toward his head. *Oh well, we got pretty damn far.* He ducked, whipped his revolver out of the holster, and fired upon the pirate. Zu waved for Owynn to run. They raced for two of the single-pilot skimmers.

The sudden attack caught the pirates off-guard. They fired on the dead, on Zu and Owynn, even on their own. A skimmer's ballast was punctured and deflated. Another windshield was cracked and the pirate who had been readying for flight crumpled against the steering column.

Zu took out two of the airship mechanics. Owynn aimed instead for the dead that were now chasing them. The armored pirates began to abandon their posts. The zomb-kin swarmed the ones who stayed, overwhelming them and ripping away the layers of armor. The pirates screamed for their fellows to help.

The chaos provided the perfect cover. Zu hopped into a skimmer at the back of the pirate fleet and strapped himself in. The engine was already buzzing. He cut the skimmer free of its tether and closed the windshield. The skimmer floated a few inches off the ground. Zu glanced over the controls. This was a bit different than flying the Wyvera. He found the thrust and sent the skimmer rocketing forward toward the town wall. He yanked the steering column up. The skimmer pivoted skyward.

He looped around, upside down, back toward the airfield. Owynn was just getting off the ground himself. *Time for those guns.* Zu found a trigger under the steering column. The skimmer rattled as the ground was pelted with bullets. He managed to burst enough balloon segments of the zeppelins that they wouldn't fly. He spotted a stack of barrels sitting off to the side of the airfield, probably so they could be loaded up. They looked like what Baako had described.

Swooping around for another attack, Zu fired on the barrels. Black powder spilled over the airfield. More skimmers launched, chasing after them. Zu hoped Owynn could handle the attackers. Zu had to get these "grenades" to the rukh.

The skimmer didn't have any portholes, just that one windshield-hatch. Zu pulled the hatch release. The windshield opened just enough to get caught by the wind. Zu struggled with the steering column to keep from crashing. He flicked his goggles down over his eyes. The windshield wobbled and twisted until it finally came free of the skimmer.

Now free to open air, Zu grabbed one of the grenades out of the bag. He pulled the pin out and dropped it onto the airfield. Just before landing, it became a magnificent fireball that sent fragments spraying all across the field. It was close enough to the black powder that the barrels exploded as well. The chain reaction sent one airship up in flames, then another. The pirates flew into a panic, some fleeing while a few tried to save what they could.

Owynn came up next to Zu. He pointed at a skimmer protecting the rukh, then behind, indicating more chasing them. Zu grinned. They had their work cut out for them. The two separated. Zu twirled and looped and rolled the skimmer as he evaded the skimmers behind him. By D'alor's grace, it felt amazing to be airborne.

Owynn brought up the rear. Zu kept the skimmers focusing on him while his brave navigator grounded the lot of them. When they were free of pursuers, the two sped off toward the rukh. They kept a pirate formation as they approached. Hiding among the enemy worked once, why not again?

Down below, Zu spotted Baako standing on a platform created when the cargo bay door was open. He had the pirate captain on his knees. But the surrounding pirates didn't look impressed. Greedy was the word that came to mind. Killing the current captain would only leave an opening each one of those scoundrels had ambitions to fill.

Zu broke off from the formation. He glanced around the streamlined cockpit for anything resembling a parachute, but found nothing. But, there was a black flag secured to the skimmer's sleek nose. Zu locked the steering column, released the restraints, and took a knife to the black flag. He cut the flag free and pulled it into his lap.

The skimmer protecting the rukh banked left until they were headed straight for Zu. Zu plunked back into his seat, unlocked the column, and shot wildly. Two of the enemy skimmers veered away. Owynn zipped past Zu's open cockpit. He shot the two-person skimmer in the right wing. Smoke billowed. The craft tumbled down in a tight spiral, crashing into a cluster of dead.

Zu fired again on the skimmers, but also kept one eye on the ground. Baako was running for cover. But where were the twins? Then, Zu noticed the rukh's cannons pivoting, aiming for Owynn's skimmer. Zu pressed his skimmer forward. The fuel tank indicator hovered at empty.

Owynn took down another skimmer. Only one remained. It broke off, probably having seen the danger of being too close when the rukh fired. Zu needed something to get his friend out of the way as well. He tried to shoot the tail off Owynn's skimmer, but missed.

The rukh's cannons blasted in sequence. Owynn's skimmer was rattled by the first cannonball arcing past the windshield. The next one struck the wing. Another tore the little skimmer in half.

The wind robbed Zu's scream from his mouth.

"Owynn!"

The cannons pivoted again, straight at Zu. He had seconds before they were reloaded. This was it. He turned the skimmer toward the center of the rukh and locked the steering column. He yanked the pins out of every remaining grenade, took the pirate flag by the corners, and leapt out of the open cockpit.

Zu plummeted toward the ground at a rate that would probably only break a bone or two when he landed. The last pirate skimmer shot at him, then at the pilotless skimmer. But it was too late. Zu's skimmer crashed against the surface of the rukh. A second later, the grenades went off. The pirate skimmer was engulfed. Zu was buffeted away.

Explosions rippled through the airship. The gasses that helped keep the flying cities aloft were efficient, but highly flammable. Every pirate on the streets below scattered. The dead weren't aware enough to move out from under the massive ship as it crashed down.

Ashes and flaming bits of debris showered down around the crash site. Zu aimed his landing for Baako and Liridon, who he spotted hiding in an alley. He made sure to kick an encroaching zomb-kin in the head before crashing into the pair. Liridon squirmed out from under Zu. Baako helped him to his feet. The man was bleeding from a bullet wound in his shoulder.

Zu groaned as he stood up. Nothing broken, but he would terribly sore tomorrow.

"Thank you, and apologies. Where are Aria and Yuri?"

Baako cast his eyes down.

"Aria was right. I should have…Those wolves, they didn't listen to me. We fought, but…"

Zu pulled Baako close until their foreheads touched.

"This isn't on you, friend. Come. Let's see that they didn't die in vain."

Liridon was watching the skies.

"Airship. And another."

Zu saw them, too. Skimmers, zeppelins, and cloudskippers, all painted the color of night, were headed away from town. His plan was working. Seeing the fireball that was once your greatest weapon is a demoralizing thing. The pirates must have decided to move on to easier targets.

When they were gone, Liridon waved Zu and Baako toward the docks.

"I heard an Automazomb this way. I'm sure we'll find Evellyn and the Corvidae wherever it is."

Zu readied his pistol and followed Liridon.

"So, this Evellyn, she's your-?"

"My friend, a genius engineer, and my light. We lost touch when Caelspyr fell, but she's back now."

They ran north through dead-filled streets. Peacekeepers and townsfolk worked together to protect their home from the infected. With the pirates largely gone, the good people of Port Fenzir were winning the fight.

A few streets away from the docks, the horde of zomb-kin began outnumbering the living. They turned onto the road leading directly to the water. The docks were in shambles. The boats that remained were either

216

sunk or burning. At the center of the swarm was a massive Automazomb with metal arms tipped with sharp claws. It let out a metallic bellow.

Zu thought he had an open shot to the thing's head. It couldn't be too much different from any other dead thing, right?

But Liridon pushed Zu's arms down.

"Look."

The Corvidae lifted a young woman over the crowd. Her arms and face were wrapped tightly to protect her from infection. She used a zomb-kin's skull like a stepping stone. She had a small gun in her hand as she jumped onto the Automazomb's back. But she didn't shoot. She touched it to the base of the monster's neck.

Then, the Automazomb did something Zu never thought he would see in his life. It reached out and ate one of its kin.

"She has the power to turn them good again."

Liridon half-shrugged.

"She injects them with a concoction that changes the chemicals that course through their guts and muscles. I read a study back at the library about how everything we eat can be determined by our, for lack of a better term, humors. Fascinating stuff. I bet it's the same principal here." He waved off Zu's stare. "Exactly as you say. She makes them good again."

With the help of the Automazomb, the living were able to clear the docks of zomb-kin. When the peacekeepers and volunteer fighters swept through, Zu reconvened with what remained of the Corvidae.

Magpie was scowling.

"Can you believe that peacekeeper? He blamed us for not keeping a better handle on the dead. Says we're to leave as soon as the dead are no longer a threat."

Zu happily put his weapons away. With any luck, this would be the last time they were ever used on this continent.

"Well, if you have nowhere else to go, you three are welcome to join us."

Crow tipped his head to the side.

"Join you where?"

Baako smiled wide.

"We have a map that will take us across the ocean to find a new land!"

Crow and Magpie both answered at once.

"What?"

"Impossible."

They sounded excited by the prospect.

Liridon shook his head and pointed back toward the center of town.

"I have a map. It's the reason I was trying to hire the Corvidae. But, there's a slight wrinkle in those plans."

Zu followed Liridon's gaze to Evellyn, who was checking over the freshly-rehabilitated Zomb.

"She could join us as well, you know."

"Her work is here, fixing the Automazombs."

Evellyn, apparently satisfied, strode over with a pleasant smile. She and Liridon laughed as they embraced, both of them expressing their utter joy at the other surviving. Zu wouldn't be responsible for breaking the two up. He wondered if the historian might part with the map, even if he weren't going on the voyage.

Rook asked Evellyn if he might inspect the strange injector gun. She agreed and he turned it over carefully, admiring it.

"I can do it."

Evellyn eyed the man warily.

"What?"

"I will take on your task, if you wish to join the historian across the ocean. As the Corvidae flock disperses, I find myself longing for a life of healing over one of danger and death."

The group erupted in questions. Evellyn plied Liridon for more about how and why he would go across the ocean. Magpie demanded to know why Rook was quitting and what she was supposed to do now. Baako begged Crow to also leave the Corvidae behind so they could be like brothers once more and adventure together. Crow was curious if Liridon knew anything about the purported sea monsters that would drown any would-be sailors.

Zu found himself unable to do anything but wait for some conclusions to be made. The unknown called to him, but only time would tell if the others heard it also. He saw a rickety wooden platform guarding over the docks. He left the others to discuss their futures.

Atop the platform, he could feel the sea breezes rolling in from the ocean. Thin clouds floated eastward. Even if he was alone in his journey, Zu determined he would fly to the lands on the other side of the world.

A deep, friendly voice pulled Zu away from his daydreaming. Baako looked up at him.

"Captain? Are you coming?"

Zu climbed down with a smile on his face.

"Where to?"

"To the crash site of the rukh. Me'n Crow and Evellyn are going to build a new airship out of the wreckage. We'll want your input."

"Best make our destination the airship field. There isn't much left of the other airship."

Baako nodded and ran off to tell the others. When Zu met up with the rest of the group, Evellyn was talking Rook through use and components of the injector, some glass vials, and how to make more of the concoction when the need arose. Liridon kept a worried grip on Evellyn's hand during the conversation, as if the woman might change her mind at any moment and leave him. She turned to give him a reassuring peck on the cheek.

* * *

Two weeks later, the new airship was complete. Liridon used the entirety of his savings to fund their new expedition. The airship was on the small side for a zeppelin, but had even larger ballasts than the Wyvera did. They could fly for months without landing; it was possible they might have to.

Baako and Crow walked up with crates stacked higher than their heads. Baako set down his crates at the bottom of the gangplank.

"We made a deal with the barkeep of Verdellen's Favor. She wanted a distiller machine and, in return, we got you a present, Captain."

Zu lifted the lid of the top crate. Inside, nestled among straw to keep the glass from breaking, were bottles of spirits. He lifted them one at a time. The labels were from all over Eysan. His lip pulled to the side. A goodbye from their home continent.

He offered to help them bring the gift aboard.

"We'll open one of these tonight. It's only right to celebrate the birth of a new airship. And doubly so when it sets off on such a grand voyage."

They brought the crates to the cargo hold, then Baako went to join Liridon in plotting their course at the new navigator's station. The man had been an eager student of Owynn's work. Both of them were students, teaching each other from the pile of books Liridon deemed necessary for the journey. It seemed there wasn't a book in the Port Fenzir library that wasn't necessary.

One of Liridon's books provided the airship with a fitting name. Zu was leafing through the crew's new library and discovered a myth about the Shifting One's monstrous pets. Yaim'allelo apparently loved strange creatures, but his-her favorite was a combination of a whale, crocodile, and a frigatebird that was so large it the deity could ride upon it. Zu thought the name Levianth fit the new ship perfectly.

Zu descended to the engineering deck to check on Evellyn and Crow. They were busy fine-tuning every little valve and gear. Meanwhile, Magpie leaned out a porthole, double-checking the rigging on the starboard side.

Zu leaned against the humming machines and closed his eyes. He was finally home again. When he opened his eyes again, he addressed his new crewmates.

"Fine work, all of you. Come to the observation deck when you finish. We'll fly at dusk."

One by one, Zu welcomed everyone as they trickled in, their tasks complete for the moment. He tried to keep his smile bright and eager, but his heart was heavy. He'd lost almost everyone these past few years. He missed his wife and children. He could still hear Henning's last words echo in his mind. He kept expecting to see the twins, Lillian, and Owynn arguing in the galley.

The sun was just above the horizon as Evellyn walked through the door, covered in grease. The sky outside the large, westward-facing windows was ablaze with pinks and oranges. Zu gave the order to launch the new ship. As the airship rose, Zu's smile became more genuine. Here was a new crew for a new adventure. He hoped that in the time to come, they would be just as close as the families he had lost.

He made sure each crewmember who wished for it was given a glass of rum. Liridon preferred water in his cup. Magpie asked for a shotglass. Evellyn suggested that perhaps champagne was more appropriate to a toast. Zu laughed to himself and went about making sure his crew was happy.

Then, he lifted his glass into the air.

"We survivors are the luckiest few. For all we've lost, fate has guided us to this point together. Let us reach out, together, into a world larger than we have ever known. I bid you welcome aboard the Levianth. May she bring us a new day in a new land. To the unknown. To the future!"

The crew all raised their glasses and cheered.

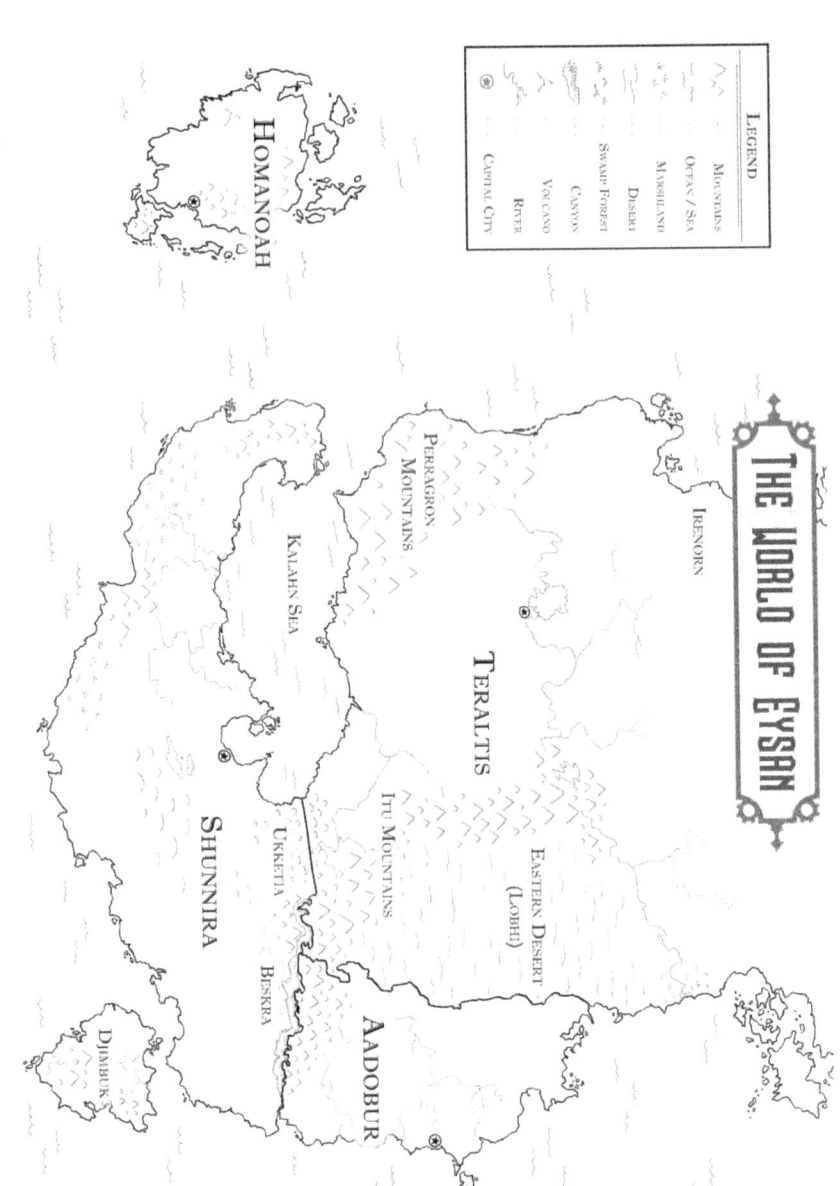

THE WORLD OF EYSAN

HOMANOAH

Perragron Mountains

Irenorn

Kalahn Sea

Teraltis

Itu Mountains

Shunnira

Ukketia

Eastern Desert (Lobii)

Beskra

Djimburi

Aadobur

Acknowledgements

As we wrap up the series, we would like to acknowledge you, the readers. A book is nothing but messy paper unless someone like you opens it. Thank you for joining us on this adventure.

And a special thanks also to Karen Bitters, beta reader extraordinaire.

About the Authors

Dex Greenbright is an illustrator as well as a sci-fi & fantasy author. He makes his home in Chicago and can usually be found writing in a cozy little corner of his local coffeeshop. For more of his writing and art, please visit dexgreenbright.com.

Victoria Bitters has been a scribbler of macabre tales since she was a kid. She is a Chicagoland librarian and practices other deadly arts, too.

Jessica L. Lim is a wandering teacher who has taught in Japan, England, and across the Chicagoland area. She would love to bring back Firefly and is the proud owner of a budgerigar named Max.

CPSIA information can be obtained
at www.ICGtesting.com
Printed in the USA
BVHW040915260622
640608BV00003BA/71

9 781088 034439